THE RECKONING

"Alix." His voice was harsh. "I haven't had a woman in a long time. God help you if this is a game."

"Hush." Her lips were warm as they pressed against his chest and moved slowly up to the hollow in his throat. "Don't talk, Dominic. You are here with me now. I'll not question the wisdom of fate in bringing us together again. Perhaps there may never be a tomorrow." Her voice dropped to a mere whisper. "There is only now. Share it with me."

"Do you know what you are asking, Alexandra?" His eyes were wary and as black as velvet.

Instead of answering, she unfastened the top button of her shirt.

"Alix." The word was almost a moan. His mouth came down on hers and the world went away. She shivered as his hands moved over her body. His kisses became harder and more demanding. The need between them was fierce and elemental.

Dominic knew he should stop before it was too late. A gentleman did not take the innocence of an untried virgin. But he was no gentleman and this was Alexandra. His Alexandra . . .

THE RECKONING

Jeanette Baker

Pinnacle Books
Kensington Publishing Corp.

http://www.pinnaclebooks.com

PINNACLE BOOKS are published by

Kensington Publishing Corp.
850 Third Avenue
New York, NY 10022

Copyright © 1997 by Jeanette Baker

Pinnacle and the P logo Reg. U.S. Pat. & TM Off.

First Printing: October, 1997
10 9 8 7 6 5 4 3 2 1

Printed in the United States of America

By the shores of Gitche Gumee,
By the shining Big-Sea-Water
Stood the wigwam of Nokomis,
Daughter of the Moon, Nokomis.

—*The Song of Hiawatha* Henry Wadsworth Longfellow

"Spanish civilization crushed the Indian; English civilization scorned and neglected him; French civilization embraced and cherished him."

—Francis Parkman

AUTHOR'S NOTE

The French and Indian War, called the Seven Years War in Europe and Canada, began in 1754 and lasted until 1763 when the Treaty of Paris was signed. This treaty gave Britain almost all French land in Canada and all holdings east of the Mississippi River except New Orleans. In order to fit my plot into the lives of my fictional characters, Dominic and Alexandra, I condensed history, setting battle sites and Indian attacks several years ahead of their time.

Governor Vaudreuil truly was governor of New France, although the character traits presented in this novel are purely imaginative. Of Louis XV and his long suffering queen, history tells us that the marriage, although fruitful, (they had ten children) was not a happy one. Nevertheless, Marie Leczynska was a faithful wife and never gave birth to children that were not her husband's.

Chief Pontiac was greatly influenced by the Delaware Prophet and struggled for years to rid New France of the English, although his attack on Detroit didn't occur until several years after the time period in this novel.

The rituals, agriculture, songs, medical practices, and religious beliefs of the Ojibwa are accurate, taken from the sources included in this note. Many of the events in this book such as the Indian attack, the treatment of captives, the murder of handicapped prisoners, the march through the forest, the adoption of women and children into the tribe, the role of French priests, the distrust of Catholicism, Native American cannibalism, ransoming captives to the French, the sugaring, and many more, were taken from the narratives of Molly Jemison and Mrs. James Johnson, who were captured by Iroquois and Algonquian Indians along with their families. Molly and a younger brother were the only family members spared by their Seneca captors. Mrs. Johnson was ransomed to the French and later reunited with her husband and children in England.

The words uttered by Marie Leczynska in chapter six, "Why bother to save the barn when the house is on fire?" were really spoken by the Minister Berryer as a response to pleas for aid to Canada. France was tired of war and she abandoned half of North America with a sense of relief, closing her eyes and ears to the enraged colonists left behind. Almost every French family had lost a husband, a father, a son. Their animals were confiscated, their land destroyed, and then, they were expected to lay down their arms and take the oath of allegiance to a country they had fought against for generations.

One has only to visit Quebec to see the drawn battle lines. Schoolchildren are taught their lessons in French. French is the official language, Catholicism the official religion. On the St. Lawrence Seaway, four thousand miles from France, rests a city as continental and sophisticated as Paris. A desire for secession burns in the hearts and minds of every native from the youngest schoolchild to the most aged citizen. Quebec is a welcoming province, provided visitors stumble through their questions and their menus in the language of the mother country, France.

I used many sources to complete this book, among them a French dictionary, *The Thorne Rooms At The Art Institute of Chicago, Racinet's Full Color Pictorial History of Western Costume,* and the patience of my husband whose retention of languages, particularly French, is truly amazing. For those who have acquired a desire to know more about this fascinating period of history, I recommend the following resources:

Journal of a Voyage to North America, Pierre Charlevoix
Travels in Pennsylvania, 1699, John Bartram
The Fur Trader and the Indian, Lewis Saum
Indians of the Western Great Lakes, William Kinietz
American Primitive Music, Frederick Burton
Pontiac and the Indian Uprising, Howard Peckham
The Canadian Frontier 1534–1760, W.J. Eccles
Montcalm and Wolfe, Francis Parkman

Prologue

Red Wing of the Owahki clan stood and stretched to his full height. He was tall and lean, and in the leaping light of the council fire, his arrogant high-boned face reflected none of the inner turmoil crowding his mind. War chief of the Anishinabe, Red Wing was known for his courage and wisdom, but he was still very young. He called upon Kitche Manido, the Creator of Life, to show him the way.

With the predatory grace of a timber wolf, Red Wing lifted his stern hawk-nosed profile to the night sky, raised his arms, and howled. Ishkoodah, the comet, stopped for a timeless instant to shake out her fiery tresses and caress the face of her worshipper before continuing her journey down the pathway of the stars. The heavens rumbled and grew dark. The sky opened and sheets of blinding rain poured down. The fire hissed and died. Kitche Manido had spoken. The Anishinabe would join their Huron and Algonquian brothers and ally themselves with the French to drive the hated English from the sacred hunting grounds of their people.

Twenty leagues to the east, across dark forests and roaring waterfalls, the Ottawa, the St. Maurice, and the Saguenay Rivers poured into the St. Lawrence. On the banks of the massive seaway, three figures, curled in beaver skins, lay on the damp ground.

With a curse, Dominic Jolliet pulled the pelt over his face and prepared to wait out the downpour. Few wraps were as effective against the wet as the dense, water-resistant fur of the beaver. There was no other shelter and it was a two-day journey to the Ojibwa village of Bowating, or as the French called it, *Sault Sainte Marie,* the Place at the Falls.

Dominic lifted his fur to glance briefly at the Indian scouts. His eyes widened. *"Sacrebleu,"* he muttered, reaching for his knife.

Wah-Wah-Tay-See and his brother, Wa-emboesh-kaa squatted on their haunches, staring at the sky. A crooked flash of light illuminated the clearing, revealing triumphant smiles on their dark, rain-washed faces. In perfect synchronization they stood and moved swiftly, silently, a combination of grace and violence, to where the white man lay.

Dominic steadied his knife against his palm and bunched his muscles, preparing to spring. Blood pulsed through his veins and pounded in his temples. His eyes narrowed. His hands were steady. For one bittersweet moment he thought of his father and felt remorse. *Henri Jolliet, Duc de Lorraine,* deserved better than the son he had been given. *"Je vous demánde pardon, mon père,"* he whispered. "Forgive me."

* * *

Two days south as the bald eagle flies, in the mineral-rich valley of the Hudson River, Alexandra Winthrop stood by the window, shivering in her thin nightgown. Wind, laced with the promise of rain, rattled at the doors and windowpanes. It stole through the cracks in the mortar of the sturdy log-framed house, rustling the curtains and whipping up the dying embers of the hearth fire.

Julia tossed restlessly in the large bedroom upstairs. Beside her, the baby slept soundly. In the loft at the back of the house, six-year-old Travis breathed the deep sleep of the unconscious. Only Alexandra was awake.

She rubbed her arms against the cold. Her skin prickled and the hair rose on the back of her neck. This ominous feeling was new to her. Why wouldn't Julia be sensible and return to England? James Graham was dead. The Duke of Leicester had long since forgiven his granddaughter for her unsuitable marriage. He wanted her home. An uncivilized wilderness was no place for a widow with two children.

Lightning streaked across the sky. Alexandra's eyes widened. Was there movement in the dark forest beyond the clearing or was it merely her imagination? Julia often teased her with the bantering affection of an older sister, saying that she saw too much. Alexandra knew it was the artist in her. Where others saw only the scene, she saw dark and light, color and shadow, movement and depth.

She had been blessed with an unusual and powerful gift. Behind the bones of a face she could detect deception and greed, character and wisdom. When she painted a portrait, her fingers moved quickly, instinctively, her brush finding the colors and shades and tints, exposing the souls of sinner and saint and those that lay somewhere between.

Thunder rumbled in the distance. A wolf howled. Beyond the trees, something glinted silver in the night. A foreboding, darker and more dangerous than anything she'd felt before, consumed her. Unshed tears burned beneath her eyelids. Alexandra turned toward the stairs. She was filled with a sudden, inexplicable urge to stop time and hold Julia in a crushing, protective embrace.

Chapter 1

"Do you think Julia is happy, Anthony?" Alexandra Winthrop's golden eyes searched her partner's face as they waited for their turn in the quadrille.

He squeezed her arm. "As happy as can be expected, my love." He smiled reassuringly. "I've seen her dance several times. I'd not expected that."

Alexandra nodded, a worried frown creasing her brow. "Will you excuse me for a moment? She is standing by herself and I don't think she should be alone."

"As you wish." Smiling tenderly at his betrothed, Captain Anthony Doddridge watched her cross the room to her sister's side.

He did not question his amazing good fortune. It was enough that Alexandra Winthrop had agreed to marry him. Why the most sought-after young lady in London should bestow her hand and heart on a titleless second son and follow him across an ocean and into the wilderness of North America was a mystery he had no desire to unravel. There were rumors that she had been disappointed in love, but he gave no credence to such gossip. Alexandra was only nineteen-years-old, much too young for a serious affair of the heart. He wished they could be wed immediately. But this business with Julia must be settled first.

Anthony mopped his brow with a handkerchief. It was late August and terribly hot. Too hot for dancing. He made his way to the punch bowl and downed two cups in swift succession.

This house party had been Alexandra's idea. The men living in the Connecticut River Territory had recently returned from trapping in the north. In their absence the women and children had retreated to safety behind the stout walls of Fort Edward. For months they had lived, worked, and slept in the stifling, crowded quarters of the English fort. Living in constant fear of an Indian attack, anxious mothers had insisted their children stay within the confines of the walls, hardening their hearts against the grumbling of healthy children lured by the brilliant blue of a summer sky and the cool green promise of the woods.

Six weeks before, when the men had returned laden with pelts, the grateful settlers had returned to their abandoned farmhouses and overgrown gardens, anxious to resume their solitary lives.

Julia and her children had returned to their home also. It was the first harvest she would be without her husband. At Fort Edward, with the men gone, the loss of James Graham hadn't been quite so unbearable. Aching with sympathy, Alexandra had watched her sister's face as husbands and fathers returned to claim their families.

Even though Julia knew without a doubt that James had been reported dead, she couldn't help hoping for a miracle. Perhaps, she confided to Alexandra, the messenger had mistaken his identity. Perhaps he would return after all, tanned and healthy, to catch her up in his arms and scratch her face with his whiskered cheeks. His hearty laugh would resound against the wooden beams of the cheerful kitchen, waking the children. He would lift Travis against his massive chest and tickle Abigail's baby cheeks until she laughed out loud, revealing the first glimmer of white protruding from toothless gums.

By the time the last group of men had returned to the fort, James had been dead for six months and Julia was reconciled to her grief. It was then that Alexandra convinced her sister to give a party. If Julia could not be persuaded to return to England, she should marry again and as quickly as possible. The wilderness was a dangerous place for a woman with two small children. Julia was still very beautiful and there were unattached men at Fort Edward.

Across the crowded room, Anthony's eyes met Alexandra's. She returned his grin with a rueful smile. The affection between them was strong and he knew exactly what she was thinking. The stamping feet and clapping hands, the calico-clad women and shaggy men were worlds away from the elegant salons and ballrooms of London and Paris.

If Julia hadn't committed a shocking mésalliance and married far beneath her, Alexandra would never known such a world existed. If the Duke of Leicester hadn't had a change of heart and a strong desire to see his great-grandchildren, Julia would have been consigned to the devil and Alexandra would have remained in the Leicester town house writing letters to her betrothed from London.

Captain Doddridge leaned against the wall and stared at the two sisters. Anyone with eyes in his head would have guessed that Julianne and Alexandra Winthrop were related. It wasn't a similarity of feature that gave away their relationship. It was a kinship of soul, an alive awareness and appreciation for life that distinguished them from every other woman of their class. Their ready laughter and swift compassion, their sparkling wit and straightforward manner of speaking, their cheerful optimism in the face of bleakness were characteristics exclusive to the two of them alone. In the jaded cities of London and Paris, they had stood out as unusual. Here in the backwoods of Colonial New England, they were unparalleled in charm and uniqueness.

Like all the Winthrop women, they were slightly above medium height and very slender. Julianne was classically beautiful, with dark eyes and black hair, while Alexandra—

Captain Doddridge paused and drew a shuddering breath. There was no describing Alexandra. One had only to see her to understand why. He watched her from across the room, her lips parted, her smooth chestnut hair and golden eyes shining in the candlelight. She was speaking earnestly to Julia. Anthony Doddridge sighed. He had given up all hope of persuading Leicester's eldest granddaughter to return to England, but obviously Alexandra had not.

"Are you pleased, Julia?" Alexandra's speaking eyes carried a silent plea.

Julia squeezed her sister's hand. "It's a lovely party, Alix. I know why you did it and I'm very grateful." Her lips twitched. "It certainly has served its purpose."

Alexandra, straightforward to a fault, didn't feign ignorance. "I hoped it would. This isn't the place for you, Julia. Perhaps, with James beside you, it would have served, but now—" she stopped, hoping she had not presumed too much.

Julia nodded. "You are right, of course." She bit her lip. "What of Grandfather? Has he truly forgiven me? I'd not want to take the children where they're not welcome."

Alexandra laughed. "Grandfather will take one look at Travis and Abigail and be so smitten that he'll hardly notice either of us at all." Her voice lowered and she turned to meet her sister's dark eyes. "The last seven years haven't been easy for Grandmother, Julia," she confessed. "She misses you very much."

Julia reached out and drew her sister into her arms. "I

imagine it was very hard for you to be the Duke of Leicester's only grandchild. Poor Alix. I'll come home and help you bear the burden."

Enveloped in the softly scented arms, Alexandra relaxed for the first time since she had sailed into Boston Harbor two months ago. Her mission had been successfully accomplished. Julianne was coming home.

The last guests were already out of sight, down the dark path toward their homes or the fort. They kept close together, their holiday spirits subdued. The men walked on the outside of the path, their muskets ready for an unanticipated Indian attack. Anthony stood in the doorway holding Alexandra's hands. He was a solidly built man and quite distinguished looking in his blue coat and white breeches. He glanced at Julia, who was blowing out the candles and pulling the furniture back into place in the drawing room.

"I won't be able to see you tomorrow," he said softly to Alexandra. "The colonial militia will be arriving from Albany and I must be there to greet them."

"Her eyes glowed with happiness. "Julia has agreed to come home, Anthony. Isn't it wonderful? We can leave as soon as transport can be arranged."

He ached to pull her into his arms and cover her lips with his own. Mindful of Julia's presence, he soothed his frustrated sensibilities by squeezing her hands and gazing into her eyes. She was so beautiful. Her copper-colored hair was pulled smoothly away from her face and caught in a bow at the back of her neck where it fell in soft waves to her waist. Her skin was pale olive, with an apricot tint on her cheeks and lips. Her features were fine-boned and clearly formed. But it was her eyes that had first caught his attention and held him still. Huge and thickly lashed, they were a color he had never seen before, somewhere between brown and gold, amber and hazel, filled with light and dark. They lit her face, illuminating her features to such warmth that he often broke off in the middle of his conversation to stare at her in fascinated wonder.

"I had hoped we could be married before you returned to England," he said.

"Oh, Anthony." Alexandra looked stricken. "I couldn't do that to Grandmother. She has her heart set on our marrying at Leicester. After Julia's elopement, I couldn't deprive her of another wedding. Surely you can understand that."

He sighed. "Of course, my dear. We'll do whatever makes you happy, but I won't be leaving for England until March. Six months without you seems a very long time."

She smiled and the still beauty of her face lit to heart-shattering loveliness. "We've all our lives ahead. Neither of us would want to deprive two old people of their greatest pleasure." She gestured in the direction of the departed guests. "Hurry now and catch up. They'll bar the gate."

Anthony Doddridge had been neatly outmaneuvered. Bowing, he bid good night to Julia and made his way down the path after the others.

"Do you love him, Alix?" Julia's voice was low and devoid of all expression.

Alexandra turned quickly and caught an unusual look on her sister's face. "Why do you ask me that?"

Julia considered her answer carefully before speaking. "He hardly seems the sort of man you would marry. He's very pleasant, of course," she amended hastily, "and it's plain that he loves you dearly, but—" She searched Alexandra's face. "—are you sure, Alix? Can you love someone so very predictable and so—" She hesitated. "—so stuffy?"

Alexandra's eyes blazed an angry gold. "How dare you criticize Anthony. He's a kind and wonderful man."

"I can see that," replied Julia. "But kindness is a poor substitute for fire, my love. Are you so anxious to be away from Leicester that you would sell your body and soul to a man who inspires nothing more than fondness in your heart? You are very young." Her face softened. "What of love, Alix, and passion?" She looked directly at her sister. "What of Dominic Jolliet?"

Alexandra's pale face, surrounded by the burnished copper of her hair, was like a pure-white cameo against the darkness of the room. She could have been carved from marble, so still and cold was her expression. When she spoke, her voice was clear and measured and filled with a bitterness her sister had never heard before. "You will never speak of him again. Do you understand, Julia? Never mention his name to me for as long as you live."

Julia opened her mouth to speak and then closed it again without saying anything. Nodding, she climbed the stairs to the room she shared with the baby. At the top of the landing she turned. "I beg your pardon, Alexandra. My intention was not to upset you."

For the rest of her life, Alexandra was to remember her sister's words, eternally grateful that Julia's forgiving nature would not allow them to part in anger.

It happened all at once—the blazing dawn heralding a lovely summer's day, the loud pounding on the wooden door, the ear-splitting yells that couldn't possibly be human, and the cold terrible, heart-shattering fear that turned Alexandra to stone and rooted her feet to the floor of the loft.

Before she could think, painted bodies swarmed through the door, filling the room. A bronzed, bare-chested red man twisted her arm behind her back, pulled her against his chest, and forced her down the narrow stairs.

Alexandra's wits returned. Anthony and Fort Edward were only footsteps away. If she screamed loudly enough, perhaps the fort would be roused. A small whimpering moan interrupted her thoughts. She turned toward the sound. Travis was cornered in the kitchen, his blue eyes wide with shock and fear. Standing before him was a savage brandishing an enormous tomahawk.

Seconds passed in agonizing indecision. What would

happen to them if her shout did not penetrate the walls of Fort Edward? Would they kill her? What of Julia and the children?

She could not bear it. She, Lady Alexandra Winthrop, the toast of London and beloved granddaughter of the Duke of Leicester, would never be an Indian captive. Twisting out of her captor's grasp, Alexandra opened her mouth to scream.

A powerful hand locked around her waist, crushing the breath from her lungs. Even through her terror, she could smell the unmistakable odor of her captor's body. He smelled of sweat and rancid bear grease. She wrinkled her nose as he dragged her down the stairs and into the sitting room. Indians, half-naked and painted beyond human recognition, were tearing apart furniture and storage chests, stuffing food and clothing into sacks and slicing open pillows and mattresses.

Alexandra tried to pull away, but a brutal turn of her arm jerked her back against the chest of her painted, rank-smelling captor. He pulled her outside into the clearing. Another Indian, his face hideously painted red and black, held Julia, while still another clutched Abigail to his breast.

With a shuddering sob, Travis threw himself against his mother and buried his face in her skirts.

"Hush, love," she whispered, trying to keep the fear from her voice. Her hands were tied behind her, her eyes on the Indian who held her baby.

They were arguing among themselves, using threatening gestures and pointing to the children. Julia's face was deathly white. Alexandra watched with her heart in her throat. It was obvious they were deciding whether to kill them or take them prisoners. Suddenly one of them, a sinister savage with a sloping forehead stepped forward and uttered a harsh command. He frowned at the two women, his flat black eyes darting from Julia to Alexandra.

Scowling at their inadequate clothing, he jerked open the sack he carried and pulled out two dresses, gesturing for the women to put them on. Their arms were released. Gratefully, Alexandra pulled on the dress over her shift. Julia had finished with her buttons and was holding out her arms for Abigail. With tentative hand motions, she tried to make the Indian understand that she wished to hold her baby.

The savage stared at her, uncomprehending, until her hand touched Abigail's blanket. He jerked the baby away roughly. Abigail began to wail. He held her away from him and lifted his tomahawk menacingly.

"Dear God, no!" Julia cried out.

Again the leader stepped in. He barked out a single guttural sound. Without arguing, Abigail's captor shoved the child into her mother's arms. Julia bent her head over the baby's coppery curls and uttered a swift and fervent prayer of thanksgiving. Unbuttoning her chemise, she put the child to her breast. Immediately, Abigail's wails ceased.

Alexandra drew a long and shaky breath. Her arm was numb from the unrelenting grasp on her wrist. She was half-carried, half-dragged into the thickest part of the forest away from any visible path. Thorns and pebbles dug into her bare feet and tree branches slapped against her cheeks. She looked longingly back in the direction of Fort Edward. The Indians were pushing their prisoners at a merciless pace and the strong wooden walls she had once despised were quickly fading into the distance. Julia was directly ahead of her. She pitched her voice low for her sister's ears alone.

"They will follow us, won't they Julia?"

There was the slightest hesitation before the answer drifted back to her. "No, they won't follow us. Even the greenest soldier knows that to do so means instant death for prisoners. Our only hope lies in our being sold to the French and ransomed back later."

The savage poked Alexandra in the back. "No talk," he ordered. "Walk faster."

With a strangled sob, she lowered he head, her half-naked captor pushing her from behind, deeper and deeper into the woods.

Chapter 2

Dominic Jolliet accepted the tobacco pipe, puffed twice, and returned it to Red Wing. It was late and the journey had been long. He had traveled more than three hundred leagues in less than ten days, an unheard of journey even for a *coureur de bois*. Inside the wigwam the furs were soft and the good French brandy potent. His eyelids began to droop.

Red Wing, War Chief of the Ojibwa, spoke in the guttural, single-syllabic language of the Algonquian. "We have smoked the pipe with our Huron and Algonquian brothers. Soon we march to Three Rivers and join with our French father, General Montcalm, to make war on the English and Iroquois. Will the *coureurs* join with their countrymen and help to regain our hunting grounds?"

Dominic's eyes snapped open. So that was the way of it. His native scouts had been unusually silent, their dark faces flat and expressionless, as they'd paddled the canoe eastward. How could they have known? Wah-Wah-Tay-See and Wa-emboesh-kah had been with him for the entire season. Nowhere during their journey had they come upon another human, Indian or white, to relay such news. He remembered the night of the storm when their faces had been transformed by a vision and he had feared for his life. Dominic's mouth twisted downward in a rueful grimace. He was closer to the Indian than most white men, but their ways were still a mystery to him.

"I know nothing of my people's plans," Dominic replied, unwilling to commit himself. "I shall leave tomorrow and seek out Governor Vaudreuil in Montreal."

Red Wing nodded and, in a gesture of friendship, used Dominic's Indian name. "Night Wind is wise to seek the advice of his elders. We will meet after the new moon in Bowating. Then you will tell me of your decision."

The young chief's face was lined with strain. With intuitive perception, Dominic realized that Red Wing was not in favor of the Ojibwa joining the alliance.

"Such a decision is not to be taken lightly," Dominic hedged, hoping to persuade the young war chief to reveal his private doubts. He had not long to wait.

"It is foolish." Red Wing shook his head sadly. "But we have no choice. Once my people were a mighty nation living near the great water of the Canadas. The white man has pushed us west to the fresh water lakes. The Anishinabe suffered and died from the white man's pox. After drinking the white man's liquor, he became worthless at hunting and fishing with the bow and arrow. Our women grew lazy. With the white man's beads and metal pots, his cloth and his needles, they have forgotten the ways of our ancestors. The white man exchanges a single needle or a handful of beads for the finest beaver pelts in the Canadas. Our lands no longer abound with fish and beaver. We must journey farther and farther into the land of the Sioux to bring back enough furs to survive."

His almond-shaped eyes looked steadily into the Frenchman's. "Once there was enough land for both the Iroquois and the Algonquian. More and more English land on our shores every day. Soon there will be room for only one of us. The French do not despise us as the English do. They marry our women and educate our children in the ways of the white man." He smiled at Dominic. "Like you, my friend, they take Indian names, stay in our villages, and learn the ways of the free people. If only one nation of white man is left in the Americas, we prefer that it be the French." With a fluid, graceful movement, Red Wing stood. "Sleep well, Night Wind. Think carefully on what I've told you." With that, he was gone, leaving Dominic to stare thoughtfully into the licking flames of the fire.

Red Wing had shown unusual wisdom at a young age. His position had been thrust upon him earlier than upon most. There had simply been no one else among the Ojibwa, or Anishinabe as they called themselves, with the combination of strategy and battle skill, of leadership and caution, as the tall young Indian with sorrow in his eyes.

Dominic stretched out his long legs and sighed. Tomorrow, he would leave for Montreal and seek audience with the governor. What would this mean for the *coureurs*? He was not foolish enough to believe there was a *coureur* alive with any allegiance to his mother country. Most were expatriots, forced to flee from their homeland for committing the unpardonable crime of insulting a nobleman or stealing a loaf of bread to feed their families. They had fared well in this new world where the old rules meant nothing. Anyone who had seen the fur-hunters at work was lost in admiration for these men of iron who combined the astuteness of the Indian with the natural ingenuity of the Frenchman. Without exception, they all shared something in their past which they preferred to keep hidden.

Dominic Jolliet was a nobleman, not a criminal. But that was the only difference between him and the sun-browned men who paddled their canoes down the St. Lawrence River. His brown, leanly muscled body and sinewy grace had grown even more muscled and bronzed as he'd waded through water up to his armpits, balancing a birchbark canoe on his shoulders and stepping over rocks so sharp and pointed that his feet ran red with blood. The taste for danger was inherent in him. He smoked the sweet pungent Indian tobacco, counting the distance between two stops by the number of clay pipes he consumed. In the waters of the great lakes, he was bold enough to cross the bays in a direct line, instead of hugging the coast, to avoid increasing the distance of his route. He could look at the horizon and forecast the temperature twelve hours ahead and, with the grim endurance of the native, he withstood cold and storms and flies and mosquitoes, shaming even the most experienced of trappers.

When he camped for the night with others of his trade, he sang the songs of the *coureur,* his dark eyes warming with laughter, his songs raucous, his jokes earthy and ribald, his teeth flashing white against the brown of his face. He entertained them with stories of Paris and London, of great lords who minced down the street wearing red-heeled shoes and touched perfumed handkerchiefs to their noses. He told of painted ladies wearing wigs of such height that birds could be seen perched on top of their heads. He told of the king and his mistresses. He told of the simpering foppishness of the royal bastards. He told of his father, the *Duc de Lorraine,* who had followed his only son to Montreal and of Adrien Jolliet, his uncle, the greatest fur trader of them all.

If anyone was ever foolish enough to question why young Jolliet never mentioned his mother or why a wealthy and extremely handsome young man would choose to forgo the delights of Paris to travel the trails of the *coureur de bois,* he soon learned to curtail his curiosity. One arctic glance from Dominic's Satan-dark eyes quickly silenced him. The heir to the ancient House of Lorraine was blessed with a noble name and a silver tongue. But there was one secret he would not share, not even with his priest.

For Dominic, raised amidst the color and culture of Paris and the glittering wonder of *Versailles,* Montreal was a simple backwoods village. Still, it was very much a French village. Tidy, whitewashed cottages dotted the St. Lawrence River and black, gabled roofs soared to the sky. Pointed church steeples and stone towers hovered menacingly over the *Rue de St. Paul,* and looming above all, was a steep, rocky hill.

Paddling his canoe to the landing beach, Dominic jumped into icy water up to his knees and dragged the vessel to shore. The harbor clerk called a greeting and Dominic responded by flipping a shiny *louis* into the boy's hand and disappearing through the gate.

It was night and the streets were narrow and dark, but he would have known his way blindfolded. Turning into a wide street, he stopped before an elegant home and pounded on the door. Moments passed and finally it opened, spilling light and warmth into the night.

The haughty features of the majordomo broke into a welcoming smile. *"Monsieur le Marquis,"* the servant began, *"Comment allez-vous?"*

"Well, Marceau. How is my father?"

"As well as can be expected, m'lord. He will be even better now that you have returned."

Something flickered in Dominic's dark, handsome face and then disappeared. "Where is he now?"

"He has retired for the night," the majordomo answered. "Shall I announce you?"

"I'll announce myself." Dominic headed for the stairs. Turning to look back, he surprised an anxious look on the servant's face. "Never fear, Marceau," he reassured him. "This time I shall not upset him. I have come only to catch up on French politics."

Relief cleared up the troubled expression on the old man's face. "Shall I send up a pot of *chocolat,* m'lord? It was ever your favorite."

The lean, hawkish face of the young man gentled momentarily. "I should like that very much," he said proceeding up the stairs to his father's room.

His Grace, the *Duc de Lorraine,* was seated at his desk

writing a letter when Dominic opened the door. He did not look up, but continued to write until he was finished.

Dominic did not expect the interview with his father to be pleasant. It never was. But he did not expect to be ignored. He felt his temper rise and set his teeth, waiting to be recognized.

When the *duc* had finished with his letter, he folded and sealed it. Finally, he looked at his son. "You may sit, Dominic."

"I prefer to stand, sir."

The cold gray eyes surveyed him deliberately, taking in the stained buckskin and unpowdered hair. Dominic flushed, wishing for the hundredth time that he could read his father's thoughts.

"You are hardly dressed for an evening visit, my son. I suppose I should consider myself honored that you have decided to call on me at all."

"There is rumor that France will go to war with England. I came to verify it."

"Indeed." The *duc's* mouth turned down disdainfully. "Where did you receive that priceless bit of information? In the hovel of a savage, perhaps?"

"As a matter of fact, that is exactly where I learned of it," replied Dominic.

The *duc* lifted his glass and surveyed his son. "You must forgive my declining years, Dominic, but am I to believe from this display of unusual interest that you are once again concerned with the fortunes of your country?"

"Not at all," replied Dominic smoothly. "I care only for the future of my business, *mon père*. If the French go to war against the English, the Indian tribes will take sides. It will be too dangerous to trap in the interior."

"I see." The older man frowned and drummed his fingers on the desk. He decided to change his approach. "Why must it always be this way between us, *mon fils?* Surely you have come to terms with your heritage by now."

Dominic's eyes darkened with anger. "We will not speak of my heritage, Father."

Pain reflected itself in the ravaged countenance of the *duc*. "How long will you continue to punish yourself for events that were beyond your control?"

"If you have nothing of importance to report to me, I shall take my leave of you now," replied his son in icy tones.

"Dominic!" The single harsh cry stopped him at the door. He waited for his father to continue.

The *duc* clenched his shaking hands. "What you have heard is correct. Already Huron and Ojibwa war parties have attacked settlements in the New England colonies. Prisoners will be taken and held for ransom. I met with Governor Vaudreuil only this morning. Montcalm is to clear the north of English forts by whatever means he deems suitable. Paris is crying out for furs and the cost has become too dear. We must prevent the English from trading with the savages."

Dominic cursed under his breath and turned toward his father. "This will mean full-scale war."

"Where will you stand, my son?"

A bitter smile touched Dominic's face. "Where I've stood for the past two years, *mon père*. With myself."

A muscle leaped in the older man's jaw. "She was only one woman, Dominic. In all of France, no other would have refused you. *Parbleu!* It is still the same. Trust me in this. Come home to Paris. One woman is very much like another."

The *duc* shrank before the blazing heat in his son's eyes. He remembered that Dominic's mother had eyes just that angry, fathomless black.

"Spare me your platitudes." The relentless voice mocked him. "We've had this discussion before. I warned you of what would happen if you spoke of it again." He opened the door and was gone.

The *duc's* head dropped into his hands. "*Adieu, mon fils.* Take care."

Dominic strode down the hall to his bedchamber. At first he considered storming out, unwilling to spend even one night under the same roof as the man who had sired him. When the angry drumming of his blood quieted, he realized it would be foolish to leave at this hour. This was his home, after all, built on profits gleaned over the past two years. His father was merely a guest, albeit a permanent one. He cursed fluently. *Sacrebleu!* The man was stubborn. It was past time for him to return to France.

Flinging himself into a chair, he stared into the welcoming fire. Dominic recognized the sweet smell of *chocolat* rising from the pot on the low table at his side. Marceau was ever efficient. He poured himself a cup of the dark brew and drank. The flames hissed and danced, curling the edges of the dry wood. The glowing firelight reminded him of red hair, Alexandra's hair. *Mon Dieu!* Would the searing pain never leave him? Would his breath catch in his throat and his eyes forever be drawn to every slender, titian-haired figure who passed him on the street? His head fell back and his eyes closed. His resistance was low and for the first time in two years he gave up the struggle and allowed the pain and the memories to flow through him.

Chapter 3

Alexandra Winthrop wasn't a beauty in the classical sense, but only a blind man would pass her by in a crowd. She was little more than a child when her grandfather brought her to Paris for the season, but from the beginning she had taken the nobility by storm. Her cinnamon-brown hair, dark in the shadows, flame-red in the sunlight, the hazel-gold eyes and honey-tinted skin gave her an elfin loveliness most unusual in that city of voluptuous, round-faced beauties.

She was fine-featured with a wide expressive mouth, a *retroussé* nose and a small, square chin. Slender to the point of thinness, she had a straightforward way of looking into a man's eyes and saying exactly what she thought. Dominic grinned. That in itself had been a daunting experience for many a simpering, high-heeled gentleman accustomed to the more conventional rules of flirtation.

Intelligent and compassionate, Alexandra was blessed with an artist's sensitivity for color and detail. Dominic had recognized her talent immediately. It had been her appreciation for art that first attracted him. *Ingénues* normally held no appeal for him. He preferred worldly, more experienced women. But he was somewhat of a patron of the arts and when he visited the royal gallery at *Versailles* and saw the glowing reverence on her face as she gazed at the exhibit of Titian paintings, he had been intrigued. It was the fashion for women to express boredom at the sights of Paris, but this young woman was most definitely not bored. Dominic, looking down into her animated face, hadn't believed she had ever experienced such an emotion.

As their acquaintance had progressed, he'd grown to respect and then marvel at her unusual ability. With her passion for perfection and the unusual way she had of contrasting light against dark, she had developed a style reminiscent of the early Rembrandts. Because she was a noblewoman, her talent could never be more than a hobby, but for Alexandra, whose every need was anticipated by her adoring grandparents, it had been enough. And before long, it had been enough for Dominic just to watch her, to drink in her passion for life, her appreciation for the unusual, to feel her hand tucked beneath his arm, to allow her low, musical voice to heal the jaded edges of his spirit.

There had been that incredible night, on the balcony of Madame De Becque's ballroom, when he had given in to the uncontrollable urge to feel her mouth against his. Their noses had bumped awkwardly and then her lips had parted. She was young, but she wasn't shy. Tentatively, afraid of scaring her, Dominic had tasted the polished smoothness of her teeth, and then, eagerness giving him courage, he'd ventured farther into the sweetness of her mouth.

He felt the start of her response and the exquisite pressure of her hands, small and cool, as they threaded through the hair at the back of his neck. Every bone in her beautiful, reed-thin body had melted against him. For the first time in his life, Dominic Jolliet, Marquis de Villiers, scion of a long line of men famous for their reputation with women, played the gentleman. He stepped back. Taking a deep breath, he lifted her hand to his mouth and escorted her back into the ballroom.

Dominic had known his feelings for this young English mademoiselle went deeper than anything he had ever felt before. Having had more than his fair share of experience, he had believed he knew Alexandra's mind as well. *Parbleu!* He had been sure of it. She wasn't a woman to give her favors without first giving her heart.

For the first time in his life, his instincts had failed him. Never before had he so misjudged a woman. He had played the fool, taken in by a breathtaking smile and a pair of golden eyes. His face burned when he recalled that incredible interview with his father and then the even more incredible one with the English duke.

Dominic would never again saunter down the *Rue de Chambreau* dressed in gold lace and faultless small clothes. Never again would he eat soft, white rolls and drink spiced *chocolat* at the *Café de Michelle*. The *Marquis de Villiers* had disappeared forever. He was now Dominic Jolliet of Montreal. Because he had committed the unpardonable crime of falling in love with Leicester's granddaughter, the entire course of his life had been irrevocably changed.

Alexandra struggled to maintain the grueling pace set by the war party. She and Julia took turns carrying the baby and pulling Travis along by the hand. The Indians were obviously in a hurry and the trail was overgrown and narrow. More than once, when she stopped to catch her breath, Alexandra felt the stinging lash of a whip against her legs. Under her breath she bitterly cursed the half-naked savage who brought up the rear.

"Alix," Travis whined and tugged at her skirt. "I'm thirsty." He glanced longingly at the small stream running beside the trail. They had marched all day without food or water, yet there was no indication that the Indians intended to stop.

"Hush, Travis," Alexandra warned him. "Don't make a sound if you can help it."

Tears filled the blue eyes and he nodded miserably. Alexandra's heart went out to him and she felt an unexpected surge of pride. He was only a child and he had stood the pace as well as any of them. His short six-year-old legs had managed the twisted trail without as much as a single complaint until now. Rage flooded through her. Who were these savages who kidnapped women and children, and drove them like dogs through the forest without as much as a bit of food or a sip of water? She hated them! The lean, copper-skinned bodies moving silently through the forest, their expressionless faces, hideously painted, their heads shaved except for a short, stiff thatch of hair sticking up on top, were the embodiment of every evil she could possibly imagine.

At last, when it was too dark to see any farther, they camped for the night on the hard ground. There was still no food or water. Only Abigail, nursing at Julia's breast, fell asleep without hunger pangs gnawing at her stomach.

To complete her humiliation, Alexandra was forced to lie down between two Indians, a rope thrown over her body and under theirs. Her slightest movement would rouse them. They smelled of rancid bear grease. The ground was cold and twigs poked into her back. As the moon rose and night settled in, swarms of mosquitoes attacked her eyes and skin, biting ravenously, drawing blood. Looking up into the star-studded blackness, Alexandra prayed for a swift and merciful death.

She awoke to a chilling drizzle. For the first time in twenty-four hours, they were fed. Rifling through the sacks filled with food and clothing from Julia's home, the red men pulled out bread and meat, dividing it equally among the prisoners and themselves. Alexandra wolfed down the hunk of bread and dried meat she was given.

"Thank God they're feeding us," Julia whispered, barely nibbling at her bread.

"Rest assured it is no great kindness on their part," Alexandra retorted. "They knew we couldn't have walked another mile without food."

Julia's eyes, as dark as midnight, were huge in her pale face. "You don't understand, Alix. If they are willing to feed us, it means they intend to keep us alive."

"Enough talk." The leader waved his tomahawk. "We go now."

Wearily, Alexandra stood and held out her arms for the baby.

"Never mind," Julia said quickly. "I'll take her until I'm tired."

Food and a night's rest had improved Alexandra's disposition. Even the Indians looked less formidable in the light of a new day. By early afternoon Travis had recovered his six-year-old nonchalance. Chattering amiably, he was not at all daunted by the fact that his tall, hatchet-faced captor remained silent.

Days turned into nights and then into days again. How long had it been? One week or two? Alexandra had lost count. Flies took the place of mosquitoes, buzzing around open eyes and noses until her arms grew tired of waving them away. Branches slapped at the tender skin on her arms and face and she tripped more times than she could count on the hem of Julia's dress. She rounded a bend in the trail and stopped suddenly. Her sister lay on the ground, her ankle bent in an unnatural angle, a white line of pain around her mouth.

"Julia." Alexandra ran to her. "What happened? Are you hurt?"

"I'm afraid my bone is broken." Perspiration beaded Julia's brow. "I can't stand on it."

Desperation made Alexandra's voice sharp. "Of course you can. Travis will carry Abigail and you can lean on me."

Julia's smile didn't reach her eyes.

Surprisingly the Indians did not force them to continue. The one Alexandra recognized as the leader left their camp with his bow and arrow and came back with a hawk which he again divided equally among them.

"Alexandra." Julia's voice was soft, but Alexandra could hear every word. Freed of the restrictive cord for several days now, she crawled to where her sister lay on a pillow of leaves.

"If anything should happen to me—" Julia hesitated and bit her lip.

"Nothing will happen to you. We'll be ransomed to the English in no time at all."

"Hush." This time her sister's voice was sharp. "This is no time for fairy tales." She clutched Alexandra's arm. "Take care of my children. Take them back to England. Promise me, Alix, promise me that no matter what happens, you won't leave them behind."

A queer trembling had taken hold of Alexandra, and her voice, when she spoke, sounded as if it came from someone else. "What are you talking about, Julia? Where are you going?"

The dark eyes stared into hers, compelling her to listen. "We are still on the English side of Fort Niagara," she explained. "I believe these Indians are a tribe belonging to the Algonquian nation. It is too dangerous for them to slow their pace before we reach the French border. Don't you see how they cover our trail?" She wet her lips, and for the first time, her voice cracked. "I cannot continue with a broken ankle, Alix. The most I can hope for is that they leave me unharmed. I must know that you won't fail me in this." Her eyes were bright with unshed tears. "It will go easier for me if you say nothing and go with the children willingly. They will have their way in the end, no matter what you do."

Alexandra threw herself into her sister's arms, weeping uncontrollably until Julia pushed her away. With dry eyes, she admonished her. "Stop, Alix. Travis will see you."

Shaking with misery, Alexandra turned over and, burying her head in her arms, sobbed herself to sleep.

In the morning, everyone but Julia was given bread and meat. Alexandra couldn't push the food past her lips, but again Julia scolded her. "You'll need strength for the journey. Please eat, Alix."

The food caught in her throat and sat like lead in the pit of her stomach. After she had finished, the Indian who had dragged her from the loft knelt at her feet. He carried a pair of moccasins. Another Indian knelt before Travis with a smaller pair, painstakingly decorated with beadwork. He slipped them on the boy's feet and Travis grinned.

A painful sob burst from Julia's lips. Travis turned toward his mother. "They've given me shoes, Mama," he said. "Why are you crying?"

"Come here, Travis," his mother said.

Obediently he trotted to her side. She pulled him into her lap and for once he didn't struggle. "You and Abigail are to go on with Alexandra," she said gently. "I won't see you for a very long time. Be a good boy and obey your aunt." She swallowed and kissed him fiercely. "Always remember who you are, Travis. Remember your name and the names of your parents. Say them," she ordered. "Say James and Julianne Graham."

"James and Julianne Graham," the child repeated dutifully.

"Remember to speak English and say your prayers. Promise me, my son."

"I promise, Mama."

Julia smiled. "You are a good, brave boy. God will bless you." She held out her arms for Abigail. Without a word, Alexandra handed over the baby. Fighting back tears, she watched Julia kiss her daughter's cheek and stroke the russet curls. When Alexandra leaned over to take the child, her sister's whisper brushed her cheek. "You carry my heart with you, Alexandra. Do not fail me."

The Indians waited in polite silence for Julia to bid

goodbye to her children. Then they moved on, pushing the captives ahead. With mounting horror, Alexandra realized the tall Indian who had walked with Travis from the day they were captured had stayed behind. That night he caught up with them.

Opening his sack, he pulled out a freshly taken scalp. The hair was wavy and fine and very dark. Julia's hair! Bile rose in Alexandra's throat and her stomach heaved. Turning over onto her stomach, she retched and retched until the world spun dizzily around her and she slipped into merciful blackness.

Chapter 4

One long miserable day ran into another. Sometimes the weather was merciful and the sun bathed Alexandra's face in comforting warmth. Sometimes it rained for hours on end, soaking her hair and her clothing and the thin blanket in which she carried Abigail. Not even the baby's pitiful wails penetrated the thick fog insulating her mind from the horrors she had witnessed. With unseeing eyes, Alexandra passed the breathtaking wonder of the falls at Fort Niagara, crossed Lake Nipissing in a flimsy bark canoe, and forded treacherous rapids at the bend of the Mattawa River. The Indians no longer bothered to cover their tracks. They were in Chippewa country. Michilimackinac, gateway to Lake Michigan, home of the Anishinabe, was close at hand.

"Alix," Travis boasted, holding up a cleverly fashioned slingshot. "Watch me shoot that squirrel from the tree. Chu-a-ka taught me."

For the first time in days, Alexandra felt a small stirring of emotion. She recognized it as anger. "Don't you dare," she said coldly. "These savages know nothing worth know-ing. I want you to stay as far away from them as possible."

The separation from his mother no longer haunted Travis. He was six-years-old and each new day was an adven-ture. He loved striding through the forests and sleeping under the stars. No one bothered him about washing his hands or combing his hair and the Indian moccasins were much more comfortable than his regular shoes. He envied the bronzed, well-muscled bodies of his captors and longed for the time when he would fit his own arrow to a bow and send it flying through the trees. Alexandra's odd behavior disturbed him. He had never seen her so cold and remote. Unconsciously he pulled farther and farther away from her side, preferring the companionship of the Indians.

Their only encounter with white men was at a French fort near Chemblec. Stopping outside the walls, the tall Indian who had first claimed Alexandra took a comb from his sack and began untangling her hair. Then he braided it in two thick plaits. Dipping his fingers into a gourd he smeared a red, sticky substance over her cheeks and chin. When he had finished he turned to Travis and did the same.

Alexandra was past caring what she looked like. Numbly, she followed the Indians into the fort. A babble of French voices penetrated the murky haze clouding her brain. It was the first civilized conversation she had heard in weeks and the sweet sounds of the familiar language made her weep.

"Why, it's a white girl with a baby," a woman exclaimed glancing at Alexandra's red braids in horror. "*La pauvre petite.*" Her eyes were warm with pity.

Alexandra heard the sympathy in her voice and turned, speaking in perfect French. "*S'il vous plaît, madame,*" she began, "can you help us?"

Travis's Indian jabbed her in the back with his finger. "No talk. White squaw keep silent."

Alexandra bit her lip and allowed him to lead her into

a small lean-to built along the inside wall. She slumped down, cradling Abigail in her arms. Later, Travis was brought in. His blond hair had been completely shaved except for a single scalp lock. This had been saturated with bear grease so that it stood up stiffly on top of his head.

"Oh, Travis," whispered Alexandra. "What have they done to you?"

Travis rubbed his scalp and grimaced. "My head hurts. I think it's bleeding."

Alexandra looked at the superficial knife wounds marking his pink skin. "You'll be all right, darling," she replied. "Don't worry. It will grow back."

The child yawned and curled up on a pile of straw in the corner. "I'm hungry. Do you think they'll feed us tonight?"

"Go to sleep," Alexandra replied wearily. "I'll wake you if they bring food."

Abigail whimpered and kicked ineffectually at her blanket. She hadn't cried for several days. It no longer brought her nourishment. Soon she was asleep, her thumb wedged firmly in her mouth. Alexandra ignored the rumbling of her stomach and closed her eyes. Moments later she was wide awake. A scratching noise accompanied by a hushed whisper called out to her. Quickly she moved toward the door.

"Who is it?"

"I am Sylvie Marcheroix," a feminine voice answered. "I saw you come in today. How can I help you?"

"Thank God!" Tears streamed down Alexandra's face. "Please," she begged. "Can you arrange for the Indians to leave us here? My grandfather will reward you well."

"Who are you, *petite?*"

"Alexandra Winthrop. My grandfather is the Duke of Leicester." The woman's gasp was audible through the wood. "He will spare no expense to repay you for your trouble."

"I will do what I can, *chérie,*" Sylvie promised. "If it

happens that you must continue with the Ojibwas, I will find a way to notify your grandfather.''

"Thank you, *madame*," said Alexandra. "Tell him that Julia is dead."

"Mon Dieu! You poor child. Are the children yours?''

"No. They are my niece and nephew. Julia's children. Travis and Abigail Graham." She stifled a sob. "The baby is ill. She needs milk and food."

"I'll arrange it," the woman promised. "Never fear, *chérie*. That I can do."

True to her word, the following morning milk and gruel were brought into the shed for the baby. Alexandra and Travis were given hot food and bread. They wolfed it down under the anxious eyes of their benefactors.

Sylvie Marcheroix laid her hand on Alexandra's shoulder. "My husband could not convince the Indians to leave you here, Mademoiselle Winthrop. They will take you to their village, which is four days to the west. There you will be adopted by the tribe, replacing family members lost to them. Do not fear, *chérie*. They do not intend to harm you.''

Adopted! The awful word hung in the air. "We are to live with them permanently?" Alexandra's face under the vermilion color was ghostly white.

"I will send word to your grandfather," Sylvie promised. "He will pay the Indians and they will release you."

Alexandra bit her lip. "You would do this for us, your enemies?''

"Our countries may be enemies, *mademoiselle*, but I am still a Christian. You would do the same for me, I am sure." She hugged Alexandra fiercely and stepped back, her eyes bright with unshed tears. "You must be very brave and eat as much as you can. It isn't good to be so dreadfully thin."

"Thank you, *madame*," said Alexandra. She was filled with hope. In time, they would be rescued.

Two days later, she knew their destination was close at hand. They no longer traveled on foot, but in four bark canoes. The Indians paddled these fragile vessels down glinting rivers and across whitewater rapids that no civilized man would have dreamed of crossing. Alexandra closed her eyes and clutched the baby tightly to her breast, praying for survival. At night, her captors danced around a fire, their faces painted, their bodies twisted into strange, animal-like contortions. Despite her revulsion, Alexandra could feel the blood pound through her veins as if some primitive, long-dormant part of her nature had finally awakened.

When they weren't dancing or traveling, the Indians took turns drilling Travis in the syllables of their language. Over and over he would repeat the meaningless phrases until the shiny, copper-skinned heads nodded their satisfaction and Alexandra thought she would scream with frustration.

Finally they reached a narrow strip of beach. Again Alexandra and Travis were painted with the sticky red dye. As they marched on, she noticed that the trees seemed farther apart. Small patches of land had been cleared and crops grew in haphazard fashion between the weeds. Soon they reached the outskirts of an Indian village.

A tremendous howling began. Alexandra hung back, terrified by the clamoring voices. Indian women, clad in deerskin, pressed forward, pulling her hair and pinching her skin. Naked children shouted words she could not understand and dogs barked and leaped at her.

A sharp command cut through the commotion and suddenly there was silence. The women and children formed two lines on either side of a tall, powerfully muscled Indian chief. Alexandra had never seen such massive shoulders. Her startled eyes moved across his bare chest down to the lean waist and breechclout-covered middle to legs as well-defined and muscled as a Greek statue. He was magnificent! The sculpted cheeks and hawkish nose, the feathered bonnet on his head, the mahogany skin and obsidian-dark eyes called out to her. Her fingers itched. If only she could paint him.

Forgetting everything but the overpowering beauty of the tall chief, she walked down the path and stood directly before him. His eyes gleamed and his lips were firm and chiseled, as if a master sculptor had carved them from granite. Entranced, she reached out to trace the iron-hard line of his jaw.

Red Wing recoiled in horror. Never had a prisoner dared so much. Who was this woman who approached him without fear? Her touch was cool and light and she stared at his face as if he were a god. One of the braves broke the silence.

"We have brought this English woman to you, Great Chief. You have been without a mate since the month of the Growing Moon. For too long we have watched your sorrow. She is young and strong and has marched many miles without complaint. The boy we will give to Yellow Moon for the loss of her son." He gestured toward Abigail. "The papoose is sickly and will probably die."

Red Wing nodded and looked again at the woman's face. Her skin stretched tightly across her bones, and her clothing was in rags. But her eyes and hair reminded him of autumn leaves and her color was not the insipid white of most of her race. Most unusual of all, she was not afraid of him. He had the strangest desire to make her smile. Perhaps, if he let her keep the ailing child, she would smile at him.

For a long moment the weight of the Indian's gaze held Alexandra motionless. Then he issued a brief order and turned away. Two older women stepped out of the crowd. One led Travis away. The other motioned for Alexandra to follow her. Through a row of rounded bark buildings and flimsy wigwams she followed the squaw. Hairy circles hung on poles near every doorway. Her stomach heaved as she realized what they were, human scalps.

The woman stopped at the door of a wigwam that looked

more substantial than the others. Alexandra stepped inside and blinked, waiting for her eyes to adjust to the dimness. The overpowering smell of dog, animal skins, and rancid grease nearly choked her. A fire flickered in the center of the dwelling and smoke, thick and cloying, filled the air.

The woman dipped a wooden ladle into a pot hanging over the fire and handed it to Alexandra. The broth was delicious. Sinking to her knees, she drained the ladle and dipped it again into the pot. She remembered the baby. Holding the ladle to Abigail's mouth she tilted it, forcing a few drops into the rosebud lips. Abigail drank greedily. Breathless with relief, Alexandra offered her more, and still more, until the baby turned her head away and closed her eyes.

After another swallow, Alexandra's food-starved stomach rebelled. The smoky heat of the room took its toll, and soon she sank back on the skins, joining her niece in an exhausted sleep.

Red Wing parted the pelts covering the entrance to the wigwam and stepped inside. Firelight threw the pale, chiseled features of the English girl into bold relief. Unlike the round moon faces of the Anishinabe women, her face was narrow, the bones sharp and clear under her skin. He frowned. He hadn't considered taking another wife, but even if he had, it wouldn't be a woman like this. His tastes ran to plump, submissive women who knew how to please a warrior beneath his furs at night. Every instinct told him this white woman would not be in the least submissive. Red Wing stretched out on his blankets. The steady throb of the drums lulled him into a restless sleep. He dreamed of blood and fire and a woman with russet hair and golden eyes.

Chapter 5

Alexandra awoke slowly. Her furs were warm and the wigwam was silent except for the deep, steady breathing of a figure wrapped in blankets on the other side of the fire. For the first time in weeks she had been allowed the luxury of sleeping as long as she pleased. Abigail lay beside her. She was so still that Alexandra knew a moment of fear. Placing her ear against the baby's mouth, she was reassured by a faint stirring of warm breath. Sighing with relief, she lay back on the furs and stretched her legs.

Sounds of daybreak reached her ears. Soft female voices laughed companionably. Dogs barked. A baby cried and was silent again almost immediately. Alexandra looked at the motionless mound covered with blankets. Could the slight body of the old woman who had fed her take up so much room?

The furs covering the entrance were thrown back, and for an instant, light flooded the wigwam. The old woman of the night before stepped inside, motioning for Alexandra to remain silent. She reached for the sleeping baby.

"No," Alexandra protested and pushed her away. The

woman frowned and placed her finger against her lips, gesturing toward the blanketed figure.

"I don't care," Alexandra whispered furiously, forgetting that the squaw would not understand. "You shan't take Abigail. I won't let you."

A movement from the other side of the wigwam caught her eye. Alexandra's eyes widened as the muscular war chief threw aside his blanket and stood up. He looked every bit as formidable as he had in the moonlight. For an instant, she thought she detected a look of surprise in his flat black eyes, but it disappeared instantly. He uttered several terse words to the squaw. She responded and pointed to the baby.

In fluent French he pointed to the woman and addressed Alexandra. "Have no fear. She-Who-Speaks-To-The-River says the papoose needs nourishment. The infant will be returned to you after it is fed."

Alexandra was speechless. She did not protest when the woman lifted Abigail into her arms and carried her out of the wigwam.

"Who are you?" Alexandra's French was more than adequate even though she'd had no occasion to use it for over two years.

"I am Wiskino, Bird-of-the-Red-Wing, War Chief of the Anishinabe." The man's eyes held hers in an unblinking black gaze. "What are you called?"

Her mouth was dry. "Alexandra Winthrop."

A whisper of a smile crossed his carved features. "Al-ex-an-dra." He pronounced it strangely, placing equal emphasis on all syllables.

"What will you do with me?" Her voice no longer cracked.

Red Wing stared at her curiously. Her words were low and musical, like the voices of the women of his people. He searched her face, gauging just how much to tell her. "You will be adopted into the tribe," he said at last.

"Her face whitened. "You mean we won't be ransomed to the French?"

Red Wing shook his head. "You have been chosen to replace those lost to us. No ransom will be asked."

Horror was reflected on Alexandra's face. "But we're English. You can't expect us to live like this." With no recollection of having moved, she stood directly before him, her hand clutching his arm. "Would you like being kidnapped and forced to live in London?"

A flicker of understanding appeared briefly in the black eyes. Red Wing considered her question carefully before answering. "It will be better for the boy to stay here," he decided.

The woman was much too close. He was uncomfortable with the flame-licking desire that had stirred to life in his loins when she touched him. The rigid moral code of his people forbade intimacies between a man and woman until they were united by the Midewiwin. It was of utmost importance that a chief obey tribal law.

Red Wing hadn't had a woman in a long time. He was a war chief, trained from birth to deny all physical needs. The joining of a man and woman drained a man of his strength and robbed him of his reflexes. Still, he had never seen a woman like this before. For one brief, wild moment he considered wrapping her bright hair around his fist, dragging her to his beaver pelts, and assuaging the burning ache she had started in his groin.

He pulled away, horrified at the journey his thoughts had taken. Nodding toward the sack filled with goods from Julia's home, he said, "Take what is yours. The rest will be given away." With a swift, cat-like grace, he glided across the rush-covered floor and out the door.

Alexandra sat down cross-legged and began rummaging through the sack. Her fingers closed around a familiar object. With a thankful cry she pulled out one of her drawing pencils. Dumping the entire contents of the bag on the floor, she soon found her oils and several precious sheets of paper. There was a jeweled brooch that Alexandra recognized as her grandmother's. This, she slipped inside her pocket. Nothing else was familiar to her. Alexandra's lip quivered. There was little left of the belongings Julia had treasured so carefully.

After replacing the contents of the sack and hiding her art supplies beneath the blankets she had slept under the night before, Alexandra ventured to the wigwam entrance and stepped outside. No one paid any attention to her. Mustering her courage, she ventured out in search of Travis. From the entrance of a wigwam close to her own, a woman called out to her in English. With a shock, Alexandra realized that beneath the sun-darkened face and Indian deerskin, the woman's eyes were blue. Alexandra walked across the clearing and sat down beside her.

"Are they treating you well?" the woman asked.

"If being kidnapped and forced to march through the wilderness for weeks on end can be considered well, I suppose I've nothing to complain of," replied Alexandra bitterly.

The woman nodded in sympathy. " 'Tis hard in the beginning. Once you've been adopted, it won't seem so difficult."

Alexandra frowned, disgust evident in the hard set of her mouth. "You can't mean that you would actually think of staying permanently with these savages?"

The white woman flushed under her tan, but her eyes met Alexandra's steadily. "My family is dead. This is the only home I know."

Tears filled Alexandra's eyes. "They killed my sister. I promised her I would take care of the children. Do you know where they are?"

"A small blond boy was taken into the wigwam of Wah-hah-nee. He lost his son two summers ago to the pox."

Alexandra swallowed. She watched the nimble fingers of the woman thread colored beads on strips of deerskin and stitch them into an intricate pattern on the hides stretched before her on the ground. "How long have you been here?" she asked at last.

The woman was silent for a long time. When she finally spoke, her voice was low. "I don't know. Seven or eight years, I think. I was brought here before my fifteenth birthday, at the time of the spring planting. What is the year?"

Alexandra's lips were dry. "Seventeen hundred and fifty-five."

"Then, I've been here nine years. I was born in seventeen hundred and thirty-one." She smiled, proud of her accomplishment.

"How can you bear it?" Alexandra burst out. "Don't you miss being with your own kind? What of books and music and decent clothing?"

The woman eyes widened in astonishment and she stared at Alexandra, noticing for the first time the long slender hands, the cultured speech, the aristocratic bones of her dirt-streaked face, and the rich material of what must have once been a costly gown. "Who are you, mistress?" she asked.

"Alexandra Winthrop."

"I'll warrant 'tis Lady Winthrop in polite society?" the woman replied, nodding wisely.

"Yes," answered Alexandra. "But here it is of no consequence. Alexandra will do nicely. What shall I call you?"

"My Christian name is Sarah, but my husband calls me Blue Jay."

"Your husband?" Alexandra was interrupted by a baby's cry.

An Indian squaw carrying a child stepped out of the doorway behind them. She handed the baby to Sarah.

"This is my son," Sarah announced, smiling into the face of a child who was unmistakably Indian. "Isn't he beautiful?"

Alexandra stared into the black eyes of the half-breed baby. Conflicting emotions tumbled over each other in her mind. She was a daughter of England, reared in a

society that believed itself to be created in God's own image
and superior to any other on earth . . . where a class system
so rigid existed that marriage between a country squire
and a baronet's daughter was considered a shocking mésall-
liance . . . where a lady's abigail did not deign to speak to
a downstair's maid and a majordomo considered himself
infinitely superior to a gardener. Nothing in Alexandra's
entire realm of experience had prepared her for the sight
of an Englishwoman beaming with pride as she held up a
child of mixed blood for another's approval.

The child cooed and waved his arms. Still, Alexandra
remained silent. She looked at Sarah. The woman's eyes
were bright and hard and filled with hurt understanding.
Something in the brilliant blue depths reminded Alexandra of her sister. This woman was a mother just as Julia
had been and she loved her child with the same selfless
devotion that Julia had shown with her children. Suddenly,
Alexandra was ashamed.

She stood. "Wait here," she said, and walked across the
clearing to the wigwam where she had slept the night
before. Pulling out her drawing paper and pencils, Alexandra returned to Sarah's side. She sat cross-legged on the
ground, balancing the paper on her knees and began to
draw using short, deliberate strokes. Within moments, the
outline of a woman with a baby in her arms was recogniz-
able.

Sarah gasped as she watched the skilled fingers bring to
life the distinctive bridge of her own nose, her short upper
lip and high forehead. She laughed delightedly when the
baby's dimple and button-black eyes stared back at her.
Thirty minutes later, she stared, speechless at what had
once been a blank page. The finished likeness was incredible. Sarah raised astonished eyes to Alexandra's face. "This
is beautiful," she breathed in wonder. "I've never seen
anything like it. How can you work so quickly?"

Alexandra brushed the question aside. "I'm pleased that
you approve. 'Tis for you to keep."

Sarah's eyes were very bright. "I've never had a likeness of myself. Thank you very much, Alexandra."

"If you like, I can finish it for you. My oils are in the bag. The Indians must have brought them from Julia's home." A stabbing grief closed her throat. She blinked back tears, unable to continue.

A warm hand covered hers. "Tell me what happened."

The kindness in the sympathetic voice released the ice surrounding Alexandra's heart. Tears welled up in her eyes and spilled over onto her cheeks. "Julia broke her ankle," she whispered. "They scalped her."

Sarah squeezed the shaking hand beneath her own. Her years with the Ojibwas had taught her something of survival. A swiftly moving war party could not stop to tend an injured prisoner. Their lives depended on covering at least twenty miles per day.

"I'm so sorry, Alexandra, but I'm very glad they spared you. The women here are kind enough, but I have waited a very long time for a friend."

The blue eyes brimmed with warmth and Alexandra managed a watery smile. Automatically reaching into her pocket, she froze momentarily and then laughed through her tears.

"What is it?" Sarah asked, disturbed at the note of hysteria in the young Englishwoman's laugh.

"I would very much like a handkerchief," Alexandra explained, "and I just realized that it may be a long while before I have such a luxury."

Sarah bit her lip. Most likely Lady Alexandra Winthrop would never see the likes of a lace handkerchief again. It was too early to break such news to her, but lodges and wigwams throughout the village hummed with rumor. The Englishwoman with the hair of a fox was intended for Wiskino, Bird-of-the-Red-Wing. It would not be a formal coupling until he gave his approval. Sarah knew that that approval would soon be forthcoming. She had been with the women the night before when Alexandra had walked toward Red Wing and fearlessly lifted her hand to touch his cheek.

Sarah had been married for over two years. She knew the meaning of the expression on the war chief's face. If only Alexandra could be prevented from showing her natural revulsion at the thought of mating with an Indian. Red Wing was a popular chief. An insult directed at him would not be taken lightly by his tribe.

"It really isn't such a bad life," Sarah reassured her. "You'll see."

Alexandra wiped her face with the back of her hand. "You're very good, Sarah. When I'm released, I shall tell my grandfather of your kindness. If you truly wish to stay here, so be it. But if you choose otherwise, you may come home with us. I'll do whatever I can to help you begin a new life."

Sarah, her cheeks stained with guilty color, bent to kiss her son's chubby fist. She had lived too long with the Ojibwa. Deception did not come easily. "Thank you, Alexandra. I shall keep that in mind."

Chapter 6

The Duke of Leicester found his wife in the drawing room. She was seated in a red-and-white brocade chair near the fireplace. Her fingers absentmindedly caressed a delicate ivory vase painted to resemble jade imported from China. The duke disliked this room excessively. The lacquered screens, richly carved furniture, and porcelain vases were done in the Oriental style made popular by Inigo Jones. Leicester was an Englishman, and like most Englishmen of his class, he preferred all things British.

He stared at the small, birdlike figure of his wife and frowned. For fifty years she had graced his home and warmed his heart. In an age of economic and political alliances, their union had been an unusual one from the very beginning. Her smile, her touch, the sound of her voice were as necessary to him as breathing. He loved her deeply, irrevocably. For most of their marriage, he had been content with the knowledge that his feelings were reciprocated.

Just as surely as he had known she loved him, he now was just as certain she did not. When had her feelings altered? What was it that had frozen her heart against him? He dismissed the idea of a lover immediately. Liane was a woman of character and high moral integrity, most unusual in her time and class. She would no sooner commit adultery than she would abandon the teachings of her faith. Night after night he racked his brain. It wasn't Phillipe's death that had changed her, nor Anne's. Perhaps it had happened when Julia ran away and married her colonial.

Not for the first time, the duke wondered how a man like himself and this woman of breeding and sensitivity could have spawned two such worthless children. When his granddaughters were born, first Julia and then Alexandra, he had dismissed them as insignificant replicas of their parents. But later, when he had taken them into his home after they were orphaned, the duke realized his mistake. They were spirited and beautiful and proud, every bit as unusual and intelligent as their fascinating grandmother.

Underneath his gruff exterior, Leicester had a healthy respect for the brilliant nuances of his wife's mind. She was gracious and lovely and politically astute. Since his marriage, Leicester's word in Parliament had carried tremendous weight. No one suspected that it was all due to the elegant little Frenchwoman the duke had brought home from Paris to be his duchess.

The fates had been kind. Through Julia and Alexandra Winthrop, he had seen that the proud Leicester tradition could continue. Then Julia had committed the unpardonable sin of eloping with a colonial. In the duke's mind, she had betrayed him. With the thoroughness characteristic of his nature, he had wiped her from his thoughts, instructed his solicitor to exclude her from his will, and centered all his hopes on Alexandra. Phillipe's younger daughter, the child of light and color and laughter, would make the correct political alliance. Her heirs would sit in the House of Lords and rule England for generations to come. Through them, the ancient House of Leicester would be immortal.

The duke looked at his wife's long fingers, at the slender, patrician hands, the fine bones and immaculate, oval nails. His palms began to sweat. How had it all become so muddled? How could he possibly tell her? How could he not?

He wet his lips. "My love," he began.

Liane de Bouvier, Duchess of Leicester, continued to gaze at the architect's table set up by the window. It was erected to serve as an easel and on top sat an unfinished canvas. The brushes, stiffly upright in their vase, carried touches of thick, white paint, as if waiting for the artist to momentarily return.

"What is it, Charles?" Her cultured voice with its trace of a French accent betrayed not the slightest tremor of impatience at the untimely interruption of her thoughts.

The duke cleared his throat. "It appears Captain Doddridge was correct. I've received a letter from a woman at *Fort Chemblec* in Canada. This Frenchwoman," he glanced down at the paper he carried, "by name of Sylvie Marcheroux, claims to have seen Alexandra and the children."

Liane's eyes, enormous dark orbs that reminded him of his granddaughter, were suddenly intent on his face.

"Julia?" she asked.

"Julia is dead. Her body was found in the woods." The gruff voice faltered for a moment and then continued. "This woman believes that the Indians have taken Alexandra to an Ojibwa Indian village near Lake Huron. From there, prisoners are often sent to Montreal or Quebec and ransomed back to the English."

His eyes dropped under her accusing stare. "Surely, you can't blame me for this, Liane. The child insisted on going to Julia."

"You really believe that, don't you, Charles?" Liane's laugh was bitter. "You sent Alexandra to her destiny as surely as you sent Phillipe and Anne to theirs. Only Julia

carved out her own fate. She alone can hold you blame-
less." The thin, beautifully molded lips drew back in a
contemptuous smile. "Julia had the courage to fight you.
She was happy. Did you know that, Charles?" The smile
disappeared and tears glittered in her eyes. "For seven
years I've hidden my granddaughter's letters for fear you
would think I'd betrayed you." The tears flowed freely
down her cheeks. "You've always condemned our children
for their spinelessness. Now you know that their mother
was the greatest coward of them all."

For a large man, the duke moved swiftly. In the space
of a heartbeat he was by his wife's side. Kneeling at her
feet, he lifted her hand to his mouth. "There isn't a cow-
ardly bone in your entire body," he murmured, pulling
her from the chair and holding her tightly against him.

She cried for a long time, her body wracked with long-
suppressed sobs. At last she lifted her head from his shoulder. What he saw in the ravaged features caused him to
squirm.

"You are overset, Liane. How can you possibly believe
I would willingly cause my children's deaths? Phillipe was
my son, my heir. Anne was my only daughter."

Her voice was a mere whisper against his cheek, but it
froze him like the slice of cold metal against warm skin.
He was no longer conscious of the cold seeping through
his joints as he knelt on the floor.

"Phillipe never had your strength, Charles. You were
hard on him, hoping to turn him into something he could
never be." She sighed. "I blame myself as well. Throughout
his life, I shielded him from your anger. I made him weak.
When he lost Wheaton Abbey, he couldn't face you. The
duel was a sham, but it was an honorable one. He never
intended to survive it."

His face was ashen. "Pray continue, madame. How did
I contribute to my daughter's demise?"

Liane looked into the face of the man she had once loved
more than life itself. It was a strong face. Many considered it

ruthless. She hesitated. Need she say more? Hadn't he also suffered? Unbidden, her daughter's eyes on her wedding day, cold and shuttered, appeared before her. The vision was replaced by Julia, proud and defiant, forced to leave her home, murdered by savages in the wilderness. Now there was Alexandra as she had been in Paris, her lovely face aglow, her eyes brimming with happiness, her conversation filled with the name of a handsome French nobleman. Then, overnight her hopes were dashed, her mouth pinched with pain, her eyes never completely free of a wary watchfulness that broke her grandmother's heart.

"Anne should never have married the Earl of Sussex," Liane continued. "He was years too old for her."

"Fifteen years is not an unheard-of age difference."

The duchess pretended not to hear him. "She was in love with Thomas Ackers," she continued. "Can you really believe that an eighteen-year-old girl with all her faculties would prefer a portly, middle-aged earl to a young man like Thomas?"

"Thomas Ackers was the son of a squire," the duke protested.

The contempt in his wife's eyes brought the red to his cheeks. "I convict myself with my own mouth," he muttered. "Why didn't she tell me?"

"Would you have behaved differently?"

Charles Winthrop was a hard man, but he was an honest one. "Perhaps not," he growled, "but if she'd had as much spirit as Julia, perhaps I would have seen things another way. Anne was such a shy little mouse. A single miscarriage killed her. Who would have believed she cared deeply about anything?"

"Spirit didn't help Julia," his wife reminded him.

"Julia left the continent. We would have been reconciled if she'd stayed in England."

Liane looked skeptical.

"Damn it, woman," the duke thundered. "I loved the girl."

"So you say." Her voice was cold. "You loved Alexandra more than anyone, Charles. Yet you sent Dominic Jolliet away. You allowed him to believe Alexandra couldn't care for him because of who he was."

"What do you know of young Jolliet?" the duke asked carefully.

"I grew up in Paris, m'lord. The *affaires* of the *Duc de Lorraine* are common knowledge among the nobility."

"If you know this, how can you possibly imagine that I would allow Alexandra to wed such a one?"

The duchess looked at him pityingly. "I thought you had learned your lesson with Julia." With a swift, graceful movement she rose to her feet and placed her hand on her husband's elegantly coiffed wig. "Know this, Charles. Our daughter was weak only when it came to defying you. She died of a miscarriage brought on by a dirty old woman who lived in the hills. Anne would not bear Sussex's child. The man was a monster." Her hand dropped to her side. She straightened her back and drew a deep steadying breath. Her next words, painful as they were, must be said. "If Alexandra is not restored to me, I shall leave you."

"Where will you go?" It was his voice that spoke and his mouth that formed the words, but the duke did not sound at all like himself.

"I still have acquaintances in Paris. Don't worry. I'll manage." With her head held high, she walked out of the room.

Stiffly, the duke stood and massaged his sore knees. He walked to the window and looked out at the huge expanse of green lawn. "You are wrong, Liane," he whispered. "It is not Alexandra I have loved more than anyone. It was always you."

Versailles, France, December 1755

She reminded him of Raphael's *Madonna*. His heart pounding erratically, as it always did in her presence, the Duc de Lorraine lowered himself to one knee and lifted her hand to his lips.

"Your Majesty," he murmured, hoping she wouldn't detect the breathlessness in his voice.

"Henri," the Queen of France chided, "surely we need not stand on ceremony with one other." Motioning for him to rise, she asked, "How was your voyage?" The word was pronounced with an accent on the first syllable, a legacy from her Polish ancestry.

"Well, Your Grace. The ship made remarkable time. I left Montreal only three weeks ago." Stiffly, he rose and seated himself on a pale-blue *bergère* across from the queen.

Placing her finger in the book she had been reading, Marie Leczynska, wife of Louis XV, reclined on a chaise lounge and lifted her eyes to the duke's face. "What brings you here, my friend?"

"Need you ask, *mignonne?*"

The queen flushed. "There is no purpose to this, *monsieur*. Surely you know that?"

"I came to bear you company, my love. That is all. Would you deny me even that small pleasure?"

"Don't." Marie held up her hand. "I am an old woman. What was once between us exists no longer. I will not speak of my sin. Long ago, I confessed and made my peace with God. Would you condemn my immortal soul, Henri?"

Her eyes were coal black and bright with unshed tears. Once again, Henri Jolliet, *Duc de Lorraine*, wondered what it was about this woman that had captured and held his heart for more than thirty years. No one would ever call hers a beautiful face. It was too pious, too serene, filled with a charm and intelligence quite unusual in the decadent, artificial court of the Sun King. Born with a gentle nature, she had been completely unprepared for the weak and faithless character of her handsome young husband.

Thirty-one years ago, the Polish Princess had been warmly welcomed by fifteen-year-old Louis. King of France for ten years, he was seven years his wife's junior. After twelve more years and ten children, the king grew tired of his Marie and sought newer, fresher game. The number of mistresses he had mounted and discarded was legendary.

Jolliet, deeply in love with the shy Marie, burned with the memory of her humiliation. In a moment of weakness, seeking to reassure her, he had declared his love, and so had begun the sweetest years of his life.

All of Paris hummed with the news of their *affaire*. Louis never mentioned it, or perhaps he didn't care. Madame de Pompadour was firmly ensconced in the palace as his mistress; and while her slightest whim was everything to him, France remained loyal to her queen. Louis was no longer called "The Well Beloved." Nobles and commoners alike cursed him behind his back for his selfishness, his timidity, his penchant for unsuitable women, and his foreign policy.

"How is the king?" the *duc* asked politely.

The queen's flush deepened. She fidgeted with the lace on her sleeve. "Well, as always."

"I'm relieved to hear it. Do Machault and The Pompadour still rule France?"

"Stop it, Henri." She turned the full force of her speaking eyes upon him. Marie Leczynska was an intelligent woman. She didn't pretend to misunderstand. "To answer as I must would be a lie, and to answer honestly would be treason. Even Voltaire and Gramont agree. France must set its sights on India and the Caribbean. We are deeply in debt. Even now, when there is no war, more than half our sums go to support the military in New France. Why should we save the barn when the house is on fire?"

Jolliet's mouth hardened. "Say no more. I understand well enough." His hand clenched on the arm of the delicate chair. "*Mon Dieu!* Have you no influence, Marie? If we lose New France to Britain, we will see the decline of our empire. The English outnumber us already. It is only a matter of time before all of Canada is within their grasp. The fur trade will be lost to us."

"That would be a great tragedy for the House of Lorraine, would it not?" The question was laced with mockery.

His mouth tightened. "I thought you had a small interest in the fortunes of the House of Lorraine, Your Grace. Perhaps I was wrong."

Moistening her lips, the Queen of France asked the question she had longed to ask from the moment Henri Jolliet first entered the room. "You are not wrong, Henri. How is Dominic?"

Henri Jolliet stared into the eyes that still haunted his dreams. They were wide and dark, so dark that he couldn't distinguish the pupil. There was only one other face in all the world with eyes of such a color.

He sighed, his voice filled with bitter resignation. "He hates us both, Marie. I fear he always will."

Chapter 7

Bowating, New France, January 1756

Dominic Jolliet, his thumbs hooked through the twisted deerskin that served as a belt, lounged against a post supporting the longhouse. Across the clearing he watched the slim straight figure of a woman as she stirred the contents of an enormous kettle. Inside the dwelling, a merchant fingered the thick beaver pelts spread on a makeshift table.

"Qu'ils sont beaux, Jolliet." The man beamed. "My journey was well worth the trouble. These are the finest furs I've seen. You will surely make a fortune this year."

"Oui," Dominic agreed, barely listening to the effusive words. From his position near the door he could no longer see the woman stirring her pot. Shifting to improve his view, his eyes moved appreciatively over her long legs, her thick, sun-streaked hair, and the sure, competent movement of her hands. He couldn't keep himself from staring. Red hair still had the power to stop him in his tracks.

She was a white woman, obviously a captive, dressed in a combination of calico rags and Indian buckskin. The fluid grace of her walk as she moved about the fire unleashed a flood of memories. He turned away, his mouth twisting in mocking self-derision. When would it end? Two years was long enough for the heart-searing pain to fade.

Lost in his private thoughts, Dominic almost missed the series of events that was to change the course of his life. Years later he would recall the incredible odds against him that day and wake in the night drenched in sweat and shaking with fear.

It began with a harsh, inhuman cry, like the howl of a timber wolf whose cubs have found a hunter's trap. Dominic turned in time to see the red-haired woman break into a run, following a small band of Indians.

His heart leaped into his throat and a memory, crystal clear and laced with pain, forced its way into his mind. A flash of speed. A streak of blue. That impossible, willowy grace. Chestnut hair flaming red against the backdrop of a Parisian sunset. He winced and shook his head. It couldn't be. Not if he lived a thousand lifetimes would he see Alexandra Winthrop running through an Indian village in the southernmost tip of French Canada.

Against his will, his legs responded, taking up the challenge. He raced out of the longhouse after the fleeing figure. *Sacrebleu!* Whoever she was, the girl could run. He grinned and increased his speed.

At the edge of the village clearing, where the stakes surrounding the wigwams and domed longhouses opened into the forest, Dominic caught up with her. She was arguing with a band of Indians, and from the looks on their faces, they were not pleased.

Afraid of what he might find, Dominic was suddenly reluctant to approach her. Positioning himself a distance away, behind a towering maple, he strained his ears to listen. The woman, speaking in halting Algonquian, gestured angrily with her hands.

"You can't take him with you," she insisted. "He's only a child."

At the sound of her voice, a strange prickling sensation raised the hairs on the back of his neck. *Mon Dieu!* Was it possible?

"The boy is Midi Nikan, our blood brother, a fine brave," the tall savage insisted. "He is young, but very strong."

"Don't be ridiculous." Her voice cracked. "He's an English boy. What use will he be to you?"

For the first time Dominic noticed that the small boy standing in the center of the band was not an Indian. His nose was small and turned up. Under the bear grease, the new growth of hair on his head was corn-tassel yellow. Eyes, blue as the summer sky, looked out from his dirty, too-thin face. He was dressed in a deerskin jacket, leggings, and breechclout, and he carried a small bow and arrow.

"Don't worry, Alix." He grinned engagingly. "I promise I won't be gone long."

"Travis," she begged. "Please don't go with them."

The child's chin tightened. "I shall go," he said in perfect English. "I've practiced and practiced. You aren't my mother, Alix."

"Enough." The Indian lifted his hand. "The boy is my son now. It is my wish that he go with me to the Village of the Three Beavers." He spoke coldly to the woman. "You have nothing more to say."

"Travis," the woman's voice quavered. She knelt on the ground holding out her arms.

The boy looked back. His lip began to quiver. "Please, Alix. May I go?"

Rising to her feet, the woman struggled to control her emotions. She managed a smile. "Go along, Travis. Behave yourself. Whatever happens, remember your mother."

Dominic watched the slim, motionless figure of Alexandra Winthrop for a long time. He wondered what would happen to the fragile threads of her self-control when she turned and recognized him. Deciding this was not the time to approach her, he melted into the shadows and made his way back to his furs on the other end of the village.

No man representing himself as a true *coureur de bois* would miss the winter's entertainment at Bowating, the Place at the Falls. One of the Ojibwa's most important trading villages, it was located at the middle of a water route between the St. Marys River and the outlet where Lake Superior fed into Lake Huron. Other tribes were also attracted to the village because of its easy accessibility, its abundant supply of whitefish, and most of all, Dominic thought disgustedly, the irresistable lure of the white man's brandy.

Hurons, from the region west of Lake Simcoe on the Ontario peninsula, traded pottery and surplus corn. The Fox and the Saux from Illinois brought buffalo hides and shells from the country south of Lake Michigan. The Ottawa and Potowatomi, People of the Three Fires from Tickenecket, Place of Little Beavers, contributed copper, furs, birchbark, and *kinnikinnick*, a mixture of dried plants for smoking.

The population of Bowating, no more than four or five hundred Ojibwas in the spring and summer months, swelled to several thousand during the winter. When ice froze the rivers solid and the cold was so intense that trees cracked like gunfire shots and bled sap through their bark, the Algonquian and their allies gathered together for warmth and entertainment. Games and storytelling prevailed and leaders met in councils to discuss war expeditions and defense strategies against the Iroquois in the east and the Sioux to the west.

Dominic had not intended to stay in Bowating this winter. Despite the tempting allure of a season spent among men who cared for nothing more than pulling the wilderness around themselves like a cloak and, when the ice melted, disappearing into the setting sun, he knew he must move on to Montreal and civilization—such as it was. To spend another winter in a mindless, drunken haze would remove the choice of his destiny from him forever. He would become a *coureur* at heart, his sole purpose in life to steer a frail canoe west through dark forests and roaring waterfalls toward a future he could neither predict nor control.

Despite his father's dire predictions, Dominic had never forgotten who he was and he had no intention of throwing away his heritage. He hadn't counted on meeting Alexandra Winthrop once again.

Cursing softly, he looked up at the darkening sky. She was an English lady, granddaughter of the Duke of Leicester, and he was a French bastard of royal blood. Two years before, she had led him on and then spurned his attentions like the most heartless *coquette* who sold her services on the *Rue de Paris*. Still, she was a white woman, helpless in the hands of savages. He could no longer consider himself a man if he refused to help her.

Reaching into his pocket, Dominic pulled out his pipe and tobacco pouch. He must find Red Wing. Bowating was an Ojibwa village and Red Wing was Chief of the Ojibwa. No man, woman, or child entered the enclosure without his permission.

Stars crowded the sky like a blanket of lights when Dominic finally found the War Chief. He was seated around a council fire with a Huron sachem and two Ottawa warriors. The pipe had been passed and the *coureur* could see that the mood was serious.

"Welcome, Night Wind." The young chief's smile was unusually welcoming as he embraced his friend. "Will the Anishinabe enjoy your company this winter?"

"Perhaps," Dominic replied, unwilling to commit himself. "I would speak with you when the time is right."

Red Wing turned to his companions. His words were polite but formal. "My brothers, the winter is long. You have spoken eloquently. I will carry your words to the Council of Chiefs. We will meet again and I will have an answer. Now, I must speak with Night Wind."

The three men nodded. Using only the muscles of their calves, they rose gracefully, in unison, disappearing into the night.

Red Wing waited until he could no longer see their shadowy figures in the darkness. Folding his legs beneath him, he motioned for Dominic to be seated.

The *coureur,* familiar with Indian protocol, picked up a dry twig and held it close to the flames. When it ignited, he lit the tobacco in his pipe and passed it to Red Wing. "It has been too long, Wiskino," he began.

Red Wing grunted and inhaled the pungent smoke.

"Five moons have passed since we last spoke," Dominic continued.

The War Chief passed the pipe across the fire to Dominic. "What did you find in the French city?"

"It was as you said," Dominic replied. "Our French father across the water will send soldiers to push the English from the Canadas."

Red Wing nodded. "Trapping the beaver will be difficult until the English and Iroquois are defeated. Many strangers seek the hospitality of Bowating this winter. They know it will be their last season to trade before the soldiers land on our shores."

Dominic saw his opportunity. "I have seen two of your strangers," he said casually. "An English woman with hair like the fox and a boy of six or seven summers with blue eyes."

"Al-ex-an-dra." Red Wing drew out the unfamiliar syllables. "She was captured by a war party outside of Fort Edward four moons ago."

"Will Wiskino ransom her to the French?"

Red Wing shook his head. "Her destiny is to remain with the Anishinabe."

The knuckles of Dominic's hand were very white as he clenched the pipe, but his voice betrayed no unusual interest. "How does Wiskino know this?"

"Under her white skin and hair of flame, she is one of

us, a painter of pictures, an *o-jib-i-weg.*" He pronounced the white man's name for the Anishinabe carefully, giving each syllable equal importance. "With her sticks and colors she captures the spirits of our people on her parchment." He held out his palm, the fingers splayed. "There is magic in her hands. I have seen it. She is one of the free people, born to those with white skin. Kitche Manido has returned her to the Anishinabe."

"Holy Christ!" The oath escaped Dominic's lips before he could prevent it. He needed time to sort out his jumbled thoughts, to think of a reasonable explanation for his interest in an Ojibwa captive. Caution was a practice he had learned to revere when dealing with Indians. To a war chief, the political ramifications of kidnapping the granddaughter of an English peer was of no consequence whatsoever. Red Wing was secure in his power and the knowledge that he could slip away beyond the Great Lakes, taking his people so far away from European civilization that neither English nor French trappers would ever find them.

Drawing deeply on the stem of his pipe, Dominic inhaled the cloying smoke, holding it inside his lungs until his eyes watered and rainbow colored-spots appeared before him. When it seemed as if his chest would burst, he exhaled and breathed in a cleansing gulp of cold air, relieved that his sudden rush of anger had disappeared and he was once again in control of his emotions.

"Her name is Alexandra Winthrop," he said, his eyes on the chief's face. "I knew her many moons ago in my country across the water. Her grandfather is a very wealthy and powerful man. He will pay in gold for her release." Dominic willed every muscle in his body to immobility. He was so still he could have been carved from the cold stone of the granite mountains surrounding the village. But his mind worked feverishly. Alexandra's only hope of freedom lay in her ransom value. Everything depended on the quality of furs the Anishinabe had gathered over the spring and summer. If the tribe had seen a successful trapping season, Red Wing wouldn't be tempted by the gold of an Englishman.

"There was no man in the house when she was taken," Red Wing announced at last. "My braves brought only the women and children."

Dominic frowned. The Duke of Leicester was a strict guardian. He would never have allowed Alexandra to make a journey to the colonies without a protector. A chill began at the base of his spine and inched its way upward, numbing him to the ever-increasing cold. Could she have married a colonial? It had been well over two years. Time enough for any woman to find a husband. He fought against the irrational jealousy threatening to consume him. There had been nothing between them. If she had a husband, all the better. Dominic's responsibility for her safety would end after he escorted her to the nearest English fort.

"I will consider your words, Night Wind." Red Wing stood and stretched to his full height. "It grows late. You are welcome to sleep inside the wigwam of Min-ni-wah-wah."

Dominic was not surprised that Red Wing referred to the dwelling that was his home as his mother-in-law's possession. He knew that the Algonquian were matrilineal. When a brave married, he moved into his wife's wigwam and became one with her family. All personal items belonged to the women of the tribe.

For an instant, he hesitated. The night was cold and the clouds hung low and dark with the promise of snow. Then he remembered the suffocating smell of unwashed bodies and the cramped discomfort of sleeping within two feet of another human being. He shook his head. "My furs are spread beside the wigwam of my guide, Wah-Wah-Tay-See."

Red Wing nodded and walked away.

The night did not pass easily for Dominic. Hours after he slid between his pelts, exhaustion finally claimed him and he drifted into troubled sleep. He dreamed of a spacious room ablaze with a thousand lights. His mother's face appeared before him. Her mouth was sad and her eyes, the deep unrelieved black of a moonless night, were shadowed with pain.

Chapter 8

The small band of women and children were in no hurry. Laughing and sharing conversation, they walked along the riverbank, snowshoes toe-in to prevent any inadvertent tumbles. Alexandra was too worried about Travis to appreciate the beauty around her. He had not returned with the hunting party and she feared he had been adopted into another village.

Climbing with the others to a group of maple trees that constituted the tribe's portion of the sugar bush, she walked, unseeing, past the glistening expanse of Lake Superior, its deep blue water as vast as an ocean, the shining stillness broken here and there by dark islands.

To the north, fold after fold of timbered hills rolled to the blue-misted horizon, a hidden lake in every crevice. Fog lay around the travelers like a blanket of smoke, and the forest beneath their feet was carpeted with a soft layer of snow. Balsams and red-barked pines soared a hundred feet overhead in a silent struggle for light. Save for an occasional golden ray breaking through an opening left by some fallen giant, the gloom beneath the canopy of boughs was deep and hushed. In wetter places, the white trunks of aspen and birch stood out vividly against the somber evergreens. Here, near the Kaministiquia River, the water was stained the color of tea by vegetable molds that grew on the rocks and white water rapids frothed with a yellow tinge.

As the women and children continued to climb, the water became clear again. Alexandra noticed that the inlets were narrow and oddly shaped, scalloped with coves and indented with sharp-nosed promontories, some wooded and some gray, with granite crags creased and scored by ancient ice. Abigail, bound securely in a cradleboard on Alexandra's back, was nearly a year old. The Alexandra of old would have balked at carrying such a precious and cumbersome burden up the narrow precipice. But six months with the Anishinabe had taught her endurance and to keep all complaints to herself.

"We are nearly there." Sarah's soft voice drifted back to her. She spoke in English, subtly informing Alexandra the comment was for her ears alone. "Usually I enjoy this, but I've never carried such a heavy load." She glanced down at her own sturdy baby and smiled affectionately.

"I thought collecting maple sugar was done in early spring," Alexandra said.

Sarah nodded. "March is the best time for sugaring. But this year the weather has been unusual. The ground froze early, followed by a deep snow. Sap runs best that way."

Alexandra knew that the Anishinabe considered maple sugar and wild rice to be their two most important vegetable foods. It had taken her a long time to become accustomed to food without salt. Within an hour they reached the lodges that would be their temporary shelters until the sap stopped running.

Immediately Mi-ni-wah-wah spread out cedar boughs in the interior of the lodge she would share with Alexandra and Abigail. Over these she laid rush mats, blankets, and furs. The storehouse was then opened, great rolls of birchbark turned back, one at a time, and bark dishes—*makuks* and buckets, white outside and warm yellow within—were pulled out. The odor of balsam and dry sweet birch bark filled the lodge. Alexandra sniffed appreciatively and watched the older woman as she carefully examined the utensils. She knew that the color of the sugar depended on the whiteness and cleanliness of the utensils.

Because the actual tapping was only done by those who were experts, Alexandra was left to her own devices. Unstrapping Abigail, she laced her into tiny leather moccasins chewed to buttery softness by Mi-ni-wah-wah's strong teeth. Taking the baby's hand, Alexandra left the lodge in search of Sarah.

She found her near a huge maple and watched in interested silence as she made a diagonal cut in the tree. Below the cut, she removed about four inches of bark in a perpendicular line and then inserted a wooden spike. Then she placed a sap bucket on the ground below the spike. Smiling with satisfaction, she turned toward Alexandra. "You can watch if you like, but I have at least two hundred more of these to do." She nodded toward her sleeping baby. "Little Elk is asleep, but perhaps there are others who need help with the children."

Glad to escape what looked like a tedious task, Alexandra led Abigail toward a small group of children huddled around a firepit. Quickly she organized the older ones into a game of hide-and-seek. Red-cheeked and laughing, they dodged around trees, mimicking the sounds of hoot owls and loons as they dared each other to find their hiding places. The younger ones, tired of making angels in the snow, were quick to learn Ring-Around-The-Rosy, that pathetic ditty born in the shadows of disease-ridden Europe. Whirling around and around, they fell, exhausted and dizzy, into the powdery softness.

Later, after a meal of boiled meat and rice, she divided them into teams and they competed in relays for the rest of the afternoon. Alexandra, lured by the laughter and friendly comaraderie of her charges, allowed herself to be drawn into the competition. Her natural grace and the hard muscles earned by life in the Indian camp worked to her advantage. Carrying Abigail in her arms, she raced to the finish line, flushed and triumphant, straight into the arms of a tall, broad-shouldered man dressed in weathered buckskin.

"So." Dark eyes smiled down at her. "The girl who can dance like an angel can also run like a deer."

"You!" Her eyes were a brilliant gold, the pupils wide with shock. She had forgotten how incredibly handsome he was. In all her memories of Dominic Jolliet, his striking good looks had faded into the background. It was the magnetism of his presence that stayed in her mind. From the moment he walked into a room, all eyes followed him, every man, woman, and child instantly aware he was there. Alexandra had only to give her carefully repressed emotions free rein and she would immediately recall the lean, cat-like grace of his movements, the irresistible charm he could summon at a moment's notice, and the piercing intelligence reflected in his amused, mocking glance.

She looked in wonder at the black sweep of lashes framing his eyes, at the straight nose and soaring brows. Her appreciative gaze drank in the perfect symmetry of bones and teeth and tightly drawn skin. She drew a deep breath. He looked very stern, his eyes hard and bright, as if he had lived for a long time on the power of his nerves.

Dominic met her absorbed stare without blinking. He searched her face, assessing the changes of the past two years. Her red-brown hair was pulled back into a single braid, revealing the pure, uncluttered line of her chin and cheekbones. She was thin and dirty, burned darker than he'd ever seen a white woman.

Dominic swallowed. His throat felt very dry. He was quite sure that nothing in the world could equal the loveliness of Alexandra Winthrop's face as it appeared to him at that moment. He realized with a sense of helpless inevitability that she still fascinated him more than any other woman he had ever known and his years in the Canadian wilderness hadn't cured him of his obsession. The pulse leaped erratically in his throat.

Brilliant color, not entirely due to her exertions of the afternoon, stained Alexandra's cheeks. "What are you doing here?"

Dominic shrugged, his eyes on the copper curls of the baby in her arms. "I'm in the business of trading furs. Bowating is my home for the winter. When I recognized you in the village, I followed you here. When the ice melts on the Saguenay, I'll take my canoe and travel west." His voice dropped to the dangerously caressing note she remembered so well. "And you, *mademoiselle*? Why are you so far from home?"

Alexandra swayed slightly. Unintentionally, she leaned against him and closed her eyes, unable to look at his face any longer. It was too much, to see him here, to see him at all. The memory of Paris was so far away, like a priceless treasure, locked away in the darkest corners of her mind. A world of grace and elegance, of scented candles and sparkling crystal. As if it were only yesterday, she could feel his eyes upon her, glinting liquid black, bold and possessive, warm with approval and something else she wouldn't allow herself to admit.

For a fleeting moment, long ago, when they had turned in the steps of the minuet at Madame De Becque's ball, she had known the dizzy excitement of being held against the whipcord strength of his chest. When her fingers closed over his arm, his muscles had tensed beneath the velvet coat. His lips were warm and firm on her hand. Alexandra burned with mortification as she recalled the shameless liberties they had shared. She had been a girl then, young and trusting. Every day had been a gift filled with sunlight and promise. She had fallen in love, naively assuming her affections were returned.

Alexandra's mouth twisted in a rueful grimace. The

woman destined to gentle the fascinating Dominic Jolliet did not exist. Her back stiffened. Lifting her chin, she stepped out of his arms. She was no longer a naive girl. She was a woman engaged to be married and responsible for two children. Perhaps Dominic could be persuaded to help her reach Anthony at Fort Edward. "I came to take my sister home to England," she explained. "A war party kidnapped us. We've been here six months."

"Julia is here with you?"

Alexandra bit her lip. "She's dead," she replied flatly. "Her children are with me." She shifted the baby to her other hip. "This is Abigail. Travis left with a hunting party. I don't know when they'll return."

Dominic released his breath slowly. The red-haired *petite fille* was her niece.

"Will you help us?" she asked bluntly.

He considered her question. "Have they mistreated you?"

Alexandra shook her head. "No. But we can't stay here forever. We're English citizens, and my grandfather is an old man. He'll be sick with worry."

"Ah, yes." Dominic's mocking smile did not reach his eyes. "The estimable Duke of Leicester. He must be worried, indeed, if he hasn't already given up hope."

Surprised at the contempt in his voice, she asked, "Why do you dislike him so?"

For a long moment, something flickered in the smoldering charcoal of his eyes, and then disappeared. When he spoke, Alexandra was sure she misunderstood.

"He took something from me." His mouth was grim.

"I beg your pardon?"

Dominic's face had assumed an implacable expression. "It doesn't matter, *chérie*. It wasn't really mine after all. Of course I'll help you."

Alexandra smiled with relief. "We can't leave until Travis returns. How long do you think that will be, m'lord?"

Dominic grinned and took the baby from her. Carrying

Abigail on one arm, he handed his flintlock to Alexandra and reached for her free hand. As naturally as if she had done it every day of her life, she laced her fingers through his and walked beside him toward the lodge.

"Surely we were on a first-name basis when we last met, Alix. My title seems a bit pretentious in this setting."

Alexandra frowned, unprepared for the rush of emotion that surged through her at the sound of her childhood name on his lips. The last thing she wanted was to dredge up memories of Paris. "You haven't told me how you came to be here," she said hastily.

"Adrien Jolliet is my uncle. For years he wrote of the unspoiled beauty and opportunities for profit here in French Canada. I came to see for myself."

Alexandra nodded. Everyone had heard of the famous Monsieur Jolliet, younger brother of the *Duc de Lorraine*. "How long have you been here?" she asked.

"Two years."

She stopped suddenly and turned to face him. "But that was immediately after I left Paris. You mentioned nothing of this to me."

"Should I have?" One dark eyebrow lifted quizzically.

The color rose in Alexandra's cheeks. "We talked of everything else," she stammered. "Why not that?"

"You presume a great deal, *mignonne,*" the amused voice chided her. "Why should I have discussed my future plans with you?"

Rage and an overwhelming desire to shame him erased her reticence to acknowledge the past. Lifting her chin, she met his gaze honestly. "At the time, I was under the mistaken impression you planned to ask my grandfather's permission to marry me."

A muscle jumped along the taut line of his cheek. "You were mistaken."

"So it seems." Alexandra turned away with a brittle laugh. "I was terribly naive, wasn't I? When you left for Lorraine without a word, I realized how tedious it must have been for you. A green girl, barely out of the school-room, infatuated with the incomparable *Marquis de Villiers.*"

"Stop this, Alix!" His hands clenched. The bones showed white through his skin. There was no trace of amusement in the face that stared down at her. "For what it's worth, you were never tedious; and despite what you think, it wasn't like that at all. Your grandfather, damn his self-righteous soul, made me understand why anything more between us was impossible."

Alexandra stood completely still as the incredible words washed over her. All at once she understood. Her eyes widened, shocking Dominic with the blazing anger he read in their golden depths.

"Damn you, Dominic Jolliet." Her words were clear and cold. "You broke my heart. It was I you should have asked."

Dominic frowned. There was pain as well as anger in her eyes. Had she really cared so much? Would it have made a difference in the end? The blood pounded in his temples. "Alix." he whispered hoarsely and reached out to cup her cheek.

Recoiling, Alexandra stepped back and reached for the baby. Settling Abigail on her hip, she stood in the doorway of the lodge, facing him. "I've learned a great deal in the past two years, m'lord. There will be no further misunderstandings between us."

Recognizing the veiled warning for what it was, Dominic inclined his head in a brief salute and turned away. All of winter lay ahead. There would be time enough to renew his acquaintance with the Earl of Leicester's granddaughter.

Chapter 9

Sarah had returned from tapping the trees in time to see the interchange between Dominic and Alexandra. Monsieur Jolliet was a familiar figure in the village of Bowating. As he moved past her, she nodded her head in response to his greeting. Moving aside the skin flap that covered the doorway of Mi-ni-wah-wah's lodge, she saw Alexandra seated on a pile of furs, staring into a small hand mirror.

"Would you believe that I was once considered a beauty?" Alexandra looked up at her friend and grimaced. "I wonder if even Anthony would want me."

"Yes, I believe it and yes, he would still want you." Sarah reached for a pot on the ledge. Moving aside the skin door, she scooped up a large quantity of snow and placed the pot on the fire burning brightly in the middle of the lodge. Ice flakes dripped down the side and hissed as they fell into the flames. "A bit of dirt and grease can't erase what you have, Alexandra."

Discarding one basket after another, Sarah searched the entire shelf until she found what she was looking for. Crumbling the dry twigs into the melting water, she squatted down until she was eye level with the younger woman. "How is it that you know the *coureur,* Jolliet?"

Alexandra rubbed her niece's frozen hands and leaned over to kiss the baby's rosy mouth. Abigail smiled, revealing four perfect teeth.

"I met him in Paris long ago during my first season." The semi-darkness of the lodge concealed her blush. "He was charming and I was very young." She stopped and stared at the water bubbling in the pot.

"Is that all?" Sarah persisted.

Alexandra lifted her eyes to the puzzled face of the woman seated across from her. There was no need for subterfuge. Sarah's clear-blue eyes shone with honesty and nothing else. The false pride and coy innuendos practiced in silk-hung drawing rooms of the English nobility had no place here. In this grim, merciless land on the frozen border of Lake Michigan, men and women measured relationships in terms of life and death. Dependency was a fact of life. Alexandra had found what she had least expected, a trusted friend.

"I loved him," she admitted.

"Why didn't you marry?" Sarah's voice was soft, the compassion unmistakable.

"At the time, I thought he didn't return my feelings."

"And now?"

"Now?" Alexandra reached for a cup and dipped it into the boiling water. "It doesn't matter. Paris was a long time ago and I am promised to Anthony."

Sarah accepted the cup of herbal tea with a brief word of thanks. She sipped the fragrant brew, agonizing, once again, over whether it would be better to confide her misgivings or to remain silent and hope she was wrong.

Alexandra was living in a state of unusual intimacy with Red Wing. She was too naive in the ways of the Anishinabe to realize that her situation was not at all normal. Women were either slaves or wives, and Alexandra was definitely not a slave. The privileges she took as her right were far above those normally granted to women. She remained serenely confident in her belief that she would be rescued.

Sarah bit her lip. What would happen when this proud English lady learned she was expected to share the bridal furs of an Indian? Another more frightening thought suddenly occurred to her. Red Wing was wise and extremely courteous as befitted his position. But he was also a man. What would the equally proud War Chief of the Anishinabe do when the white woman spurned him?

The women did not return to Bowating until after the sugaring off. Alexandra was grateful when it was over. Her arms ached from stirring the heavy paddles and filling the wooden *makuks*. She wasn't experienced enough to be trusted with the reboiling. This entailed waiting for exactly the right temperature when the syrup, slick, with deer tallow, was transferred into the granulating trough where it was rubbed or worked with the back of the ladle. It had to be done very rapidly or the sugar would cool too much and the entire batch would be lost.

Instead, Red Wing's mother-in-law set her to the task of making gum sugar. This was a sticky substance and was kept in packets of birchbark tied with basswood. The syrup was taken from the kettle just before it was ready to grain and poured directly on the snow. It was backbreaking work, requiring full concentration. When night fell, Alexandra crawled into her furs and fell immediately asleep.

The sugaring had taken almost an entire month, and in that time, she had seen little of Dominic Jolliet. Occasionally he came to the sugar camp only to report that Travis hadn't yet returned to Bowating. He made no effort to seek her out or spend any more time with her than he did with the other women. Alexandra, always completely honest with herself, admitted that his impersonal behavior annoyed her. He had changed. It wasn't only his lack of interest in her that was different. It was something else. Something she couldn't quite put her finger on.

On one of his rare visits, she watched him bank the fire and set a rabbit-skewered spit at exactly the right distance from the flames. He sat back on his heels, speaking fluent Algonquian to Straw Basket while offering her daughter a sugar cone. When the child reached for it, he laughed, his teeth flashing white against his dark skin. Alexandra's knees weakened at the sight. Then it came upon her, suddenly, without warning, like a bolt of lightning. It was gone. The blazing flame that lit him from within and separated him from every other man of his class was missing. Had Alexandra been less sensitive to every nuance of his expression, had she know him less intimately, she would not have noticed. Even so, it had almost eluded her.

Her hands trembled as she reached for her paper. She could no more suppress the urge to sketch him than she could still the intake of her own breath. Gripping the chalk, her hand moved expertly across the page. Within moments, she had blocked out the contours of his face, the leanly, muscled strength of his arms, the width of his shoulders. His features came easily, from memory. She had dreamed of those dark, chiseled features every night for more than two years.

It wasn't Dominic Jolliet, the *coureur*, she drew. It was the young *Marquis de Villiers* of Paris, his eyes aflame with laughter, his face darkly beautiful in its austerity. A shock of black hair fell across his brow. His lips smiled up at her. Alexandra smiled in return. She was quite pleased with herself. Her memory and talent had served her well.

Time passed unnoticed. If she had been using water colors, the waning light would have warned her of the passing day. As it was, she remained absorbed in her task, oblivious to the activity around her.

The lace showing at the sleeves of his coat was finished. She started at the outline of a hand. Her pencil faltered. Dominic had beautiful hands. They were lean and brown and long, the hands of an aristocrat. It was one of the first things she had noticed about him.

A shadow fell across her paper. Alexandra looked up and blinked. The light was behind him.

"I'm flattered," said Dominic. Something in his voice triggered her memory and caused her breath to shorten.

With shaking fingers Alexandra pulled the cover over her sketchbook. Her cheeks were unusually pink, but her eyes were steady on his face. "You needn't be," she replied. "I'm an artist and deeply appreciative of beauty. You are, after all, a very beautiful man, *monsieur.*"

A flicker of something crossed his face and then disappeared. Alexandra waited for him to speak. For endless seconds their gazes locked. At last Dominic smiled. "Good night, *mademoiselle,*" was all he said. Alexandra stepped into the lodge and moved the deerskin flap into place.

Dominic turned away and walked back to the fire, a thoughtful look on his face. Once again, her unconventional behavior had startled him. He was a man both comfortable and familiar with women. Two years ago, he would have sworn there was no situation involving the fairer sex to which he had not been initiated. That was before he had been introduced to Alexandra Winthrop. There wasn't another woman in all the salons of Europe who would have responded as candidly as she had. *Mon Dieu!* There wasn't another woman in all the world like Alexandra.

Dominic fell into step beside Alexandra as she walked along the narrow trail. The women had completed the sugaring and were on their way back to the village. Remarkably graceful in the awkward snowshoes, Alexandra defied custom by carrying her bedding, instead of the baby, strapped to her back.

Balancing the child on her hip, she stopped occasionally to catch her breath and switch Abigail to her other side. Dominic would have offered to lighten her burden, but he knew the Indian women would disapprove and take out their displeasure on Alexandra. Caring for infants, food preparation, and erecting a shelter was woman's work.

"When the ice melts and canoes can again travel on the St. Lawrence, I'll leave for Montreal," he said. "From there, I'll send word to Leicester and bring back enough gold to secure your release."

"Does that mean we'll belong to you, like slaves?"

"Don't be ridiculous, Alexandra." An angry red stained the prominent bones of his cheeks. "The money is merely a loan. I trust the duke will reimburse me."

Alexandra's lips twitched. "Don't be so sure, m'lord. You may be burdened with an Englishwoman and two children for longer than you imagine. How will you explain us to your father and the good citizens of Montreal?"

"My father is wise enough not to meddle in my affairs," Dominic snapped, annoyed that the prospect did not seem at all as daunting as it should. "And the citizens of Montreal can go to the devil for all I care."

"Why haven't you married?" Alexandra shifted the baby to look directly at him.

"How do you know that I haven't?" he countered.

"Have you?"

The straightforward query unsettled him. A French woman, a French lady, would never have posed such a question.

"No," he answered shortly. "I haven't found a woman whose company I can tolerate for any length of time."

"A *coureur de bois* isn't home for any length of time," she argued reasonably. "I don't see the problem."

His eyes glittered dangerously. "You are very eager to see me take a wife, *mademoiselle*. Perhaps you would care to apply for the position?"

She reddened under her tan. "Don't be absurd."

"Perhaps you would feel safer in my presence were I married." His smile mocked her.

The gold-tipped lashes hid her eyes. "I'm not afraid of you, Dominic."

"Then, you are a fool." His voice had gone dangerously soft. "I'm not married, Alix, but it wouldn't make a difference if I were. We are no longer in Paris. You would be wise to hold on to your fear, *chérie*—if not of me, then of yourself. Passions run deep in this frozen land. A man has only to sail down the river to escape his past. New France is a dangerous place for a beautiful woman and two children."

Alexandra shivered, feeling the extent of the cold for the first time since their journey had begun. His words were eerily familiar. She had voiced those same sentiments to Julia last summer. Had it only been two seasons ago? It seemed like another lifetime.

She looked at the lean-hipped, wide-shouldered man who walked by her side. He carried his flintlock as easily as he had once carried a lace handkerchief. Whether she liked it or not, fate had once again placed her in his hands. A secret smile touched the corners of her mouth. He had called her beautiful.

Chapter 10

Red Wing pushed aside the flap of the wigwam and sniffed appreciatively. It was good to have Mi-ni-wah-wah home. As an unmarried warrior, he had been welcomed at many of the hearth fires belonging to his tribe during the sugaring. But it wasn't the same as having a kettle full of hot food available whenever he felt hungry. He glanced over at the pile of skins where Alexandra sat absorbed in her work. The child slept peacefully at her side. A slight frown wrinkled his brow. He had never known a woman to have such patience. She could sit perfectly still for hours, concentrating on creating the image before her.

Alexandra had used up her supply of pencils long ago. Red Wing had shown her how to use charred embers from the camp fires to replace her charcoal. Traders on their way to Quebec had supplied the paper. He could still remember the surprised glances on the faces of the merchants when he had expressed interest in the sketchbook. At first they were reluctant to part with it. Drawing and painting were considered necessary accomplishments for ladies in New France, and the book was intended for Governor Vaudreuil's wife. When the War Chief had thrown a prime beaver pelt into the bargain, the precious paper had immediately changed hands.

Red Wing had never regretted the cost. It had been enough to see the smile light Alexandra's face when he'd placed it in her hands. He had thought long and hard about Dominic Jolliet's words. He was chief of his people and he took his responsibility seriously. His tribe needed gold to see them through the lean winters when the traps yielded few furs. But he was also a man without a mate and a selfish part of him wanted the white woman for himself. He had grown accustomed to her presence. Time and again, like a moth to a flame, his eyes were drawn to her slender figure, her bright, sun-streaked hair, and the way the firelight played across her golden skin. It was past time to take a wife, and none of the women of his tribe appealed to him nearly as much as this too-thin girl with her straight back and brilliant smile. He would wait awhile longer. The women of the Anishinabe, not the men, chose their mates.

Feeling his eyes upon her, Alexandra looked up and smiled. He felt the licking flames of desire deep in the pit of his stomach. Weakness invaded his knees. With a swift, fluid motion, he lowered himself to the skins by her side and looked at her drawing. Red Wing was startled and then touched. It was a picture of himself as he had first appeared to her on the riverbank. The sketch exuded tremendous power. No one looking at the taut, bunched chest muscles and powerful thighs of the Indian chief could doubt that this was a man of importance. Pride and wisdom were stamped in every feature of his face. It was clear that the artist held her subject in great affection.

"It is good." Red Wing nodded solemnly.

Alexandra smiled. She was genuinely fond of the young chief. Rolling up the paper, she handed it to him. "I drew it for you."

Red Wing sucked in his breath. The blood sang in his

veins. A gift of such magnitude could mean only one thing. It was the signal he had waited for. She was ready to accept him as her mate. He grinned boyishly and brushed her arm with his hand. "I accept your gift with many thanks, Al-ex-an-dra."

Abigail was ill. Alexandra knew immediately that the child was not herself. Her pale skin was flushed and her appetite gone. By nightfall, a raging fever consumed her and convulsions racked her small body.

Alexandra was terrified. She would have feared for her niece's life even if she had been safe at Leicester; but here, in the bitter cold and filthy conditions of the Indian village, the baby's chances for survival were slim. Alexandra choked back a sob. A comforting hand rested on her shoulder. She turned to gaze into Sarah's sympathetic face.

"How is she?"

"I'm afraid it's the fever, Sarah. You shouldn't be here."

Sarah bit her lip. "The shaman is on his way. 'Tis best not to make a fuss, Alexandra. Many times his remedies are successful."

Alexandra nodded. She had heard that the Anishinabe were skilled with herbs. "What will he do to her?"

Again, Sarah hesitated. "He will do what an English surgeon would do, bleed her to remove the poisoned blood."

"She's too small," Alexandra protested. "No English doctor would bleed a child not yet a year old."

Sarah stared down at the tiny rigid body of Abigail Graham. "There really isn't much hope for her, my dear."

Alexandra turned on her fiercely. "How dare you say such a thing! Are you God that you can decide whether a child should live or die? She can't die. I won't let her." Alexandra was close to hysteria. "I promised Julia I would keep the children with me. Travis is gone. I can't lose

Abigail now. You must help me, Sarah. You have a child. How would you feel if it were he lying here?"

For an endless moment, Sarah stared into the desperate face before her. "Wait here," she ordered. "I'll be back."

Alexandra pressed a kiss on the small forehead and thought longingly of the rocking chair in the nursery at Leicester. There were so many things she had taken for granted. Voices drifted through the skins covering the door. Suddenly they were flung back and Mi-ni-wah-wah entered with Red Wing and a hideously painted man. Alexandra clutched the child to her breast.

"What is he doing here?" she asked in halting Algonquian.

"The child is filled with evil spirits," answered the Indian woman. "She must be purged."

"How?"

The shaman lifted a small pointed blade in one hand and a clay bowl in the other. "One cut on either side of the head will relieve her pain." He nodded toward Mi-ni-wah-wah. "Old Mother will spread medicine over the wound. If Kitche Manido wills it, the child will live."

"No." The word was no more than a whisper, but to Alexandra it seemed as if her voice carried to the far corners of the village. She felt faint. Where was Sarah? The shaman stepped forward and held out his arms.

Suddenly, as if in answer to a silent prayer, the skins parted and Dominic Jolliet stepped into the wigwam. Immediately, his dark eyes flickered from Alexandra's pale face to the child in her arms. Assessing the situation correctly, he spoke quickly, too quickly for Alexandra to follow. Even though she couldn't make out his words, the authority in the clipped voice was unmistakable. Unbelievably, the shaman dropped his arms and stepped back.

Dominic lifted the skins and nodded toward the child. "Wrap the baby and come with me."

She did as she was told. The night air was bitterly cold. Her breath came in deep white gusts. Without a word, she followed Dominic as he led the way to a lodge on the far side of the village. Alexandra recognized it immediately. It was the women's hut. Every month, when a woman had her courses, she would stay isolated in the lodge until the shaman pronounced her clean again. She looked around. It was empty and unusually clean. Alexandra wasn't surprised. Most of the women were either pregnant or nursing infants, and the ones that weren't had husbands who were loathe to give up the warmth of a human body on a winter's night.

She watched Dominic kindle the fire. "What are we doing here?" she whispered.

"I convinced Red Wing that a white infant wouldn't respond to the shaman's medicine," he replied without looking up. "He agreed because he knows that if anything happened to the child, you would blame him." Dominic stood and turned to look directly at her. His eyes were shuttered and hard, like a wall between them. "It appears that your opinion is of great importance to him."

"What are you saying?" Alexandra was truly confused.

Dominic looked down into the face he knew as well as his own. Layers of dirt couldn't mar the beauty of her delicate bones and clear, amber-colored eyes. He hesitated. Perhaps she really was unaware of Red Wing's intentions. Alexandra had been cossetted all of her life by adoring relatives. Her grandfather, conscious of the loose morals of the English aristocracy, had guarded her well.

Dominic recalled the first time he'd met Alexandra Winthrop, and his mouth lost its hardness. She hadn't had the least idea of how to carry on a flirtation. Her smile was friendly without a hint of artifice, her gaze direct and unself-conscious. When she asked for a handkerchief and proceeded to sneeze heartily in his presence, he'd fallen deeply and irrevocably in love.

Alexandra felt faint. The lodge was very warm and the look in the dark eyes staring into hers gave her a curious, light-headed feeling. The baby stirred. Alexandra looked down, horrified that for even a few short seconds she'd forgotten the child.

"Can you help her?"

"I don't know," Dominic confessed. "She has a better chance than if she were an Indian child. They don't stand up well to illness. I'll boil some water and add mint bark. We'll take turns holding her over the fumes to clear her lungs."

"I remember my nurse giving me barley water and tea," Alexandra offered.

Dominic grinned reassuringly. "It's worth a try. Cheer up, *mignonne.* We've all had the fever, and your niece is a healthy child. There's a good chance she'll be over this in no time."

Alexandra settled herself on the furs and watched him as he set a kettle filled with snow over the flames. He rested easily on his haunches, waiting for the water to boil. If he were concerned over the turn of events, he hid it well. Alexandra felt renewed just by looking at him. She wondered how many women had been caught in that web of attractive self-assurance he alone possessed. How many others had swept that shock of shining, black hair away from his forehead? How many had believed in the promise of those dark eyes or heard his words of love, muffled and passionate, murmured against their throats? Alexandra bit her lip. Probably too many to count.

Within moments, the water bubbled and Dominic crumbled a handful of mint into the liquid. He reached for Abigail and, without hesitating, Alexandra gave up the baby. Unwrapping the blanket from around the child's body, he handed it back to her.

"Drape it over both of us," he ordered. "Be sure it covers the kettle, and for God's sake, don't let the ends fall into the fire."

With swift, efficient movements, she pulled the blanket over the two bodies, carefully avoiding the licking flames. When Dominic and Abigail were completely covered, she sat down to wait. It was late and she was tired. Soon, her eyelids drooped and she slipped down into the warm comfort of the furs and slept.

A voice awakened her. Alexandra opened her eyes. Gray light filtered in through the opening in the top of the lodge. She was in this strange place for a purpose, but she couldn't remember what it was. Why was Dominic here and why was he holding Abigail? All at once everything came back to her. She sat up immediately.

"How is she?"

Dominic smiled and Alexandra caught her breath. She was suddenly very aware of her disheveled appearance.

"She has spots, but the fever is gone."

With a sob, Alexandra reached for the baby and buried her nose in the auburn curls. "Thank God," she murmured.

"I've been up all night," Dominic announced. "It's your turn. Give her liquid only, no food. If she coughs, hold her over the mint fumes." He pulled off his coat and shirt and crawled between the pelts. "Wake me if the fever comes back."

Alexandra stared at his deeply tanned shoulder lying across the beaver skins. She had never seen Dominic without clothing, but she suddenly recalled the feel of lean, hard muscles hidden beneath the softness of a velvet coat. Her cheeks flamed. Quickly she stood and knelt by the fire. A meat soup simmered over the flame. Dipping a ladle into the broth she tasted it. Her eyes widened in surprise. It was delicious. Her sensitive taste buds detected the familiar flavor of salt. It had been so long since she'd had spice in her food. It appeared that Dominic was a man of many talents. Who would have thought an aristocrat weaned on the delicacies of a French chef would be so adept at cooking?

After Abigail had been fed and the lodge swept out completely, there was nothing more to do. Her drawing materials were in Mi-ni-wah-wah's wigwam, but she didn't

want to leave Abigail and it was much too cold to be outside.
Alexandra looked down at her hands and frowned. They
were filthy. An idea formed in her mind. Both the baby
and Dominic were asleep. When she picked up his clothing
from the ground she had smelled the strong clean scent
of lye soap. Again she looked at the furs. He was sleeping
soundly.

Quickly, before she lost her nerve, Alexandra dragged
a large cooking pot outside and filled it full of snow. Her
knuckles showed white through her skin as she lifted the
heavy container back to the fire. Praying Dominic would
not awaken before she was through, Alexandra rifled
through his pack of belongings until she found the precious soap. When the water was hot enough, she tore off
the hated Indian clothing and, with shaking hands, began
to bathe her face and arms. Hesitating, she looked down
at her body and then at the kettle. It was large enough.
Stepping into the water, she held her knees against her
chest and managed to sit down. She soaped her hair and
scrubbed every inch of skin until her eyes stung and her
flesh smarted and every trace and smell of Indian was gone.
Then she rinsed her hair and, stepping out of the water,
began toweling it dry with a blanket.

Unwilling to put on the filthy clothes, she rummaged
through Dominic's belongings until she found a comb and
a clean linen shirt. It was much too long for her, but it
would serve well enough as a nightshift. She cleaned and
rinsed the pot and placed the soup kettle back on the fire.
Abigail awoke once more and greedily drank down the
sustaining broth.

Alexandra soothed the baby to sleep. She was combing
out the tangles from her hair when Dominic awoke. The
day was almost gone. He looked at her from beneath his
eyelashes. Her long legs were bare beneath his shirt. The
fire outlined her body beneath the thin linen. His breathing altered.

She sensed that he was awake and turned to face him.

Whatever words she had been about to utter were forever silenced at the look of raw hunger in his eyes. Slowly she approached the bunk where he lay. As if they had a will of their own, her fingers reached out to caress the strong column of his throat, moving to the flat muscles of his chest and the dark, archangel beauty of his face.

Dominic hadn't breathed the entire time her fingers moved across his skin. His eyes were closed, his jaw rigid with the strength of his control. Suddenly, the bunk dipped and he could feel the warmth of her breath. He opened his eyes and exhaled in a rush of helpless need.

"Alix," his voice was harsh. "I haven't had a woman in a long time. God help you if this is a game."

"Hush." Her lips were warm as they pressed against his chest and moved slowly up to the hollow in his throat. "Don't talk, Dominic. You are here with me now. I'll not question the wisdom of fate in bringing us together again. Perhaps there may never be a tomorrow." Her voice dropped to a mere whisper. "There is only now. Share it with me."

"Do you know what you are asking, Alexandra?" His eyes were wary and as black as velvet.

Instead of answering, she unfastened the top button of her shirt. She had moved to the second when he pulled her down beside him.

"Alix." The word was almost a moan. His mouth came down on hers and the world went away. Everything disappeared—the fire, the fur-lined walls, the baby sleeping on the other side of the lodge—everything but him. She shivered as his hands moved over her body. Slowly, her mouth opened and she arched against him. The flaming heat beneath his sweat-soaked skin was more potent than a drug. His kisses became harder and more demanding. Alexandra was conscious of nothing but his hands and lips as they pulled the shirt away and moved across her skin. The need between them was fierce and elemental, rising from untapped wells deep inside them both.

Dominic knew the savage violence of the past year played a part in the depth and passion of Alexandra's response. He knew he should stop before it was too late. A gentleman did not take the innocence of an untried virgin. But he was no longer a gentleman and this was Alexandra. His Alexandra. His lips were on her breast. She shuddered and he knew it was too late. Nothing mattered any longer but the silk of her skin beneath his hands, the feminine softness of her breasts against his chest, and the low, whispered cry of pain and pleasure when at last he entered her.

Chapter 11

Dominic lay on his back, completely relaxed, stroking the red-brown curtain of hair covering his chest. His eyes were closed but he couldn't sleep. All of his senses were filled with the woman resting beside him. The magnitude of what had just occurred overwhelmed him and his mind grappled with unanswered questions. Alexandra stirred against his shoulder and his arms tightened around her. He wasn't ready to let her go.

She lifted her head and looked directly at him. "Is it always like that?"

Dominic looked down at the gaunt beauty of her face. "It will be better the next time," he answered shortly.

Alexandra believed him and it terrified her. Never in her wildest dreams would she have imagined her body could react the way it had. "My goodness," she whispered.

"Yes," he replied, his voice huskier than usual, and bent his head to kiss her. He intended it to be a tender caress, sweet and lingering, but when her lips clung and opened beneath his, he found he wanted more. Without releasing her mouth, he ran his hands down her back, reveling in the smooth skin and delicate bones. He shifted her beneath him. The delicious feel of her under his hands threatened to destroy his sanity. He wanted it to be different this time. The raging need of an hour before was gone. Now he wanted her to feel the building tension, experience the ache of desire. He wanted to touch every inch of her until she was strung as tight as a bowstring, vibrating at his touch. Tomorrow no longer mattered. The past was forgotten. Every fiber of his being cried out for this woman who, by all the laws of God, should belong to him.

His mouth moved from her lips to the smooth line of her jaw and then to her breast. Moisture beaded his forehead. A muscle jumped in his cheek. She moaned and he lost control. Waiting no longer, he slid his legs between hers, uttered a deep guttural groan and thrust deeply into her.

Alexandra arched against him, delighting in the urgent demand of his lean, hair-roughened body. She wanted nothing past this night. It was enough. The horrors of the last several months were wiped clean. Nothing existed but the warmth of the furs, the clean smell of soap, and the hard, probing flesh joining them together.

Holding his head to her mouth, she greedily kissed his lips, his eyelids, the hard line of his chin. The aching tension in the pit of her stomach mounted. Instinctively she moved against him wanting more, her fingernails digging tiny half-moons into his shoulders. He groaned and a warm surging wetness exploded inside her. She strained against him toward her own rising tension and when it peaked she arched and cried out as unfamiliar tremors racked her body.

Dominic gathered her in his arms and collapsed on top of her. Burying his head in the space between her neck and shoulder, he closed his eyes and slept.

Gently, her fingers sifted through his thick black hair until she found the strip of rawhide tying it back. She worked at the knot until it came loose. Silky dark waves fell across her face. She inhaled the scent of tobacco and leather. Tears welled behind her eyelids.

When Dominic awoke, Alexandra was dressed in her combination of soiled rags and Indian deerskin. His shirt was neatly folded on top of his bag. Her fingers moved quickly, plaiting her red-brown strands of hair into a single braid.

Dominic sat up, leaning on his elbow. "Will you marry me, Alix?" he asked abruptly.

She straightened her back and looked at him steadily. "Why didn't you ask me before?"

"I did."

"How curious." Her eyes mocked him. "I don't remember. Could I have forgotten such a momentous event?"

With an impatient shrug, he threw the fur covering aside and sat up. "Don't play with me, Alexandra. You know the rules. I spoke to the duke and he refused me."

"My grandfather had nothing to do with us," she said coldly. "Why didn't you ask me?"

Dominic stared at her, his face set in grim, forbidding lines. Was she really as innocent as she seemed? He waited for a long, interminable moment before speaking. When he did, the missing pieces of the puzzle finally fell into place for Alexandra.

"I was told that, due to the circumstances of my birth, I was not a fit mate for the granddaughter of the Duke of Leicester." There was no mistaking the pain in his voice.

Alexandra's eyes widened in incredulous disbelief. "Your birth is better than my own."

He laughed a short bitter laugh. "So I thought, until I spoke with my father. It appears that his late wife was not my mother."

"Who was she?"

He drew a deep breath. "Marie Leczynska," he said deliberately. "It appears that I am a royal bastard."

Alexandra almost collapsed with relief. To steady herself, she sat down beside him and wondered if he could hear the pounding of her heart. "Kings and queens do not wed for the same reasons as the rest of us," she said softly. "There is no shame in having a parent of royal blood. The Prince de Conde rules all of Paris."

"Conde is the king's son."

She moved her hand in a swift, frustrated gesture of denial. "You are your father's heir, his only son. Your mother isn't a peasant or a woman of the streets. It makes no difference to anyone that they weren't legally wed."

"It made a great deal of difference to your grandfather."

An arrested look appeared on her face. "Is that why you went away, Dominic? Because you thought I felt as he did?"

He shook his head. "It no longer matters. Life is different here. A man is what he makes for himself with his own two hands."

Alexandra smiled sadly. "You should have trusted me."

"Give me another chance." His voice was low and controlled, as if the emotions between them were too great to be given free rein. "Marry me."

She sighed. "You don't have to ask because of what just happened between us. I am every bit as responsible as you are."

She laughed shakily, and for a moment, he was reminded of the girl he had once known.

"Perhaps, even more so." A hint of red colored her cheeks, but she did not look away. "I don't regret any of it."

"I'm glad to hear it," he replied promptly, "but you know very well that what happened here has nothing to do with my question. I fell in love with you long ago, Alexandra. My feelings haven't changed."

"I'm flattered, but it isn't possible."

"Why not?"

"Because you're too late. I'm betrothed."

She had never seen him angry. He was known among the inhabitants of Bowating for his cool reserve, his steady nerve and icy control. In Paris, he had been an attentive, considerate suitor, teasing her with his mocking smile and the lazy, masculine charm that set him apart from everyone else she had ever known. Anger was an emotion completely foreign to the Dominic Jolliet she remembered.

He was angry now, with a white-hot blazing fury that darkened his eyes to pinpoints of smoldering charcoals and deepened the slashing grooves that ran down both sides of his face. Alexandra was suddenly afraid.

"Do you make a habit of this, *chérie?*" He ran his hand brazenly down the length of her body.

She refused to be baited. "You are experienced enough in the art of seduction to know that I do not."

"Then why now, when you belong to another man?"

She drew a long breath. "Because I may never belong to him. Because nothing has turned out the way I expected." Her voice lowered, but she refused to look away from the fury in his gaze. "Because I wanted to know what it feels like to love you."

His eyes softened and some of the terrible anger seemed to leave him. "I hope you weren't disappointed," he said at last.

For some inexplicable reason, she felt like crying. "You know better than that."

Cursing softly under his breath, he reached for her. She went willingly into his arms. "I don't know if I can give you up again, Alix," he murmured unsteadily. "It almost destroyed my sanity the last time." His lips were against her hair. "I can't help but think there is a reason we met again."

She buried her face in his shoulder, unable to keep back the traitorous tears any longer. If only it were possible. But now, there were even more obstacles to overcome than before. She was an Ojibwa prisoner and there were Julia's children to consider. England and France were at war and, of course, there was Anthony. Alexandra did not believe for a single moment that her grandfather had voiced the only objection to their marriage two years ago. The Duc de Lorraine had ambitions for his only son. The grand-daughter of an English aristocrat did not fit into his plans.

Alexandra had stopped thinking about the future months ago. Each new day stood alone, an isolated incident in her life, to be endured until it was over and she could lose herself in the blissful unconsciousness of sleep. If her traitorous mind occasionally wandered back to England or to Julia, she deliberately repressed the thought and threw herself into a regime of endless activity. Dominic was a part of her present. Alexandra would take her comfort and her pleasure in his company for as long as possible without recrimination or concern for a future she no longer believed in.

Each day they spent together in the women's lodge, Dominic watched in amazement as new facets of Alexandra's character were revealed to him. This woman he thought he knew, slender as a shadow and born to opulent luxury, cracked the ice of frozen rivers and laughed with delight when she gaffed a whitefish and lifted it bare-handed from the rushing current. He saw her slip without complaint from beneath the furs they shared each night into the arctic air to place more kindling on the fire. He wondered, as he gazed at her coppery head bent over a piece of deerskin she had chewed to softness with her own saliva, if he had ever really known her at all. Who was Alexandra Winthrop? The sensitive, fascinating English debutante or the golden-skinned siren who climbed into his bed and gave of herself with such abandon that all his defenses were stripped away. Long after she slept in his arms, he lay awake, shaken and humbled, every nerve on edge and exposed.

Mist veiled the hills like a blanket of smoke. Dominic pushed open the door of the lodge and stepped outside into the bitter cold. It was daybreak. Not a sound broke the silence. He breathed in cautiously. The frigid air stung the sensitive insides of his nose. Hunching his shoulders, he walked swiftly, purposely, across the frozen ground to the makeshift shelter that was the *coureur's* camp at the edge of the village.

The nagging worry that had surfaced in his mind for the past several days could no longer be swept aside. The baby was completely well. There was no sign of fever or the frightening pox that had covered her small body. Alexandra was Red Wing's captive. If she didn't return to his wigwam soon, he would grow suspicious. Dominic's time with her was limited. There was a chance, although slight, that the War Chief had considered his words. Perhaps he would ransom his prisoners to the French after all. Dominic cursed under his breath. Red Wing wasn't the only one who needed convincing. Alexandra, sure that her nephew would return, was determined to wait for him.

With a desperate sense of inevitability that grew stronger every day, Dominic heard the ice crack on Lake Huron and the snow turn to slush. He felt the warmth of lingering daylight and watched as flocks of geese and wild turkeys darkened the skies on their journey north. Green buds appeared on the trees and the fur of the hare and fox and marten were no longer white. When the first *coureur* braved the freezing current and paddled his fur-laden canoe up the St. Lawrence to Montreal, he knew that his time had run out. The decision was no longer Alexandra's to make. The Anishinabe would march north as soon as the weather permitted. Unless his instincts had failed him, unless he could bribe the young chief with enough gold to part with his captive, Dominic knew that Alexandra would make the journey as Red Wing's bride.

He needed money and he needed it quickly. There was only one way to get it. For the first time in two years, he would put his trust into the hands of another human being. He stepped into the rude hut and looked around. Four men, filthy and reeking of brandy, were huddled around a miserable fire, staring at the cards in their hands. They looked up as Dominic entered. "I win again, Gervaise."

The tall, sharp-nosed *coureur* smiled and laid down his hand.

Gervaise grunted and threw his cards down. "Luck is with you, Marcel. I owe you two pelts."

Marcel frowned. Dominic noticed that his eyes were small and set very close together.

"Come, Gervaise," the man protested. "You've only lost two pelts. Is your reputation as a gamester undeserved?"

"I am not a fool, my friend," Gervaise replied softly. "If you are wise, you will take the furs and say nothing more." He held the beady-eyed *coureur's* gaze for a long moment. The man flushed and his eyes lowered.

"Dominic." Gervaise grinned affectionately at the lean, black-haired young man leaning against the door post. "We are honored by your presence. Tell us how we can serve you?"

"*Oui,*" sneered Marcel. "Tell us what has lured you away from the bed of the beautiful Englishwoman, Jolliet. Have you tired of her or has someone told you of the Ojibwa Chief's plans to make her his squaw."

"Marcel!" Gervaise snapped a terse warning.

Dominic pushed himself away from the door. "Your questions are impertinent, *monsieur,*" he said. "I do not care to have the lady insulted. Apologize at once or you will have cause for regret."

There was complete silence around the fire. Dominic's words were low and hard, his eyes narrow and bright with anger.

"I speak the truth and owe no one an apology," the man grumbled.

"Marcel." Gervaise again intervened. He had known Dominic for two years and understood the meaning of that dangerous tone in his voice.

"You've the devil of a temper, Jolliet." Marcel laughed shakily. "I had no idea you had feelings for the woman—"

"Silence!" Dominic ordered. His hand moved to the knife at his belt. "I'm waiting, Marcel."

Marcel swallowed. His eyes moved to the slim, wicked blade of the nobleman's knife. He wasn't a fool. To face Dominic Jolliet, his hand already holding the handle of his knife, was foolish to the point of insanity. "I meant no harm," he said gruffly. "I beg your pardon, *monsieur.*"

Dominic slid his knife back into its sheath and waited. Marcel stood and reached for his coat. "I'll see to those pelts."

Gervaise nodded and waited for him to leave. With a slight movement of his head, he signaled for the others to follow. "Now, Dominic," he said after the room was cleared of all but the two of them. "How can I help you, my friend?"

Dominic stretched out on the beaver pelts and warmed his hands at the fire. "I need you to take my furs to Montreal and sell them for me. You will be well paid." The firelight played across his face, shadowing the hollows and emphasizing the high aristocratic cheekbones.

Once again Gervaise wondered what it was that kept this handsome young nobleman who could have all of Paris at his feet in the savage wilds of New France. "May I ask why you cannot take them yourself?"

Dominic grinned. "You may. But it will serve no purpose. My reasons are my own, Gervaise. You won't be sorry. I'll reward you well."

"Does this have anything to do with the Englishwoman?" the *coureur* asked bluntly.

"Tread carefully, *monsieur.*" Dominic's voice was once again dangerously soft. His black eyes glowed with a warning light. "If I wished you to know, I would tell you." Suddenly he smiled, exercising the full force of his charm. "Will you do it or not?"

Gervaise sighed. "*Oui, Monsieur de le Marquis.* When have I ever refused you anything?"

Dominic reached out and gripped the older man's shoulder. "That is precisely why I trust you, my friend. There is no one else I would ask."

Gervaise grunted, acknowledging the compliment. He would take on the task and be true to his word because of the love and respect he felt for Adrien Jolliet's young nephew. Deep in the recesses of his soul, he knew that even if he had no affection at all for the young *coureur de bois,* he would do as he asked. Only a fool would attempt to deceive Dominic Jolliet and expect to live.

Chapter 12

Salisbury, England

The Duke of Leicester stared in amazement at the array of huge traveling trunks cluttering the marble floor of his hall. "What the devil–!" His eyes met the anxious glance of his butler. "Searles, ask my wife to join me in the library."

"Of course, Your Grace." The butler hurried away.

Thirty minutes later, the duchess hesitated at the door to the book-lined room. Taking a deep breath, she turned the knob and stepped inside. Her husband was pacing the floor.

"I suppose I should be grateful that you deigned to obey my instructions at all, my lady," he growled.

Liane smoothed the rose-striped fabric over her enormous panniers and crossed the room to stand before him. "I was under the impression that I was mistress in my own home, Charles. Your instructions sounded rather like an order. You should know by now that I'm not fond of orders."

The duke gritted his teeth. Damn all exasperating

women! He fought to control his temper. "May I ask where you are going, Liane?"

"I thought I'd told you."

"You know very well that you did not."

They stared at each other. "I'm going to Portsmouth," Liane announced at last. "I've arranged passage to Boston. Captain Doddridge will see me to Fort Edward."

"I see." He sounded very unlike himself. "And if I should forbid it?"

Her dark eyes glinted with something he had never seen before. "That would not be wise, Charles."

Charles Winthrop, Duke of Leicester, sank heavily into the nearest chair. He knew the meaning of the word defeat. "No, I suppose not. When will you leave?"

Surprised at her easy victory, Liane sat down on the stool at his feet. "We leave for Portsmouth tomorrow."

The duke raised his eyebrows. "We?"

"Fanny will be traveling with me."

"Good God!" He looked horrified. "However did you convince my sister to make such a journey?"

Liane's laugh, pure and rich as a choirboy's soprano, warmed his heart. "It wasn't that difficult really," she explained. "Worth has mounted another mistress. I think Fanny feels that in her absence her husband will grow to appreciate her."

"More likely he'll enjoy playing the bachelor," the duke muttered.

"What of you, Charles?" Liane's face was serious again. "Will you enjoy playing the bachelor as well?"

Hope flared in Leicester's breast. Reaching for her hand, he lifted it to his mouth. "You should know the answer to that, my love. What we have together cannot be compared to the arrangement between my sister and her husband."

"Do you mean that?" Her eyes demanded the truth.

He hesitated. How could he explain what her coldness of the past several years had meant to him? He was a hard man. Displays of affection did not come easily to him. Only with Liane had he felt comfortable enough to open his heart and expose the vulnerable, tender side of his nature. Even his own children had never known him as anything other than a dispassionate disciplinarian. It was this woman, his companion and confidante, his duchess of nearly fifty years, his wife, who owned his soul.

Suddenly it was too much. Julia's loss, Alexandra's and the children's disappearance, the untimely deaths of his own son and daughter were as nothing compared to this. Liane, his Liane, was abandoning him. He gripped her shoulders fiercely. "Don't go," he pleaded.

"I must, Charles," she replied gently. "Alexandra and the children are all I have left. This waiting to hear old news is no longer tolerable. I shall go mad unless I do something."

"What of me? You are my wife, Liane."

She closed her eyes and felt his bitterness work itself deeply into her very bones. Did she dare suggest it? "You could come with me," she whispered.

"Yes, I could."

She opened her eyes and stared at him in disbelief. "Will you, Charles? Will you leave all this and come to the colonies with me?"

The light in her eyes wiped away his last lingering doubt. "I didn't think you would have me," he replied gruffly. "I shall be delighted to accompany you, madame, on one condition."

Liane frowned. "What is your condition, *monsieur*?"

"Fanny must remain here."

Liane placed her hand inside her husband's. "I accept your condition, my love."

The Sealark, a solid British merchantman built entirely of English oak, rose on a wall of water. Seconds later, the oaken hull with its towering masts, plummeted into a valley of menacing darkness, much like a matchstick helpless in the current of a mighty river. Liane clung to a post and watched from the safety of the companionway as the crew reefed the sails and tied down the masts. They had tried to outrun the storm, but now it was upon them and she was afraid.

"Liane." Her husband came up behind her. "You should go below. Everything that isn't tied down will be washed overboard."

"Please," she protested, "I cannot. I know it sounds absurd, but I'd rather die than stay shut up in that cabin again." Liane shuddered. Her bout with seasickness had been like nothing she'd ever experienced before. There had been moments during the worst of her retching when she'd believed her life would surely end in this world of keening wind and straining canvas and surging waves.

"It isn't safe," Charles insisted. "Come. I'll stay with you. Perhaps a drop of laudanum will help you sleep."

Liane allowed herself to be coaxed down the hatchway into her cabin. Lowering herself onto the narrow cot, she opened her mouth obediently for a measure of the sleeping draught.

She lay awake for a long time, her eyes wide open in the dimness, her hand tucked reassuringly inside her husband's. The deck swung, hovering in a slanted position and then righting itself once again as *The Sealark* rolled in the wake of the turbulent ocean. The blanket was comfortably warm. Not a word was spoken. Liane forced her mind into deliberate blankness, refusing to succumb to the panic that hovered on the edge of her consciousness. She focused on the swinging oil lantern hanging from the ceiling. Finally, it blurred and faded into mindless darkness.

She awoke with a sudden jolt. Pain brought tears to her eyes. Her forehead ached, and for a moment, she couldn't remember where she was. The flickering oil lamp hurt her eyes and the roar of the thundering waves pounded in her ears. She had fallen off her cot and Charles was gone. When she tried to sit up, the cabin tilted and she was thrown against a bulkhead. Frustrated with her unsteadiness, Liane grabbed hold of the door handle and pulled herself up. She opened the door and stepped out into the hall. Step by step, she managed the difficult climb up the slanted deck. The ship rolled and pitched, throwing her from one side of the companionway to the other until, by the time she reached the entrance, her frail body was purple with bruises.

Liane heard a loud drumming overhead. With a shock, she realized it was rain, a deluge of the kind she'd never experienced before. Waves roared and pounded against the sides of the ship and mountains of water washed across the deck. The wood creaked and groaned as if an angry master craftsman were tearing it apart, plank by plank, timber by timber.

The ship reeled just as she grabbed the railing, saving herself from being thrown backward down the path she had taken. The ladder was slanted at an impossible angle. Somehow she climbed to the top and peered out from the hatch. Her eyes widened and she stared, shocked at the terrible carnage. Broken and battered, the ship floundered on the heaving seas. Screams of agony could be heard above the cry of the wind as the main mast suddenly gave way, sweeping men off the deck. The dead were piled high at the masts, their bodies caught in the sails lying limply on the decks. Through it all, the eerie wailing of the wind whistled across the ship.

A wounded crewman was hanging on to the rigging with one good arm. The other dangled helplessly at his side, blood seeping from a jagged wound at the shoulder. Reacting instinctively, Liane lifted her skirt and ripped a wide strip of fabric from her shift. On hands and knees she crawled to the injured seaman and stuffed the linen into his wound, attempting to staunch the steady flow of blood.

Thundering mountains of water swept over the bow and across the deck, knocking her aside and washing the wounded man over the railing into the churning waters of the angry Atlantic. Bowing her head, she prayed fervently. Out of the corner of her eye, she could see the horrified face of her husband as he slipped and struggled his way across the broken rigging to reach her side.

Charles. She smiled. He was so very dear. Despite everything, she couldn't help loving him. The action around her assumed a dream-like quality. It would all be over soon. They would find Alexandra and bring Julianne's children back to Leicester. She would make it all up to Julia through her children.

"Liane!" The duke's face twisted in anguish. His hand reached out, clutching the edge of his wife's ruffled underskirt. The deck tilted once more. The fabric came away in his hand. A mountain of water swept across the deck. When the wave receded, the deck was wiped clean.

"No!" Charles thought he had shouted the words, but they were barely a whisper. Desperation wiped away his caution. He rushed to the foredeck, frantically searching the dark water. Shrugging out of his jacket, he stopped to remove his boots.

A strong arm clasped him about the waist. "What the devil do you think you're doing?" The captain's merciless stare demanded an answer.

"My wife," Charles croaked hoarsely. "She's been washed overboard."

Captain Bennett's eyes darkened with pity. "I'm sorry, sir," he said. "We'll do our best to find her, but in a storm like this I can't offer much hope."

"For God's sake, she can't swim," pleaded the duke. "Release me." He struggled against the arms that bound him like bands of steel.

"You won't find her, m'lord," the captain insisted. "Would you end your own life as well?"

"There is no life without her," shouted the duke.

"In that case, Your Grace, you leave me little choice." With a sharp, well-aimed blow to the side of the older man's head, the captain knocked him senseless. Dragging the heavy body, made heavier by his water-logged garments, into the safety of the companionway, he motioned to a nearby seaman. "Take the duke to my cabin and lock him inside. When the wind dies, climb the mizen and see if you can spot a body in the water."

The seaman was very young. His eyes widened. "Who is it I shall be looking for, sir?"

"The Duchess of Leicester," was the clipped reply.

The Sealark had sustained heavy damage. Repairs were going forward as quickly as possible. Captain Bennett squinted at the gray light of a new day and decided it was time to see how his prisoner fared. Making his way to his cabin, he turned the key in the lock, pushed open the door, and stepped inside. The duke was seated near the table.

"Good morning," said the captain.

Leicester didn't answer.

Captain Bennett cleared his throat. "I'm sorry, Your Grace. We found no sign of your wife."

The duke nodded.

"I don't mind telling you," the captain continued, "that it's a miracle we survived the night. The main mast is down."

Again, the duke did not respond.

Bennett tried once more. "You look as if you could use some brandy, my friend. Will you join me?" Without waiting for an answer, he walked over to a large cabinet. Opening the door, he removed a bottle and two glasses. He filled one and held it out to the duke.

Slowly, as if it took enormous effort, Leicester reached for it. Lifting it to his lips he drained the glass. The frightening grayness disappeared from his skin.

The captain leaned against the bulkhead. "Were you married long?" he asked.

"Yes" was the brief reply.

"I'm terribly sorry, sir." The honest blue eyes of the captain were bright with sympathy.

Leicester's good manners reasserted themselves. "Thank you," he replied, "for the sentiment and for the brandy. It appears I needed it more than I realized."

Bennett poured more brandy into the duke's glass. "What will you do now?"

It was several moments before Leicester answered. The captain, believing he hadn't heard, was about to repeat himself when the duke spoke. "I must go on, of course. This journey was Liane's idea." He stared into the amber liquid in his glass. "Our granddaughter and two great-grandchildren were captured by a tribe of Algonquin. We believe she was taken north to New France. It was my wife's dearest wish to find Alexandra. I cannot fail her now." A lump formed in his throat. It was hard to speak. "If I turn back, it would be as if she had died for nothing."

"So be it." The captain drained his glass. His face was smooth, revealing none of his inner thoughts. Traveling the woodlands near the Hudson River was difficult enough for a white man born and bred in the colonies. For an English duke, familiar with the comforts of clean sheets and featherbeds, it would be impossible. The only white men who could successfully negotiate their way through the thick pine forests and rushing rivers of New England and France were the French *coureurs,* and they were nearly as Indian as the red men themselves. There wasn't a prayer of a chance that Alexandra Winthrop and the children would be found. Bennett sighed. He hadn't the heart to tell the Duke of Leicester that he was on a fool's errand. Christ, the man needed something to do. Perhaps, by the time he realized the futility of his mission, he would have become reconciled to the loss of his family.

*   *   *

Leicester stood on the ramparts of Fort Edward and looked out at the panoramic view of North America. To the west were the breathtaking peaks of the Adirondacks, to the east lay the Green Mountains. Running north and south of the fort were the gleaming waters of Lake Champlain, claimed by both the French and the English. It was enough to make a man who had never seen anything larger than the Grampians catch his breath in wonder.

Fort Edward was much more primitive than the duke had expected. Surrounded by an outer wall, the fort was four-sided with pointed bastions jutting out from each corner. Captain Doddridge had explained that these allowed the defenders of the fort to deliver flanking fire down the length of the four curtain walls which lay between each bastion. A storehouse, square with a cannon mounted on its flat roof, stood southeast of the entrance arch. The walls, great squared timbers laid horizontally and filled behind with earth, were the fort's best defense against enemy artillery and could easily be repaired when damaged.

The duke looked down uneasily from his position on the ramparts. The garrison, built to quarter only four hundred men, did not look large enough to withstand a sudden raid. Perhaps they could hold out against a war party of redskins armed with only tomahawks and spears; but against French rifles and cannon, they would surely succumb. He watched Captain Anthony Doddridge climb the crude steps toward him.

"Good evening, m'lord." The young man removed his tricorne and tucked it under his arm. "I would be honored if you would join me for dinner."

The duke's bushy eyebrows drew together. He stared at his granddaughter's betrothed. What on earth had the girl seen in him? "Is there anything worth eating in this hovel?" he asked haughtily.

"Nothing that you are accustomed to, I'm afraid," answered Doddridge. Our rations consist solely of salt pork, some dried peas, and bread. We don't even have wine. But the spruce beer tastes surprisingly like ale and 'tis comfortably warming, besides keeping the scurvy away. I'm sorry sir, but it's all we have and it is better than starving." Doddridge flushed . He knew he was babbling, but Leicester always had this effect on him.

The duke sighed. "Well then, I suppose it must do. Go on, lad, lead the way."

With relief, the captain turned away and moved toward the stairs. Damn the man! He always made him uncomfortable. Why had he come at all? The duchess had specifically said that she intended to travel alone. It was the worst sort of luck that she had been killed. Her tragic death had made the old man more difficult than ever. When he had learned that despite months of searching there was still no news of Alexandra and the children, he had been furious.

Anthony Doddridge was an officer in the British army. He was familiar with surly-tempered men who vented their wrath on underlings. Loud voices and red faces were necessary evils that accompanied his position. The duke's anger was something entirely different, like nothing Anthony had ever experienced before. It was an icy stillness, a frozen contempt, a coldness so complete that the victim of that silent rage was never the same again. He wondered, not for the first time, how a woman like Alexandra, a woman of light and heat and laughter, could have grown up in such a household and come out unscathed.

Chapter 13

Dominic kicked at the beaver pelts in the *coureur's* lodge and swore under his breath. Ever since Alexandra had returned to Min-ni-wah-wah's wigwam, time had hung heavily on his hands. He resented the circumstances that kept him in Bowating long after he should have been on his way up the St. Lawrence. Gervaise had departed the week before. Dominic counted the hours. It would take another day to reach Montreal, a week to sell the skins, and then seven more days to return. Each evening, he marked off another notch on a wooden post in the lodge, breathing a prayer of thanksgiving that Red Wing still had made no mention of moving his tribe farther north.

"Dominic," Alexandra's voice called to him from outside. "Are you in there?"

Quickly, he opened the door and pulled her inside, closing it tightly behind her. They were alone for the first time in a week. His arms closed around her. Hungrily his eyes moved over her face, burning into memory every detail, every angle and curve of her still, autumn-colored beauty. Twisting the sun-streaked braid around his hand, he pulled her head back. Muttering under his breath, he set his mouth against hers, hard.

Welcoming the lean, muscular feel of him against her, Alexandra parted her lips. His kisses deepened. She moaned, a soft contented sound in the back of her throat.

"*Mon Dieu,* Alix," he gasped, lifting his head. "I can't get enough of you." His eyes darkened with desire. "How long do you have?"

Alexandra did not pretend to misunderstand his question. She had long since come to terms with the fire between them. Pressing her mouth against the line of his jaw, she breathed deeply. He smelled of soap and tobacco and leather, all things distinctively masculine. "Not long enough, I'm afraid," she replied regretfully. "I only came to tell you of the council fire tonight. There will be stories and dancing. Red Wing is to make an announcement." Her tongue touched his ear and her voice lowered. "Perhaps tonight we'll have more time."

Dominic forced himself to return her smile. Tenderly his callused fingers traced her sun-browned cheek and beautiful, sensual mouth. He bent his head and brushed his lips lightly against hers. No trace of the icy fear that clutched at his heart was revealed in his expression. "Until tonight," he murmured. The wooden door creaked as she left the lodge and closed it behind her.

Calmly, Dominic gathered his belongings and tied them together. He walked to the embankment where a single birchbark canoe rested on the shore. The water of Lake Huron, now completely free of ice, was a dark gun-metal gray, as still as glass under the cloudy sky. Dropping his belongings into the fragile craft, he knelt and ran his hands lovingly over the thin, durable bark. "Tonight, we leave," he whispered. "The waiting is over."

Alexandra listened as Sarah revealed the purpose of the evening celebration.

"The Feast of the Dead," she explained, "is a ceremony held for those who have died during the previous year. When an Ojibwa leaves the earth, a period of mourning is observed after the burial. The body is placed upon a platform where it remains for four days. The spirit leaves the body and travels to the afterworld. Then the body is wrapped in birchbark and buried with his feet pointing westward."

Alexandra was fascinated by Sarah's demeanor as she repeated her tale. She sat primly, her hands folded in her lap, her face perfectly composed, as if she were a child reciting her catechism. "Beloved possessions such as a medicine bundle or weapon are buried with the corpse," continued Sarah. "The grave is marked with the person's clan totem, turned upside down to indicate death. Small wooden spirit houses are erected over the graves. Each family who has survived a death during the past year holds a feast for the entire village. At the feast, a place is set for the deceased, whose spirit will remain in the family. Everyone who comes dines in honor of the family and in memory of the dead."

Alexandra's mouth dropped open. "You mean people actually *celebrate* death?"

Sarah stiffened and settled her son more comfortably in her lap. "It isn't so terrible. If heaven is truly a reward, why are the white man's funerals so mournful and dreary? It seems to make a great deal more sense our way. At least the living are allowed some pleasure."

"I suppose you're right," Alexandra replied slowly. For the first time, she realized the insurmountable chasm that separated her from the other Englishwoman. Sarah had cut all ties with her own people. She considered herself an Ojibwa. Alexandra smiled at her friend. "I won't question anything that gives us cause for celebration. This winter has been the longest I've ever known."

"Surely the time spent in the woman's lodge went quickly," Sarah teased.

A tinge of apricot stole across Alexandra's cheeks. "I'd rather not speak of it, Sarah," she said softly. Her time with Dominic was hers alone. It would have to last a lifetime, and she would not share it with anyone.

A strange figure stopped in front of the wigwam. He was a white man dressed in the black of a clergyman with a wide hat and a long tunic that closed around his throat and hung in long filthy pleats to the ground. He wasn't old, but his face was lined with deep suffering. "I have heard that your *enfant* was very ill, mademoiselle. Is she better now?" He spoke in flawless French.

"Yes, thank you," replied Alexandra in the same language. "She is completely healed. May I ask who you are, sir?"

"I am Father René Gerard." He held out his hand.

"You are a Papist?" The dislike in Alexandra's expression was unmistakable.

The priest hesitated briefly and then withdrew his hand. Nodding to Sarah, he moved away.

"Father Gerard is a kind man, Alexandra," Sarah reproved her. "Perhaps someday you will realize that goodness and generosity exist outside of England."

"In England, we do not care for Catholics," Alexandra pronounced stubbornly.

"Neither did I," Sarah replied. "Father Gerard is a Christian, no matter what his denomination. When my daughter was stillborn–" She bit her lip. "When one is alone, one learns to take whatever comfort is available. Many of his kind were tortured by the Iroquois, and still he walks among them, bringing the word of God."

"Why did you never tell me you had another child?" Alexandra asked softly.

Sarah didn't reply. Lifting her baby to his feet, she waited until he found his balance before releasing him. "I've much to do before tonight." She stood. "Goodbye, Alexandra."

Everyone in the village was present at the council. Braves,

young and old, sat in a circle around the fire. The women and children arranged themselves behind the men. Alexandra searched for Dominic. He was seated with the braves, directly across from her. She smiled and smoothed down the skirt of her tunic. Min-ni-wah-wah had presented it to her that morning. It was new and soft and felt deliciously warm after her threadbare clothing. The pale fawnskin had been dried, bleached, and chewed to buttery softness. Then it had been stretched and sewn into a close-fitting tunic with breeches that showed the slimness of her waist and the long, lovely lines of her legs. The hem and sleeves as well as the matching moccasins were covered with dyed porcupine quills arranged in the pattern of a timber wolf.

Overcome by the magnitude of such a gift, Alexandra had kissed the squaw's wrinkled face and immediately heated a kettle of water to bathe and wash her hair before putting on the garment. Unbound and smelling of the wind, her hair rivaled the glowing flames of the fire as it floated and crackled with a life of its own. Alexandra knew she looked brown and healthy and very lovely. She was glad of it. She wanted to appear at her best tonight. The reason had everything to do with the lean, stone-faced young man sitting across the fire from her. Dear Lord, he was handsome.

In the leaping light of the council fire, his chiseled, high-boned features looked untamed and fiercely primitive, very unlike the French aristocrat she remembered. With the uncompromising honesty that was part of her nature, Alexandra realized that she preferred him this way.

The blood drummed through her veins and her cheeks felt hot. She was sure that Dominic had not yet noticed her. The Indian brave sitting in front of her was very large. She shrugged her shoulders. It wasn't important. Before the evening was finished she intended to make very sure that the young *coureur de bois* noticed little else.

Red Wing lit the pipe, drew on it deeply, and then passed it on. Each man sucked in the acrid smoke and then gave

it to another beside him. Alexandra wrinkled her nose
against the sweet, cloying smell and waited for something
to happen.

The Grand Sachem, impressive in his feathered head-
dress, rose and, using as many gestures as he did words,
began to speak.

"What is he saying?" Alexandra whispered to Sarah, who
sat beside her."

"Hush." Sarah laid her finger across her lips. "It is
the Midewiwin Origin Tale. Listen carefully and you will
understand."

Obediently, Alexandra concentrated. She knew enough
Anishinabe to make out most of what the old man said.
Soon, she forgot everything but the magical words of the
story of creation told in the melodic cadence of the Ojibwa
holy man.

"The Great Spirit, Kitche Manido, created the first
Indian. He picked up the dirt from the earth and closed
his hand. Something moved and he opened it and saw a
woman. The Great Spirit was pleased. Her skin was the
color of the earth, and her hair and eyes the dark of the
night sky." The silence was complete. Not a child moved
nor a dog barked. *"Breathe,* commanded the Great Spirit,
and the woman breathed. He gave the woman seeds of
many kinds to raise gardens, and he gave her a bow and
arrow. *The seeds will nourish you in greater ways than ever the
bow and arrow will,* Kitche Manido warned her. The woman
looked around and realized that there were two of every
bird and fish and animal. *Where is my companion?* she asked
the Great Spirit."

Alexandra shifted her body to look around the Indian
who blocked her view. Dominic's eyes met hers, black and
burning with intensity. It was almost as if the Sachem's
words were intended for the two of them alone. She could
not look away.

"The woman slept," the Sachem continued. "Kitche
Manido moved around her. Reaching down, he removed

the woman's lower rib. When she awoke, she found herself lying with another person, made like herself. That is why a woman has fewer ribs than a man." The Sachem dropped his arms and bowed his head. "The legend is finished. I have nothing more to say on the subject."

When he spoke again, his voice had changed. He was no longer the harbinger of the Great Spirit. He was a man, pleased with his role in this celebration. "Our Great Chief, Wiskino, Red Wing of the Owahki clan, has once again chosen a bride." He spoke formally, cognizant of the importance of his announcement. "After the dancing and the exchange of gifts, the marriage ceremony will take place."

Alexandra was stunned. Neither Mi-ni-wah-wah nor Red Wing had mentioned that he was thinking of marriage. Who could the woman be and how would it affect their living arrangements?

This time the pipe was passed to the women. Alexandra inhaled the thick, sweet smoke and immediately experienced a rush of dizziness. Experimentally, she inhaled again. It was suddenly very warm and the night darkness exploded with flashing color. She felt weightless, as if she floated on water. Caught up in the heady, unfamiliar sensations, she didn't notice when the pipe was removed from her hand.

Somewhere, from a distance, the sound of drums beat its even toneless rhythm through her head. Human voices chanted softly and grew steadily louder. Hazy figures gathered into a circle and moved to the music, slowly at first and then, as the tempo increased, faster and faster, until Alexandra could no longer distinguish between the pounding of the drums and the throbbing, fevered cadence in her brain. It was too much! She was afraid. Afraid of the primitive gyrating movements of the dancers, the mindless freedom brought on by the drug-laced tobacco, the music that could have but one purpose, and the wild, sensual singing of her blood.

Sarah was no longer beside her. A bare-chested brave had thrown his blanket around her, pulling her into the circle of dancers. Alexandra's eyes widened. She struggled to focus. A tall, dark figure materialized before her. His features were blurred, but she knew who he was immediately. Even if she hadn't recognized the blanket that had warmed her for so many nights, she would have known that masculine, predatory grace anywhere.

Dominic held up the blanket. As if she had no will of her own, Alexandra stood and moved into his arms. He closed them around her, capturing her in the welcoming gray wool. For the space of a heartbeat, he held her against him, breathing in the intoxicating scent of clean, wind-blown hair. His arms tightened possessively. She lifted her head, her mouth a hair's breadth from his own. Dominic stepped back to unwrap the blanket from around her body and, imitating the other dancers, threw it over his own shoulders. Holding the ends, he pulled Alexandra back into his arms and drew the concealing wool completely around them both.

The drumbeats softened. A single voice began to chant. Others joined in. The eerie, melodic notes flowed through Alexandra's mind, consuming it completely, sweeping away the last of her fears. She was completely relaxed. Her head rested on Dominic's shoulder and her body molded against his as he guided her in the strangely familiar movements of the ancient love song.

"Nia nin-di—nen—dum nia nin-di-nen-dum me—ka a—nin nin—i—mu—ce sa nia nin-di-nen-dum," the voices sang.

Dominic translated, his voice low and husky, his breath warm against her ear,

"Oh, I am thinking, Oh, I am thinking. I have found my love. Oh. I think it is so."

Alexandra smiled into his shoulder and closed her eyes. She was comfortably warm and very drowsy. If only they could stay like this forever, just the two of them, hidden from curious eyes by the concealing folds of the blanket.

She burrowed against him, straining for even closer contact.

Dominic drew a ragged breath. The feel of her skin, the smell of her hair, the delicious softness of her breasts pressed against his chest were driving him insane. His senses were heightened by the potent tobacco and the disturbing, erotic melody of the mating dance. Impossible images formed in his brain. As clearly as if it were truly happening, he could see it, the two of them, on the ground in the warm darkness, locked in a passionate embrace, her sun-gold body naked and welcoming beneath him, her lips begging him to take her quickly.

With a muffled curse, Dominic pressed his lips to the pulse leaping in her throat. At the same time, he pulled her tightly against the aching hardness between his thighs.

Alexandra was drowsy no longer. She was deeply and passionately aroused. The darkness and privacy of the blanket gave her courage. Following her instincts and the wild surging of her blood, she slid her palms under his shirt, stroking the taut skin of his chest. Rewarded by the sudden tensing of his muscles, her fingers moved down to his stomach. Tilting her head back to give him greater access to her throat, she continued her tactile exploration, moving ever downward. When she had almost reached her goal, Dominic gave a low, strangled cry and caught both her hands in a viselike grip. She waited in expectant silence.

"Enough, Alix! This is torment." He laughed unsteadily. "In another moment I shall be unmanned, *chérie*. Either that, or I'll take you here in front of them all and damn the consequences." Bending his head, he nuzzled her throat.

Alexandra smiled. Reveling in her power, she gave herself up to the feel of his mouth on her skin and the incredible, heart-stopping pleasure of his hand on her breast.

It seemed as if they had been together only a few moments when the drumming stopped. Dominic swore softly and gave her a swift, hard kiss before lowering the blanket. The dancers moved back to their places in the circle. Alexandra sat down beside Sarah. She was surprised to find the space in front of her empty. The large brave was nowhere to be seen. It was as if everyone had moved back several spaces, leaving her exposed and alone. Involuntarily, she shifted closer to Sarah.

The Sachem was speaking again, very quickly. Alexandra couldn't make out the words. She leaned toward Sarah, a question on her lips. Before she could discern the meaning of the holy man's words, Red Wing rose. He carried something in his hand. Alexandra's eyes were drawn to his magnificent, almost-naked body and the arrogance stamped on his boldly shaped features.

To her surprise, he caught and held her gaze. Slowly and with great deliberation, he crossed the empty distance between them to stand before her. In his hand was a beautifully fashioned necklace made of rare white wampum from the inside of a conch shell. He offered it to her.

Completely confused, Alexandra reached for the necklace. Across the silent council fire, all eyes were upon her.

"I thank you," she said formally. "What does it mean?"

Red Wing spoke at last. "When the last snows melt on the lake, the Anishinabe will travel north to the Rainy River Country. Before we go, you will become my woman, wife of Wiskino."

Wife! The word sank into her drug-dulled consciousness. She worked to concentrate, to understand the full implication of his speech. Her blood froze. A squaw! Red Wing's woman! An Indian squaw! Visions, unbidden and painful, danced before her eyes. Julia, serenely beautiful as she doused the candles of the home she had shared with James. Julia, a tower of uncomplaining strength on their nightmare trek through the woods. Julia, knowing her fate and heartbreakingly brave as she kissed her children goodbye and begged Alexandra to stay with them. The Indian brave, his fingers stained with blood and Julia's scalp in his hand. Bile rose in her throat. She was going to be sick.

"I shall never be your squaw!" Alexandra's voice came out in a whisper.

Red Wing heard her and saw the undeniable loathing in her expression.

Hurt and something else, something she couldn't bear to read, burned brightly in the almond-blackness of his eyes. Nothing of his thoughts were revealed in the grim, pagan-carved austerity of his face. He simply waited, motionless, in complete control, to see what would happen next.

In that one endless moment that lasted a thousand lifetimes, Alexandra knew she must leave or disgrace herself. In a wave of anguish, she covered her mouth with her hands and fled, leaving the necklace in the dust.

Chapter 14

Alexandra ran through the darkness to her wigwam and threw herself on a pile of beaver skins near Abigail. The baby stirred, searched for her thumb, and then settled back into sleep.

Wiping her nose with the back of her hand, Alexandra sat up and thought. Her mouth turned down in bitter self-condemnation. She had been a fool to think that the many kindnesses, the light chores and new clothing, her unusual freedom within the village had come with no thought of compensation. These were Indians, the same evil tribe that had callously murdered Julia. Red Wing and Min-ni-wah-wah had planned this from the beginning. Alexandra knew, with a terrifying sense of hopelessness, that she would never be ransomed to the French. Tears filled her eyes. Burrowing into the warm skins, she sobbed herself to sleep.

Dominic pushed aside the pelts and stepped into the wigwam. Alexandra's eyes were closed. Her breath came unevenly in deep broken gasps. He stared down at her for a long moment, the tear-streaked cheeks clearly visible in the firelight. His face was iron-hard, reflecting none of the concern and exasperation he felt. Kneeling beside her, he reached out to shake her awake.

"Wake up, Alix," he ordered, his voice low.

Immediately her eyes opened. When she saw who it was, she threw herself into his arms. He held her, stroking her head as if she were a child.

"Come," he said gruffly, holding her away from him. "There is no time to waste. Listen to me, Alix. Your actions at the council have changed everything. You can no longer wait for Travis to return."

She stared at him in confusion. Her eyes were wide, the pupils still dilated from the drug. Dominic shook her harder than he intended. "You've insulted an Anishinabe chief, Alexandra. Do you realize what that means?"

He could feel her shoulders stiffen under his hands. "What should I have done? Pledged my troth to an Indian and stayed in this cursed village forever?"

Resorting to his native tongue, Dominic cursed long and fluently.

Alexandra frowned. "What did you say? I've never heard those words before."

Despite his foul mood, Dominic grinned. "I should hope not." Then, his smile disappeared. "If you had not shown your feelings so undeniably, we might have had a chance. As it is, we cannot wait for Gervaise to return." His hands tightened on her shoulders. "I must leave you, Alix. With luck, I'll be back before the tribe moves north. I have a feeling that Red Wing will be only too grateful to part with you now." He pulled her against the wall of his chest. "Be careful and do whatever you must to survive. Your life will not be easy for the next several weeks, but if you do as I say, you will live." He breathed in the clean scent of her hair. "Trust me, love. I'll return as soon as I can." His lips brushed her temple and then he was gone.

When Min-ni-wah-wah returned to the wigwam, Alexandra lay on her skins pretending to sleep. A painful kick in the ribs caused her eyes to fly open. She sat up immediately.

The old woman's eyes flashed with anger. She pushed Alexandra toward the water buckets. Hurriedly, the girl complied. She realized the truth of Dominic's words. She was no longer a favored captive. She must look to herself to survive.

In the morning, her misery was complete. She was no longer allowed to care for Abigail. The baby was given to Sarah to replace the infant daughter she had lost long ago. Alexandra breathed a sigh of relief when she learned who the woman was. Sarah would care for the child as if she were her very own. Min-ni-wah-wah had taken the baby to her new home, refusing even to allow Alexandra to kiss her goodbye.

Returning from her errand, the old woman found Alexandra sitting by the fire, her sketchpad in her lap. With a wicked slap that made the girl dizzy, she ordered her back to work. From then on, there were no more long afternoons chatting with Sarah or drawing by the fire. Her days were spent scraping the nauseating flesh from animal skins, grinding corn to a fine powder, and scrubbing cooking pots with pebbles and sand from the lake. Her hands blistered and bled and grew callused as handles from heavy buckets dug deeply into her palms. Her head pounded, and occasionally she sported a black eye from the indiscriminate blows of the old woman who had once smiled at her so kindly.

Red Wing no longer looked at her at all. He avoided her gaze completely, behaving as if she didn't exist. Alexandra regretted the coldness that had sprung up between herself and the young war chief, but not once did she wish to reverse the decision she had made at the council fire. She was an Englishwoman. In her mind she could see the gables of Leicester Manor as clearly as if they stood before her. She was not like the other captives. She had promised Julia to take her children back to England. Not for one moment did she believe she would spend the rest of her life as an Indian squaw. Dominic would come for her. He had given his word. For a fleeting instant, she wondered what price he would demand for giving her her freedom. She pushed the thought to the back of her mind and picked up a broom. Whatever it was, as long as she could return to England, she would pay it.

Alexandra was pouring water into a cooking pot when a man, his face marked and lined with age, hobbled up to her. Smiling a toothless grin, he reached out and ran his hand up and down her arms. She jerked away, dropping the precious water, and ran into the wigwam, her face flushed with anger.

Min-ni-wah-wah did not look up from her sewing. "Worthless one," she snarled, "why have you left your work?"

Alexandra sank gracefully to the ground in front of the old woman. "Who is that man?" She pointed to where the ancient sannup still waited.

Min-ni-wah-wah's eyes glittered with contempt. "For a white slave, you are very particular. Since my son does not appeal to you, I thought you would prefer a different type of brave."

Alexandra shrank back in horror. "You can't mean to give me to him."

"I will do as I please," replied Min-ni-wah-wah coldly.

Sick at heart, Alexandra stumbled from the wigwam toward the woodpile. She needed a quiet place to think. In the waning light of late afternoon, she faced her dilemma squarely. For the first time in her life, she was without a man's protection. Her smile was bitter. Dominic had known what her fate would be even before she knew it herself. She would not think of Dominic now. He alone would understand what she must do. He had told her to survive.

She thought of Abigail's coppery curls and the incredibly baby-sweet smell of her. She thought of Travis as she had last seen him, defiance brimming in every line of his sturdy, six-year-old frame. Alexandra dropped her head into her hands. "Oh, Julia," she sobbed, "I can't. Don't ask it of me." In her mind, Julia's dark eyes reproached her.

It took less than an hour for Alexandra to come to a decision. Ignoring the taunts and malicious whispers of the Indian women, she walked through the village with her back straight and her head held high. She would survive.

Red Wing and Min-ni-wah-wah were inside their wigwam. She stepped inside and sat down before them. "I would speak with Wiskino," she said in a firm, clear voice.

"Insolent one." Min-ni-wah-wah lifted her hand to slap Alexandra's face. With lightning speed, the girl grasped her wrist and forced it to the ground. The woman whimpered with pain.

Alexandra's haughty voice reflected centuries of command. "Leave us, old woman," she ordered. "My business is with the chief."

Min-ni-wah-wah looked at her son-in-law. He nodded. Alexandra waited until she had left the wigwam before speaking. She looked at the dark, implacable face of the war chief and swallowed. She must do this. She had no choice. For long moments they stared at each other. Red Wing made no move to speak. She had requested this audience. He would wait as long as necessary for her to begin.

Alexandra cleared her throat. "At the council you told me I would be your wife," she began. His flat black eyes held her own, neither encouraging nor discouraging her words. "Why do you give me to another?" she whispered.

Red Wing's brow furrowed. Was the woman weak-minded? She had insulted him before his entire tribe. "You refused me," he replied woodenly. Not for the world would he allow a mere woman to see his shame.

Alexandra pretended amazement. "Does the chief of the Anishinabe require a woman's permission to take her?"

The firelight shadowed his face, illuminating the carved

planes and prominent cheekbones. He nodded. "It is our way. A woman may accept or refuse the brave who seeks to wed her."

The tension in the wigwam was thicker than cold honey. Inside her mouth, the sensitive skin was bitten raw. Alexandra tasted blood. Moving closer to Red Wing, she laid her hand on his arm. His muscles bunched under her touch. She breathed a silent prayer of relief. The man was not immune to her presence after all. "Must a woman be wed before the war chief can claim her for his own?" Her fingers trailed across his chest.

Red Wing's shuddered with the effort it took to control himself. He did not understand this fascinating woman, so different from any other he'd ever known. He still wanted her, but according to the laws of his tribe, because she had spurned him, he could no longer take her as his wife. Red Wing watched her warily. Her face was very close to his. Her eyes were the gold of sunlight on brook water. Did she know what the flames in those dancing depths promised? Were the honeyed words the invitation he sought? Her hands moved across his skin. Desire licked at the pit of his stomach and below. His loins ached. He clenched his jaw, determined to wait until he no longer doubted her motives.

Alexandra grew bolder. She leaned forward and touched her lips to his mouth. He didn't respond. She frowned. Again her mouth moved over his. This time, she flicked her tongue over the firmly sealed lips, demanding entrance. They parted immediately. Slipping the tip of her tongue inside his mouth, she slid it over the polished smoothness of his teeth, danced into the hidden hollows near the roof of his mouth, and finally, teasing and tasting, she coaxed his tongue into a ritual that simulated another, much older one that he understood very well.

Red Wing was astonished. The laws of his tribe forbade this, but his body was on fire, his nerves exposed. This strange mating of the mouths fevered his blood and pushed the doubts and questions from his mind. No longer could he mistake her meaning. This woman with hair of flame and skin like silk wanted him to take her. Untying his loincloth, he threw it aside and reached for her. Without releasing her mouth, he lifted her into his arms and carried her to the bunk where he slept.

Alexandra's mind separated itself from her body. She knew, as surely as she knew her own name, that her actions this night would damn her in the eyes of her world forever. Lady Alexandra Winthrop, London debutante, granddaughter of the Duke and Duchess of Leicester, and harbinger of the bluest blood in England, would no longer exist. Within moments, the tightly muscled body of the young war chief would join with hers and she would become Red Wing's woman.

His hands were on her thighs, urging them apart. Alexandra dragged her mouth from his and placed her hands on his chest. Whispering into his ear, she waited for him to move away and then sat up and removed her tunic and leggings. Closing her eyes, she lay down beside him and waited.

Red Wing stared in wonder at her body. He had never seen such skin. From her neck to her knees, it was as clear and pale as the sweet virgin flesh of a conch shell. Not a mark or blemish marred the purity of its color, the poreless perfection of its texture. Tentatively, his fingers moved across her shoulders, her breasts, the flatness of her stomach. No mortal woman could look like this, as if she had been touched by moonlight. Was she a spirit sent to test him? He felt the delicate fluttering of her muscles under his hand. Her eyes were tightly shut. Red Wing touched her sun-browned cheek with the back of his hand. She did not open her eyes. Suddenly he understood. She was afraid. His lips grazed her ear. His breath was warm against her skin.

"You are as beautiful as the dawn," he whispered, moving his hand between her legs, "as warm as the summer sun, as graceful as the red deer, as delicate as a woodland flower." His fingers dipped into her moist warmth.

Alexandra gasped. What was happening to her? Red Wing's lyrical words had woven their magic. She had relaxed her guard, imagining herself far away in another place, with another man. The blunt fingers moving inside her and the heavy weight of the massive, hairless chest crushing her breasts forced her back into the present. Blood drummed in her temples. Alexandra gritted her teeth. She must do this. She must mate with a savage for her own survival and for the sake of Julia's children. Turning her face into the Indian's bronzed shoulder, she parted her legs and drew a deep sobbing breath.

Red Wing frowned and lifted his head. He looked down at the woman in his arms. Her brow was furrowed, her eyes shut and her teeth clenched as if she suffered from a deep inner pain. He waited. After a moment, she opened her eyes. They were filled with tears and something else that Red Wing had seen in the face of every white man who had ever looked at him.

With a snarl of rage, he thrust her from him and leaped to his feet. White with shock, Alexandra stared at him. Never, in her entire time with the Ojibwa, had the war chief lost his implacable mask of self-control. His hands were clenched into fists and his chest moved in and out with the force of his fast, furious breathing. His face was dark with anger and his lips were drawn back over his teeth like a rabid timber wolf.

Frightened as she was, she couldn't help admiring the primitive beauty of the man before her. Dripping with sweat, Red Wing's tightly muscled body gleamed in the firelight. Every taut inch of him was fighting to master the rage that threatened to wipe away the learned discipline of a lifetime. How she would love to paint him just as he was at this very moment! Her fingers itched for her charcoal, but she didn't dare move. Every instinct of self-preservation told her to lie still.

Within moments the chief was calm. Without looking at Alexandra, he dressed and walked out of the wigwam. She heard him utter a curt command. Min-ni-wah-wah answered. Their voices grew softer. Alexandra frowned. They were walking away. She could no longer hear what they said. Swinging her legs over the bunk, she reached for her clothes and pulled them on. The smell of cooked meat made her mouth water. She looked longingly at the soup kettle. Min-ni-wah-wah would box her ears if she ate without permission. With a regretful sigh, Alexandra sank down onto the blankets that served as her bed.

The next morning it was barely daybreak when a harsh foot kicked her awake. Clutching a blanket, Alexandra rose to her feet and followed Min-ni-wah-wah through the village, past the Council circle, and down the rocky bank to the river. A canoe sat in readiness in the water and two Indians waited beside it. Sarah, her face lined with worry, stood by the water holding a bundle in her arms. The bundle stirred and Alexandra could see a hint of copper curls. Abigail!

She held out her arms. "What is happening, Sarah?" she asked in English. "Why are we here?"

Sarah handed the baby to Alexandra and laid both hands on the younger woman's shoulders. "Do not ask any questions, Alexandra. Red Wing has persuaded Min-ni-wah-wah to let you go. You are to travel to Montreal. Once you are there, it will not be difficult to send word to your grandfather." She hesitated. "Be careful, Alexandra. An Englishwoman, alone and unprotected in a French city, will have a difficult time of it."

Alexandra's smile was radiant. "Thank God! I've prayed for this moment. Anything will be better than this. The French, at least, are civilized people."

Sarah hugged her. "I hope you may be right. You won't be a nobleman's granddaughter in Montreal. Remember that, and take care. I'll watch for Travis."

"You've been a wonderful friend, Sarah. If there is anything I can ever do—"

Sarah's eyes misted. She shook her head. "My life is here. Goodbye, Alexandra."

Min-ni-wah-wah stepped forward. "Go now. It is time." She nodded to one of the Indians, who immediately stepped into the canoe.

"You must leave now, Alexandra." Sarah's voice was surprisingly firm.

The frail craft rocked beneath her. She swayed and clung tightly to Abigail. With one mighty shove, the Indian pushed it away from shore and within moments they had reached a fork in the river. Alexandra, looking back, watched Sarah's thin figure standing on the shore, her arm raised in farewell. The canoe rounded the bend, and she disappeared into the mist.

Chapter 15

Alexandra's eyes widened at her first glimpse of Montreal. She had expected a primitive village, a rustic fishing and fur-trading center. Instead, she saw a bustling metropolis similar in size and sophistication to the cities of England and France. Set on the banks of the broad St. Lawrence, steep, black-gabled roofs and two huge stone towers dominated the skyline. She remembered that the island had been discovered and named by the explorer Cartier more than two hundred years before. Churches designed in the image of French cathedrals were everywhere, and even Alexandra had to admit that the stained-glass madonnas smiling tenderly down at her were lovely. An impressive stone wall several feet thick surrounded the city, giving it a brooding, fortress-like quality, undeniable evidence that the forest and danger lurked a mere stone's throw away. She shivered and pulled the blankets around her niece.

It was late, well after the dinner hour, and terribly cold when the canoe finally reached the landing beach. Biting winds pierced through Alexandra's clothing. Numb with fatigue, she climbed out of the canoe and buried her face in Abigail's blanket. One of the Indians disappeared, returning a short while later with two soldiers. Alexandra, her arms aching from Abigail's weight, was pushed up the bank, through a fortified gate, and into a flimsy hut.

Outside the Indians and French soldiers argued loudly. She strained to hear, but the moaning wind and the cabin walls muffled their voices. The arguing stopped and Alexandra heard footsteps walking away. Then the door swung open and a man in a blue-and-white uniform studded with brass stepped inside, followed by the two soldiers. They stared at Alexandra. Aware of how she must look, she flushed and lifted her chin. She was Alexandra Winthrop, and they were no more than boys. One of them grinned and gestured crudely to the soldier by his side.

She could contain herself no longer. In perfectly clear, perfectly contemptuous French, she spoke. "You need a lesson in manners, sir. However, I'm convinced that it wouldn't be worth my time to attempt it."

The young soldier's mouth dropped open and his ears reddened. The officer looked at her in astonishment. "Who are you, *mademoiselle?*"

"My name is Alexandra Winthrop," she replied haughtily. "I am the granddaughter of Charles Winthrop, Duke of Leicester."

"*Mon Dieu.*" He frowned and his eyebrows drew together over piercing blue eyes. Alexandra was reminded of her grandfather after an unpleasant experience with his gout. There was something steady and uncompromising in the man's glance. Stroking his chin, he turned to the soldiers behind him. "Why was I not made aware of this?"

The young soldier shifted uneasily. "We were told she was English, m'lord. Nothing else."

"My apologies, *mademoiselle.*" The officer bowed stiffly. "Under the circumstances, I must make other arrangements for you." He nodded toward Abigail. "The child will go to my sister, the wife of the Chevalier de la Champlain. She is unable to have children of her own."

"This child is English. She is also my niece," replied Alexandra coldly. "She cannot be given away like a lapdog."

He rubbed his forehead and grimaced, mentally damning the incompetence of the soldiers assigned to him. "You are an Englishwoman," he reminded her, "alone and unprotected in a country at war with yours. It is hardly a position from which to make demands." He reached for the child. The look on Alexandra's face stopped him. He reconsidered. Dropping his arms, he tried to reason with her. "Do not be difficult, *mademoiselle*. The child will be well cared for. You cannot take her where you are going."

"Where is that?"

"I had intended to send you to *Les bonnes Soeurs de la St. Marie*," he replied. "They are a teaching order and take all English prisoners until we can arrange accomodations for them." His lips twitched. "Despite your bedraggled appearance, *mademoiselle*, I hardly think that would suit you. You are most definitely not a servant. Unless you have a strong desire to become a postulant and enter the holy order, another accomodation must be found for you."

Alexandra's eyes widened. "I am no Papist."

The officer laughed. "I thought not. Come." He held out his arm. "I'll take you to the governor's lady. Madame Vaudreuil will know what to do with you."

Reluctantly, Alexandra slipped her arm through his. He seemed a kind man and she had little choice. At least he had told her whom Abigail would be staying with. It was a great deal more than she knew of Travis.

Stepping carefully over uneven cobblestones, Alexandra looked around. All she could see were close, dark walls blocking her view of the city. Turning into a wider street that led to a steep hill, she could see that the houses had become very grand. At the top of the hill, they stopped and the officer knocked loudly on the wooden door of a large château. The door opened and he led Alexandra across the threshold and into a room. She gasped with shock and pleasure.

A fire blazed in a stone hearth so wide it filled the entire length of the wall. Pewter pots and cooking utensils hung from brackets mounted above the mantel. Blessed heat and golden light and the unmistakable smells of yeast and cinnamon filled the room. White cloths covered a table that Alexandra recognized as sturdy English oak. To her comfort-starved eyes everything about the kitchen of the Château de Ramezay was like waking from the nightmare of her life to find everything restored to its own familiar beauty.

Three women, obviously servants, gaped at her in silence, their dark eyes wide with surprise. Then, as if on cue, they all spoke at once, hands lifted, voices raised, shrill and unfamiliar and terrifying.

"Silence," ordered the officer. "This woman is a lady. She needs food and clothing." The corner of his mouth turned up. "And perhaps a bath. See to her while I inform your mistress of her arrival."

Alexandra flushed. It was no wonder their glances were suspicious. Her skirt was filthy, her hair impossibly tangled, the skin of her face roughened and burned dark from the sun. In the warm brightness of the kitchen she looked odd and foreign and terribly out of place. Involuntarily, her arms tightened around Abigail. Uncomfortable in the stranglehold embrace, the child whimpered and lifted her head. The firelight reflected off the coppery curls, surrounding the baby's head in a golden halo.

Cries of astonished delight came from the women. Before Alexandra could protest, one of them had lifted Abigail into her arms and pulled back the blanket. "*Comme tu es belle, ma petite,*" she crooned to the child.

Alexandra relaxed. The woman meant no harm. Abigail *was* a beautiful baby. Turning to the officer, she held out her hand. He took it. Ignoring the dirt, he lifted it to his lips. Color rose in her cheeks. "Please assure Madame

Vaudreuil that my grandfather will repay her for her kindness."

"That will hardly weigh with her, *mademoiselle,* but I shall do as you ask." His blue eyes smiled down at her one last time and then he was gone.

Thankful that she was no longer the object of the French servants' curious stares, Alexandra leaned against the wall and closed her eyes. It seemed less than a moment had passed when she heard a step in the hall. The door opened and immediately the women leaped to their feet.

The French officer was accompanied by a diminutive woman with very pale skin; small, delicate features, and a thin, haughty mouth. Her clothes were incredible. Blue silk swayed when she moved and white ruffles lined her throat and the hem of her dress. Gold gleamed from her neck and wrists and her hair was powdered and piled high on her head. Alexandra gasped with admiration. It had been such a very long time since she had worn anything soft and beautiful.

The woman's smile did not reach her eyes. "Welcome, my dear." Her voice was light and frosty. "We shall try to make you very comfortable during your stay with us."

Alexandra lifted her chin and met the Frenchwoman's gaze steadily. "Thank you, *madame.* I'm very grateful."

"Take the child, Lucien." Madame Vaudreuil waved her hand at the officer. "Mademoiselle Winthrop needs a bath and food. I'm sure every moment must be agony for her in those—" She wrinkled her nose. "—inconvenient clothes."

Alexandra's lifted her chin. "They are really quite practical, madame," she said.

"They are also dreadful," snapped the governor's wife. "You are too filthy to come upstairs. After you've bathed, Marie will show you to your room."

Alexandra bit back a scathing response, realizing that the woman was under no obligation to help her. "You are very kind, *madame.*" Under her breath she muttered in English. "I hope it doesn't choke you."

"*Pardon, mademoiselle?*" The elegant, powdered head turned toward Alexandra.

"Nothing," the girl replied quickly. "Nothing at all." With a nod, the woman left the room. Tears crowded Alexandra's throat as she watched the door close behind Abigail and the kindly French officer. At least she knew the child would be well-treated. Tomorrow she would insist on visiting Madame de la Champlain to see for herself if she was a fit guardian for Julia's daughter.

Immediately the kitchen servants fell to work. A large tub was pulled into the room and filled with hot water from the stove. Then, lowering their eyes, they laughed among themselves and waited.

Alexandra crossed her arms against her chest and shook her head. "I prefer to bathe in private," she explained in flawless French.

The women looked at each other and shrugged at the fastidious modesty of the English. After leaving a towel and robe, they left the kitchen in single file.

Alexandra's rebelliousness vanished. Untying the deerskin thongs, she dropped her clothes on the floor and stepped into the steaming water. Moaning with pain and pleasure, she scooped out a handful of soap from the dish on the floor and lowered herself into the tub. The soap burned her eyes. She scrubbed until her skin turned an angry red and then she rubbed the soapy suds into her mud-encrusted hair.

Thirty minutes later, a plump-cheeked servant returned to the kitchen to find Alexandra wrapped in the soft robe, seated by the hearth, working a comb through her hair. After smoothing out the last tangle, she stood up. The maid's eyes widened. "I had no idea a bath could make such a difference," she said.

Alexandra smiled and wondered what her grandmother

would think of the sinewy, dark-skinned skeleton she had become. *"Merci,"* was all she said.

"My name is Marie." The servant bobbed her head and grinned engagingly. "I have taken a tray to your room, *mademoiselle.* If you will come with me, we will go there now."

Alexandra followed Marie through wide hallways and long staircases, conscious of curious eyes following her as she passed by. Lifting her head, she refused to be intimidated. Leicester was every bit as lovely, she thought loyally. It was just older and less elegant. Turning down another hallway, Marie stopped suddenly and threw open a narrow door. Stepping back, she motioned for Alexandra to enter.

Never before had she set eyes on such a room. It was white with touches of yellow. Thick white rugs covered the painted floor. Yellow hangings embroidered with fringe framed the windows and the dressing table. Against one wall was a huge canopied bed complete with white draperies and yellow draw curtains. Against another was a white-marbled fireplace. The walls were decorated with delicate wallpaper artfully painted with white and yellow flowers.

Alexandra's artistic soul responded to the pristine beauty of her surroundings with the reverence of a holy man suddenly and unexpectedly confronted by his God. Tentatively, she ran her hands over the fine moldings, the embroidered coverlet, the ruffled pillows. Lovingly, her fingers traced the edges of the porcelain pitcher and the carved elegance of the chaise longue.

Marie watched, her eyes twinkling in amusement, her head tilted to one side while the Englishwoman looked her fill. Finally, she clapped her hands. *"Allons!* The food will be cold. Sit down, *mademoiselle,* and eat." Not until Alexandra was seated and her mouth stuffed full of hot, soft bread, did the maid nod her head in satisfaction and disappear from the room.

Alexandra stared at her plate in amazement. How could she possibly eat so much food? There were fish and carrots and steamed potatoes piled high on the white, china plate. She ate several bites and tasted a delicious, dark brew that she recognized as chocolate. She couldn't begin to eat it all. Alexandra rubbed her aching stomach. Her months in the wilderness had taken their toll. She felt light-headed and dizzy. The plates wavered before her eyes. She gripped the edge of the table and stood. A white lawn nightgown lay on the bed. She hadn't the strength to remove her robe. The bed had been turned down and a warming pan placed between the linen sheets. Crawling under the covers, Alexandra curled up in the luxuriant warmth. For the first time in months, her sleep was dreamless.

Chapter 16

Under his breath Dominic swore a vile oath, careful to voice the expletive in English. He was certain Chief Pontiac spoke only French in addition to his own Ottawa tongue. It was common knowledge that this infamous priest of the Midewiwin was illiterate and trusted no one. He had all messages verified by at least three French scouts before taking action on the notes' contents.

Pontiac wore a French officer's tunic over his own native garb. The costume had been presented to him by General Montcalm after the slaughter of the English at Fort William Henry. This charismatic war chief of the Ottawa was determined to unite all the tribes of the Great Lakes, Ohio, and Mississippi territories. His plan was to force the whites to abandon the land west of the Allegheny Mountains. Although Pontiac hated all Europeans and agreed with the Delaware Prophet that Indians should refuse all future trade with white men, he was also shrewd enough to know that his people's future lay with the French.

It was Dominic's misfortune that the war party had discovered him. It never would have happened if his mind hadn't been miles away, in the Ojibwa camp with Alexandra.

Fresh from his victory over the English at Fort Michilimackinac, Pontiac and his warriors were on their way to attack Fort Edward. Every available man, French or Indian, was recruited. Dominic Jolliet, steely-nerved and dangerous, expert tracker and marksman, was an agreeable surprise. Dominic, noticing immediately the guns and tomahawks hidden under the Indians' blankets and matchcoats, did not refuse.

He chafed inwardly at the delay in his plans and mentally damned Pontiac to eternal hell for further endangering Alexandra's life. He refused to think of what she must be enduring, forcing the images from his mind with concentrated discipline. It had been well over a fortnight. Perhaps she believed he wasn't coming back for her. He winced and closed his eyes, remembering the pain of such a betrayal. To lose her twice in a lifetime was more than he could bear. His jaw tightened and he opened his eyes. A determined light glinted in the night-dark depths.

Nodding his head, he reached across the campfire and took the pipe from Pontiac's hands. The *coureur's* lean, shadowed face betrayed none of his emotions. The tobacco was strong and sweet. He inhaled sparingly. The war chief was known for his uncanny ability as a conjurer. He was a priest of the Metai and had a reputation for correctly predicting the future. Dominic believed it had more to do with the drugging effects of the tobacco than from any unusual talent on the part of the chief. Pontiac would learn nothing from him.

They sat in silence for a long time. Finally, in flawless French, Pontiac spoke. "Does My-Father-Over-The-Water have new plans for his Indian brothers?"

Dominic hesitated. How much could he safely reveal? Pontiac was a butcher. He was also completely unpredictable. Every French man, woman, and child would be in terrible danger if the rumors were true.

Keeping his voice free of all expression, he answered, "Our French father across the water has great regard for his Indian brothers." He doubted that the selfish, greedy Louis XV was even aware that Indian tribes existed in New France.

Pontiac nodded and sucked on the pipe. Dominic continued. "He believes that it is wrong for the white man to stay in New Canada. But there are powerful men in his council who disagree. When he can convince them that his way is the right way, the French will leave the Canadas."

Dominic held his breath. With luck, Pontiac wouldn't grasp what he had left out. It would inflame the chief to new heights of barbaric cruelty when he realized that he would no longer have French support in his fight against the English to preserve Indian land west of the mountains. Dominic knew there was a powerful movement in France led by Rousseau and de Fleury, the king's minister, to give up its North American colonies. It was simply too expensive to provide for soldiers so far from home, especially when France itself was in danger of being overrun by Britain. He also knew, as surely as he drew breath, that when the troops withdrew from Canada, the slaughter would begin. Rivers would run red with the blood of the colonials left behind to fend for themselves.

As Dominic suspected, Pontiac's scarred face harbored a shrewd mind. He sliced through the sweetened words, straight to the heart of the matter. "General Montcalm promised that the English would be driven into the ocean before the French soldiers left us."

Dominic refrained from pointing out that the elegant Marquis de Montcalm had also promised the British safe escort from Fort William Henry after their surrender. Their massacre by the Huron and Ottawa while Montcalm's troops stood by and did nothing would go down as a shameful blot on the pages of French history. He shrugged his shoulders. "If the general is a man of his word, all will be well."

Across the fire, Pontiac stared at him, an arrested expression on his face.

The following morning the Indians smeared themselves with yellow and black paint—Iroquois, not Algonquian colors. Under the pretext of engaging in a friendly contest of lacrosse, they tossed a ball into the stockade. The gates of the fort were thrown open, and three hundred Indians managed to insinuate themselves inside the walls.

The inhabitants of Fort Edward were somewhat isolated and hadn't heard of the fate of the nine English forts along the Allegheny River. Otherwise, they would never have been tricked by the war chief's ruse.

Dominic, hidden behind the west gate, his flintlock engaged, war drums throbbing in his temples, refused to participate. He had seen more than enough of the hundred varied and ingenious ways in which the Algonquian could torture a man. But even he was sickened by the bloodbath that followed. The English were hopelessly outnumbered. Their commander was either terribly inexperienced or a complete fool. Soldiers screamed and fled from their tormentor's hacking tomahawks with no thought of defending themselves. Women and children, begging for mercy, had their skulls crushed into bloody, unrecognizable pulps, their bodies writhing in silent agony on the ground. A soldier, his cheeks still as smooth as a boy's, was split in two with a tomahawk. His executioner cut out his heart and ate it on the spot. Howling for English blood, the Indians continued their senseless butchery for three more hours.

Finally, Pontiac called a halt and assessed his prisoners. Walking from one to the other, he peered into each face, studying it closely before moving on. With an abrupt gesture of his hand, he turned and stalked out of the fort. The dozen English soldiers who remained alive were stripped and tethered by their ankles to poles high above the ground. Dominic, watching from his position at the gate, knew that in moments their faces would be a deep purple and swollen with blood.

"Poor devils," he muttered to himself. The Englishman in civilian clothes was an old man. He was also disturbingly familiar. Dominic concentrated on remembering where he had seen the man before.

In a piercing flash of memory, the cobwebs disappeared from his mind. It all came back, as familiar as if the past two years had never been. With a vile curse, Dominic pushed away from the wall and strode forward, only to stop in midstride and turn back. It would not do to seem overly concerned with the fate of the prisoners. He would wait until nightfall.

Piles of wood were stacked neatly beside each prisoner's post. Acrid-smelling fires were already blazing in dirt pits dug into the ground. Dominic recognized the odor. It was a powdered herb of a deep red color used in death rituals. Red had a particular significance for the Algonquian. It was the color of blood and war and rebirth. He eyed the prisoners uneasily. Which one of the poor unfortunates would be the first night's entertainment?

A red-haired soldier, barefooted and stripped to the waist, was cut down and brought forward. Five Indian braves, their hatchets and knife blades glowing orange with heat from the firepits, approached the prisoner. One stepped forward and pressed the flat of the blade against the soldier's side and held it there. There was a hiss, a scream, and the sharp, unmistakable odor of charred flesh.

Dominic turned away. He had seen it all before. Indians were not inherently cruel. They inflicted no punishment on others that they did not welcome and endure for themselves. Still, it was more than most white men could sit through without losing the contents of their stomachs.

Most of the prisoners still tied to the poles were unconscious and unguarded. Dominic laid his finger against the side of the old man's neck. Satisfying himself that he was still alive, he cut his tethers and pulled him into the shadows.

"Please," another prisoner whispered in English. "I am Captain Anthony Doddridge, commanding officer here at Fort Edward. Cut me down."

All at once Dominic understood the reasons for the old man's presence. The Duke of Leicester had come for his granddaughter. Naturally he would be accompanied by Alexandra's betrothed.

"Je regrette beaucoup, monsieur. J'en suis désolé," Dominic replied with clenched teeth. "One half-dead man is all I can manage." Straining, he lifted the body of the duke and slung it across his shoulder.

"Wait, please." The captain's frantic plea stopped him. This time he spoke in French. "The man you have is the Duke of Leicester. He is searching for his granddaughter. She is captured by the Ojibwas. I am her betrothed. Help us both and you will be greatly rewarded."

Dominic hesitated. The desperation in Doddridge's offer shamed him. Money he didn't need, but only someone completely without principle would leave a man to the tender mercies of Chief Pontiac. Depositing the still-unconscious duke on the ground, Dominic cut Anthony Doddridge's tethers and stretched him out beside the old man.

"We don't have much time," he warned. "They'll be coming for another prisoner soon."

Doddridge nodded and rose unsteadily to his feet. "I'll be all right. Do you have water?"

"There's a stream not far away," Dominic replied, once again hoisting the duke to his shoulder. "Follow me."

Three hours later, Captain Doddridge was completely spent. His breath came in harsh, painful gasps. He looked with amazement at the French *coureur*. The man had averaged more than six miles an hour carrying the duke's dead weight across his shoulders. Doddridge frowned. Who was this mysterious Frenchman who spoke English like a gentleman and knew the land as well as an Indian? He intended to find out immediately. *"Monsieur,"* he called out. Dominic turned around impatiently. At this snail's pace, they would never reach Fort Ticonderoga by morning. "What is it?"

The Englishman sank to his knees. "We must rest. I can go no further."

"Force yourself," ordered Dominic. "Pontiac's Ottawa braves can run forty miles without stopping. We are not yet safe, Captain Doddridge. Never doubt that they will follow us."

"Nevertheless," the captain insisted, "I must stop, at least for the moment."

"I didn't save your life back there only to watch your heart being cut out, *monsieur*. You will do as you are told."

"Why did you save my life?" The question leaped out, a desperate bid for time, but even more than that, an overwhelming curiosity that grew stronger with every mile.

"Because of Alexandra Winthrop."

The impossible words sucked whatever breath remained from the captain's body. Could he have heard correctly? What had this man to do with Alexandra? Rising to his feet, he stumbled after the lean, maddening, buckskin-clad figure of the *coureur de bois.*

Five hours later, they reached the French fort of Ticonderoga. Reclining on a military cot and propped up with pillows, the Duke of Leicester stared in shocked wonder at the man before him. He needed no introduction. The lean, chiseled features; the iron jaw; the lazy arrogant grace and raven-black hair; the smoldering anger in those mocking dark eyes were exactly the same as they had been in Paris more than two years before. True, his snow-white linen and satin breeches had been exchanged for stained buckskin, but the effect was still the same. Dominic Jolliet's very presence warned all but the foolish to proceed with caution.

Leicester wet his lips. He owed Jolliet his life. It was not often the duke found himself in such an awkward position. "It seems I am in your debt, Monsieur Jolliet."

Dominic said nothing. There was satisfaction in watching the Englishman squirm. At least the duke admitted to recognizing him. It was more than Dominic had expected.

"How did you happen to be at Fort Edward?" Leicester asked.

"Pontiac's war party found me. He hoped I might be useful." The terse words revealed nothing more than absolutely necessary.

Long moments passed. Leicester fidgeted with the torn edge of the blanket. The silence was oppressive. "You haven't asked about Alexandra," he said at last.

Dominic's mouth tightened. "You made it very clear that Alexandra is no concern of mine."

The duke lifted his hand in a feeble gesture of protest. "She is here in America, a prisoner of the Ojibwa. Will you help me find her?"

The dark eyes burned like angry coals. "Would you trust your precious granddaughter to one such as I, Your Grace?" Dominic's voice was hard and taunting. "Think of it. The granddaughter of the Duke of Leicester forced to endure the company of a royal bastard."

Leicester's lips trembled. "Is there no mercy in your heart, Jolliet? She is all I have left. I do not ask it for myself. Think of Alexandra. She had no knowledge of your visit to me that day in Paris. Can you bear to do nothing when you know she is the prisoner of savages?"

Dominic, his face impassive, said nothing.

"My God, man," the duke cried desperately. " 'Tis an odd sort of love you offered my granddaughter. I would have braved the fires of hell for my wife."

Something dark and elemental flashed in Dominic's eyes

and then disappeared. "I, too, would brave the fires of hell for my wife, *monsieur,*" he said softly. "Perhaps we can strike a bargain, you and I."

"I'll give you anything you ask."

"If I find Alexandra and bring her safely back here, I want you to agree to a marriage between us."

Leicester bowed his grizzled head in despair. "You're a stubborn young man, Dominic Jolliet. Why do you always ask the impossible?"

"Is your granddaughter's life worth so little that you would rather see her dead than married to me?" Dominic asked contemptuously.

The duke lifted his head to look directly at the young man before him. "I would do anything to save Alexandra," he replied, "but it isn't that simple. She is almost of age to make her own decisions, whether I give my approval or not." His face looked old and defeated. "She is also promised to Anthony Doddridge, the officer you rescued from Fort Edward. I know my granddaughter well, Jolliet. She will not break her word of honor."

"Nevertheless, Your Grace, I would like your permission to persuade her." Dominic waited, tense and as coiled as a spring, for an answer. He knew the duke's approval would mean a great deal to Alexandra. It might even turn the tide in his favor.

The two men stared at each other for an endless moment. Leicester was the first to break. "You ask me to betray Alexandra's betrothed."

Dominic turned and walked to the door. "There are other scouts, *monsieur*. If you pay enough, someone will be happy to search for your granddaughter."

"Wait!" The harsh command stopped Dominic. He did not turn around.

"Very well, Jolliet. Find Alexandra and persuade her to marry you. If you do that, I'll give you the finest wedding in all of England."

Dominic did not realize he had been holding his breath.

Quietly, he released it. He would find Alexandra Winthrop and he would marry her whether or not she was willing. But he had no intentions of ever allowing her to set foot on the other side of the Atlantic again.

Chapter 17

"But, *madame*," Alexandra protested. "I don't understand why I cannot take my niece and leave for England on the next ship. My grandfather will see that you are repaid for everything." She was on her way out the door, ready to accompany the governor's wife on yet another endless round of afternoon calls.

Madame Vaudreuil smiled thinly. "There is no guarantee, my dear, that once you are in England, we shall ever see a single *louis* of your grandfather's money."

Alexandra flushed and lifted her head. "The company here in Montreal must be very common, indeed, *madame*. In England, we keep our promises."

Madame Vaudreuil whitened under her face powder. The girl was insufferable. She lifted her hand to strike Alexandra's cheek. Something in the topaz eyes made her hesitate.

"A wise move, *madame*," Alexandra said softly, "a wise move, indeed." She nodded her head at the carriage waiting at the foot of the steps. "The horses await. I do not think I feel well enough to call on anyone today. Please give my excuses to your delightful friends."

Before the older woman could protest, Alexandra stepped inside and shut the door tightly behind her. Untying her bonnet, she examined it with distaste, her eyes a hot, angry gold. It was dreadful, last year's fashion and an unbecoming one at that. Had the woman no shame to allow a guest, even an impoverished one, to travel about in such a creation? Perhaps she had no taste. Alexandra considered the salmon-pink lustring that Madame Vaudreuil had worn that morning. Salmon did not suit her. It was obvious that the first lady of Montreal lacked an eye for color.

Climbing the stairs to her room, Alexandra threw herself on the bed, burying her head in her arms. Four weeks she had been in Montreal with no word from Dominic. She was not foolish enough to believe he had gone back on his promise. Her fear was that she had missed him, that he had returned to Bowating only to find that the Ojibwa had traveled north and he had followed them. She could not bear another endless length of days and nights in this foreign city of tall, stone houses and iron gates and disapproving eyes.

Each new day stretched out before her, an endless combination of tension and boredom that left her white-knuckled and drained, too exhausted to do more than pull the covers over her head and pray for the blessed relief of mindless sleep. Mornings were spent preparing one's self for embarking upon or receiving calls. Gowns were inspected, each one more unbecoming than the one before. Hair was powdered and curled, nails buffed, cheeks rouged, patches placed until every detail of Alexandra's toilette was deemed perfect. When she was pronounced ready, she would accompany Madame Vaudreuil in her handsome carriage with its sleek horses and gold-braided footman.

They would travel to another elegant house where

another exquisitely coiffed woman graciously welcomed them. The afternoon would be spent in mindless gossip, usually concerning a woman who was absent, and harmless wagering until it was time to go home.

Alexandra could never feel comfortable with these women. Their eyes followed her, noticing the too-dark skin and work-roughened hands, whispering softly about the atrocities she must have endured at the hands of the Indians. Too polite to come right out and ask if she had been ravished, they contented themselves with sending slanted glances in her direction when they thought she wasn't looking.

As the granddaughter of a nobleman, Alexandra was accustomed to town life. In London, ladies lay abed all day and spent their nights at balls or the opera. Her own interests had been different. For Alexandra, London had meant visiting friends, riding in Hyde Park and, most of all, improving her painting skills. By day, she would paint or frequent galleries and artists' haunts. At night, after a play or the opera, she was home before midnight.

The perpetual idleness of her new life was disturbing. Her healthy young body cried out for exercise. She found it difficult to sleep. At dinner, sitting between the governor and his wife, it was torture to swallow more than a morsel of food. Even the adoring eyes of Pierre Vaudreuil, the governor's son, set her teeth on edge.

At first young Vaudreuil's attentions had been a salve to Alexandra's wounded pride. His admiring smile was the first truly friendly face she had seen in Montreal. Never before had she considered her striking good looks or the effect her golden eyes and slim, straight figure had on a man. Now, when she compared the soft white complexions and smooth hands of the French women to her own, when she intercepted their pitying glances and sly smiles, she burned with angry humiliation. Once, a lifetime ago, she had been the toast of London.

Pierre Vaudreuil, the son of the governor and his first

wife, was a pleasant, sandy-haired young man with level blue eyes. By accident, he had encountered Alexandra at breakfast. Usually he ate alone. His father and stepmother preferred their morning *chocolat* and soft white rolls in the privacy of their separate bedchambers. It was something of a shock to see this slender, red-haired woman, dressed in his mother's outmoded gown, seated at the table, sipping coffee.

"*Bonjour, mademoiselle,*" he said quietly. "I believe we have not yet been introduced."

Startled, she turned toward him. His eyes widened and he caught his breath. The morning sun filtered through the windowpanes, illuminating her face in a halo of sunlight. Her brow was wide and intelligent, her lips full, her chin narrow and chiseled. But it was her eyes that held him. They were large and clear with thick, curling lashes. What he saw inside the golden depths moved him more deeply than anything he had ever experienced before. There was pain inside this woman. Suffering of such an agonizing torment that he could never begin to imagine it.

With no thought but to help, Pierre moved swiftly to her side and knelt at her feet. He took her hand in his. "May I help you, *mademoiselle*?"

She smiled and Pierre was lost. Alexandra had no idea how her brown, too-thin face changed when she smiled. She only knew that the young man's blue eyes were kind and admiring and she very much needed a friend.

No one seemed overly concerned that the two young people spent a great deal of time in each other's company. By the time Alexandra realized the full extent of Pierre's feelings, it was already too late to spare him. He had declared himself in love and offered her marriage. She refused him, explaining as gently as possible that she was already betrothed.

Since then, white-lipped and silent, he worried his stepmother by refusing to show up for meals. Later, he would disappear into the library with a bottle of claret and drink himself into oblivion. If, during his nightly wanderings about the château, he happened to see Alexandra, he would stare at her with such tormented longing that her folded hands would tighten in white-knuckled anger while she prayed for patience. Hurrying back to her chamber, she would compose yet another letter to her grandfather, knowing full well there was no possibility of an answer for months. Where was Dominic? Why didn't he come?

It never occurred to Alexandra to consider the nature of her dependency on the French nobleman-turned-*coureur*. She never questioned the strength of her own feelings or the impropriety of the bond that existed between them. The days in the women's lodge at Bowating had happened in another life, to another woman. In the back of her mind she considered herself fortunate. She had known the delicious, aching torment of Dominic's lean, beautiful hands bringing her body to the edge of passion and beyond. She had tasted his cool, rain-wet lips on her mouth and heard the heart-healing wonder of his words, low and muffled, against her throat. It was enough. When she left this place, she would return to England and marry Anthony Doddridge and never look back. But she would remember and be content. For in those few blissful days, she'd had more than most women had in a lifetime.

Madame Vaudreuil's ball was the social event of the season. Alexandra hadn't wanted to attend, but *Madame* accused her of being ungrateful and wanting her stepson's attentions all to herself. In the end, Alexandra succumbed to her own guilt. Albeit grudgingly, the Vaudreuil's had opened their home to her. The least she could do was appear gracious and show them she was just as anxious to see Pierre find an appropriate wife as they were.

For once, Alexandra's dress would be stylish. The dress-maker appeared one week before the ball. When the

woman had finished with *Madame,* she turned sparkling
brown eyes on Alexandra. It wasn't often that a seamstress
found such a promising client. The young Englishwoman
had style and her coloring was breathtaking.

"It will be a pleasure to design a gown for you, *mademoiselle.* Your posture is lovely and your figure perfect for the
new styles."

For days Alexandra stood and turned while the chattering seamstress fitted and pinned, snipped and sewed.
At last it was finished. Alexandra turned her back to the
mirror and looked over her shoulder. The heavy yellow
silk molded her small waist snugly, falling back to reveal
a petticoat of golden lace. Full sleeves, slitted and deeply
gored, foamed with lace to her wrists. She drew a deep
breath. So, this was the newest fashion from Paris. For the
first time she smiled at the little dressmaker. "You have
surpassed yourself," she said. "The gown is a masterpiece."

Beaming with pleasure, the woman thanked her, honest
enough to admit that the golden silk creation was doubly
enhanced by Alexandra's wide, topaz eyes, skin the color
of warm honey, and glorious red-brown hair.

The night of the ball, Alexandra sat at her dressing table
while the *friseur* worked. For hours she sat motionless as
the curling iron sizzled and steamed and the thick mane
of shining hair was piled high into an intricate coiffure of
puffs and curls. When the quail pipe was brought in, she
closed her eyes as scented white powder was blown into her
hair, completely concealing its red color. A maid applied a
hint of rouge to her cheeks and lips, took up the haresfoot
and brushed powder over her entire face, and at last,
applied a fascinating patch at the corner of the girl's
mouth.

Finally, it was time to dress. Alexandra stood up in her
petticoat. Ruffle upon ruffle of gold lace fell over a giant
hoop to her feet. The maid shook out the folds of the
yellow silk and carefully, so as not to disturb a single hair,

pulled it over the powdered head. "*Voilà*," she beamed. "You will be the belle of the ball, *mademoiselle*."

Alexandra turned toward the mirror and stared. Only two months ago, she had slept on animal skins in an Indian wigwam. It had been too much to hope that she would ever look like this again. Her skin had faded to its normal creamy pallor. Curls clustered about her head with just one falling over her bare shoulder. The jewelled tips of her shoes peeped from beneath the yellow-silk gown. Her eyes were brilliant, her lips parted, her cheeks slightly flushed.

She was very thin. The weight of her hair seemed too heavy for such a delicate neck. Still, she acknowledged, it was not unbecoming for her to be slender. It gave her a fragile quality, an elegant grace, like transparent Chinese porcelain.

With her back straight and her head held high, she walked down the broad staircase. Candle branches set inside niches in the wall lit the way. In the hall below, Pierre Vaudreuil waited, splendid in a flowered waistcoat. When he saw Alexandra, his mouth formed a circle of surprise. Recovering quickly, he moved forward to the foot of the stairs and held out his hand. "*Mon Dieu*, Alexandra!" he gasped. "You are the most beautiful creature I've ever seen."

She barely heard him. Tonight she had been restored. She was Alexandra Winthrop again and she meant to enjoy every moment.

The ballroom was ablaze with light. Crystal chandeliers hung from molded ceilings. Across a shining marble floor, exquisitely dressed dancers moved to the tune of soft violins. Ladies in beautiful clothing and exquisitely coiffed gentleman bowed and smiled as each new set began. The air was thick with the perfume of flowers.

It was altogether right that the eyebrows of French matrons lifted in astonishment and that French gentleman raised their quizzing glasses and begged for an introduction as she walked by. It was also right that handsome young men vied for her attention, offered her champagne, and claimed every dance on her card. It was instinctive that her slender, satin-gowned body moved effortlessly, with consummate grace, to the elegant, never-forgotten steps of the quadrille and minuet.

Alexandra glowed. She was a creature of radiance and light restored to the world in which she belonged. She did not stop to consider that her unusual popularity was due to the foreign appeal of her long-legged, chiseled English beauty. She forgot that she was English and a hostage in a foreign land. She forgot England and her grandfather and Julia's children. She forgot that she was unhappy and an unwelcome guest in the home of a cold man and his shrewish wife.

It wasn't until a strong hand captured her arm and she turned to stare into the twinkling eyes of a tall, handsome older man that everything came rushing back.

"Well, *ma petite,*" said Henri Jolliet. "It appears you have landed on your feet after all."

"Good evening, Your Grace," Alexandra said, holding out her skirts in a graceful curtsey.

"So, you do remember me." The duc nodded his head with satisfaction. "I wondered if you would."

The color deepened in Alexandra's cheeks. "I could scarcely forget, sir," she murmured.

His arm encircled her waist. "What brings you to Montreal, *mademoiselle?*"

"Haven't you heard?" Her eyes flashed. "I am a prisoner of France. The Vaudreuils are my gaolers until a ransom can be agreed upon."

He looked pointedly at her exquisite gown and elegantly coiffed hair. "If all prisoners were treated so well, your soldiers would desert in droves. We would be rid of the English for all time."

Alexandra lifted her chin. "I spent two seasons with the Ojibwa, *monsieur*. They killed my sister. Her son is still

with them. Her daughter is here in Montreal, but I am
forbidden to see her. I cannot believe there are many who
would willingly take my place."

The Duc de Lorraine's eyes were warm with sympathy.
"I am profoundly sorry, my dear. Is there anything I can
do?"

"There is nothing anyone can do, *monsieur*, except wait.
Dominic was on his way to Montreal to buy my release
from the Indians. That was weeks ago. Before he could
return, I was brought here."

Jolliet stared at her incredulously. "Dominic knows you
are here in New France?"

"*Oui, monsieur*. We were in Bowating together for the
entire winter."

"How long ago did he leave you?"

"Over three months ago." Neither one noticed that the
music had stopped. They stood, conspicuously alone, in
the middle of the floor, the tall man staring anxiously
down into the young woman's face.

"Dominic was always the fool," said his father. "Most
likely he is in terrible danger."

With unusual perception, Alexandra noticed the deep
lines carved in the old man's cheeks, the pinched mouth
and pain-filled eyes. "I think, *monsieur*," she said softly,
slipping her arm into his, "that you know very little of
your son."

His eyebrows, coal black and beautifully arched, flew
together in astonishment. Then he threw back his head
and laughed. "Come, *mademoiselle*. Have supper with me.
You must tell me everything that I do not know about my
son."

Chapter 18

"May I ask what is so interesting about the Duc de Lorraine that you virtually ignored every other man in the room?" The governor's cold voice punctuated the silence of the salon like the neat stabs of a stiletto.

Alexandra's eyes widened. No one had ever before spoken to her in such a tone. It was after four in the morning. The last ball guests had departed and she was very tired. "I beg your pardon?"

Vaudreuil walked to the marble-topped secretary. Resting his hands against it, he crossed one elegantly shod leg over the other. He was a small man, and unless he straightened to his full height, Alexandra's eyes were on a level with his own.

"Has it occurred to you that unless your grandfather sends word, you are entirely dependent upon our charity?"

Her expressive eyes flashed with contempt. "Never fear. My grandfather will pay you well for my release."

He lifted a gilded snuff box from the table, opening it with an expert flick of his wrist. Alexandra grimaced as he placed the tobacco on his wrist and inhaled. She did not approve of snuff. A pipe and the sweet pungent scent of tobacco, now that was something else.

"The Duke of Leicester is an old man," said Vaudreuil. "What if he is no longer alive?"

Alexandra swallowed. Her hand moved to her throat. She had never once considered such a possibility. "There is my grandmother," she whispered. "It would be unlikely that an accident could befall both of them."

"Perhaps." Vaudreuil considered the woman before him. She was uncommonly lovely. Why had he never noticed it before tonight? A thought, quite different from his original plan, formed in his mind. His voice was no longer cold. "Should your guardian not claim you, we must look to your future. There are several possibilities to consider."

Alexandra did not like the way his calculating blue eyes raked her body. He pushed away from the secretary and moved to stand before her. Pride and the paneled wall at her back kept her from moving away. She stiffened as he reached out to stroke her arm. His hands were dry and unusually cold.

"We could deal better together than this, *chérie*." His cajoling words filled her with dread.

Sure she had mistaken his meaning, Alexandra stared at him in horrified silence. Encouraged by her lack of response, Vaudreuil pinned her to the wall by placing both arms on either side of her. With a triumphant smile, he lowered his mouth to hers.

Alexandra gasped indignantly. With furious determination, she pushed at his arms. His mouth slid across her cheek and down her jaw.

"Take your hands of me," she said through clenched teeth. "How dare you offer me such an insult?"

He nuzzled the sensitive skin behind her ear. "Come, *ma petite*. There is no need for games. We understand each other. I will be good to you. Much better than your Indian lovers."

Alexandra struggled against the strength of the arms that held her in an iron grip. "I'll scream," she warned him.

Vaudreuil chuckled. "No, you won't. There isn't a soul in this entire house who would believe you. Accept it, *chérie*. You will be my mistress. Surely such a proposition is better than the kitchens or the streets."

"You flatter yourself, Monsieur Vaudreuil." Desperate to be free of the probing lips, Alexandra lifted her hand and raked her nails across his face. At the same time, the door opened and Pierre stepped into the room.

Cursing, the governor backed away. Reaching for his handkerchief, he dabbed at the blood running down his cheek. Pierre took one look at Alexandra's disheveled clothing and another at his father's blood-streaked face. With a growl he crossed the room, drew back his fist, and knocked Vaudreuil to the ground.

A horrified shriek came from the door. Madame Vaudreuil ran to her husband and knelt beside him. "What is the meaning of this?" she demanded.

Pierre pointed a shaking finger at his father. "He tried to attack Alexandra."

"Don't be absurd," *Madame* replied, turning back to her husband. "My darling, what has happened to you?"

"The woman is a viper," Vaudreuil snarled. "She tried to seduce me. When I would have none of her, she clawed me."

Shaking with rage, Madame Vaudreuil looked at Alexandra. Her voice was cold with hate. "After everything I've done for you. Leave my house at once or I'll have you thrown in gaol."

"No!" Pierre leaped to her defense. "I'll not have it. She has nowhere to go."

"How dare you take this—" She struggled for the word. "—this *salope's* side over that of your own father?" Madame Vaudreuil cried. "Leave with her, if you wish, but never set foot in my home again." She turned her furious gaze on Alexandra. "To think I was prepared to find a husband for you. And this is how you repay me."

Alexandra's lip curled with disdain. "I would sooner wed with a savage than marry one of you."

Pierre gazed at her, the anger changing to disbelief. "Alexandra?" His voice quavered, hoping she hadn't meant it. He stared at the mask-like beauty of her frozen expression. Her back was very straight, her chin tilted in defiance. Despair, swift and hurting, consumed him. He knew, as surely as he drew breath, that Alexandra Winthrop would never belong to him. With one last contemptuous glance at the three of them, she swept out of the room.

Throwing open the armoire, Alexandra pulled out the dresses given to her by Madame Vaudreuil, discarding one after another. Finally she found what she was looking for. Unlacing the silk ball gown, she stepped out of it and pulled the older, more serviceable wool over her head. Then, with a curse unbecoming to a lady, she took it off again and pulled on a linen nightdress. Even Madame Vaudreuil wouldn't expect her to brave the streets of Montreal at this hour.

The next morning, while everyone slept, Alexandra made her way down the stairs and into the street. She had taken nothing with her except two modest dresses and a woolen cloak. Once outside the door, she leaned weakly against the wall, overcome by a rush of dizziness. In her hurry to be away from the château, she had forgotten to eat. No matter. There were shops down the hill at the *Rue de St. Paul.* Surely, when she found work, someone would feed her.

The first shop she tried belonged to the seamstress who had fitted her for the ball gown. Her eyes widened in amazement at Alexandra's first words. "Work? Don't be absurd. Why would I give work to an Englishwoman?"

Time after time, Alexandra's request was met with incredulity. It seemed there was no one in all of Montreal who would give shelter to the enemy. Up on the hill, in the elegant, brightly lit mansions, war had seemed very far away. Here, in the streets of the city, men and women fought and sacrificed and died in their struggle against the English. Alexandra shuddered. She mustn't panic. Her accent was perfect. If shopkeepers wouldn't hire an Englishwoman, she would be French.

It was nearly June and the day was balmy. Doors were opened wide and wares displayed late into the afternoon. More than one shopkeeper was taking advantage of the long, sunlight-filled hours. A small crowd, mostly children, gathered about a man, intent on something before him. Alexandra craned her neck and stifled a gasp. It was an easel. The canvas was almost completely filled with the sketch of a young, dark-eyed matron who sat quietly in the chair by its side. The artist's other subject, a mischievous boy of about two years, bearing a striking resemblance to his mother, was giving him difficulty. Squirming in the woman's lap, he turned his head and changed expressions so frequently that the artist's patience was at an end.

"Madame," he protested, "if the child will not be still, I cannot paint him. Perhaps you would like a portrait of yourself? You can bring the boy back when he is older."

The woman shook her head emphatically. "Our arrangement was for the child as well. I'll not pay you a single *louis* unless my son is included."

The man sighed and began again.

Alexandra stepped forward. *"Monsieur,"* she began boldly. "Let me paint the child. If you are pleased with my work, a bowl of soup is all I require."

The man's eyebrows lifted in surprise. He was older than she expected. Almost as old as her grandfather.

"Do I know you, *mademoiselle?*"

The color swept across her cheeks, but her eyes met his steadily. "No, *monsieur.* I am a *habitante* and I need work. Perhaps you know of someone who can help me?"

The man hesitated. Then he stood and handed her the chalk. "If you can draw, perhaps I may have use for you."

Weak with relief, Alexandra sat down in the chair. She looked at the canvas and then at the baby. He smiled engagingly. Alexandra looked at his mother and held out her arms. "May I, *madame?*"

The woman hesitated for the briefest of seconds before depositing the baby in Alexandra's arms. There was something reassuring and honest shining in the warm, golden eyes.

Tightening her arms around the child, Alexandra breathed in the sweet baby scent of him. She missed Abigail dreadfully. Her rumbling stomach reminded her of her task. With gentle fingers she explored the tiny face, feeling the rounded cheeks and dimpled chin, checking the position of each sturdy bone and the smooth perfection of poreless, baby-soft skin. When she was completely satisfied, she handed the child back to his mother and began to sketch with firm sure strokes.

Within moments, Alexandra could hear excited whispers behind her. With one last stroke, the drawing was finished. She leaned back to survey her work. It was good. Very good. One of her best. She had needed it to be so.

The young mother looked over her shoulder. *"Tiens!"* she exclaimed. "My child is beautiful, is he not?"

Alexandra smiled and nodded. "He is indeed, *madame.*"

"You have an unusual talent, *mademoiselle.*" The artist looked at her thoughtfully. "It seems that I owe you a bowl of soup."

Her heart sank. "I paint much better than I draw," she said quietly. "Perhaps my skill with the oils would please you."

"If you paint one half as well as you draw, *mademoiselle,* I shall be more than pleased with my new employee."

Alexandra lifted shining eyes to his face. "I will not disappoint you, *monsieur.*"

"I am sure you will not, my dear. Come inside. My wife has prepared dinner."

The house was little more than two rooms attached to the shop where candles, tinder, and flint were displayed. A neat secretary complete with quills, ink, and precious paper stood in one corner. An easel and desk with oil paints and brushes stood in another. A short, solidly built woman with curly black hair and deep lines around her eyes beckoned Alexandra to the table. The meal of smoked eel, turnips, and boiled potatoes was far more satisfying than the soup she had expected.

When she rose to leave, the woman spoke directly to her for the first time. "Do you have a place to go, *mademoiselle?*"

Alexandra flushed and looked down at her hands. The woman clucked sympathetically. "Our cottage is small, but we have room enough for one more. You are welcome to share it with us."

Tears stung Alexandra's eyelids. She nodded her head. Who would have thought she would find such kindness in the home of a French family?

Through the days that followed, Alexandra sat before the easel in the modest shop, her fingers moving lovingly across the canvas, capturing the features and expressions of appreciative patrons with astonishing accuracy. Monsieur Brionne, the proprieter, watched in wonder as Alexandra's slim, capable fingers worked their magic again and again. Never did a customer leave dissatisfied. Trade increased. His clientele improved.

Occasionally a well-dressed lady or gentleman from a house on the hill would step into his shop. Madame Brionne would bustle about offering tea and sweetcakes while Alexandra sketched and painted. Late into the night, Monsieur Brionne would lie awake wondering how a homeless French *habitante* with the manners of a lady could converse with noblemen and paint in the style of a master. Who *was* this elegant, young girl?

On several occasions he attempted to question her, but

the haunted expression in her eyes dissuaded him. Finally he put his curiosity aside. The girl was polite, well-mannered, and an asset to his business. She also ate sparingly. He would not question fate when it worked to his advantage.

The cozy warmth of the small cottage, the simple but abundant food, the trusting nature of the Brionnes, served as a balm to Alexandra's troubled soul. She began to heal. The painful memories of the past year receded. She slept peacefully, without nightmares. Her appetite improved. Her cheeks glowed a golden apricot and her figure regained its slender curves. It was enough to sit in the Brionnes' doorway, basking in the warm summer air, a pencil or brush in hand, a clean canvas before her. She rarely ventured from the shop, content to look at the inhabitants of Montreal with the eyes of an observer, storing images in her brain, recreating them, true and larger than life, on paper and canvas. Soon the small shop was filled with colorful still lifes, as well as portraits. Monsieur Brionne beamed happily as a steady stream of customers commissioned paintings or walked away with small replicas of the city under their arms.

Weeks passed. The weather grew cooler. Alexandra noticed that the city was different, more crowded. Soldiers in gold-braided uniforms walked the streets. Rough, bearded faces lurked in the alleys and shops. Indians, more than she'd ever seen in Montreal, bartered moccasins, beaded vests, and baskets in exchange for gunpowder and French brandy.

In the back of her mind, Alexandra's peaceful sense of preoccupation was slowly being replaced by nervous anticipation. It was almost as if she were biding time, waiting for something inevitable to happen. She refused to delve too deeply into her own thoughts. If she had, she might have remembered that in winter, it was too cold to trap. *Coureurs* who did not spend the season in Indian villages were on their way back to Quebec and Montreal.

From inside the doorway, she watched uneasily as a group of Indians walked drunkenly down the middle of the street. They were young, mostly boys. One of them, younger and smaller than the others, wove through the crowd, expertly stealing fruit from the vendors' open carts. He turned around and laughed, his face under the dirt lighting with mischief. From across the road, Alexandra could see the piercing clarity of his eyes. They were blue!

"Travis!" she screamed, forgetting everything but her need to verify the child's identity.

The boy hesitated, looked around, saw her and ran.

"Travis. Come back," she cried out again, this time in English.

Back in the kitchen, Madame Brionne's cooking spoon clattered to the floor and her mouth dropped open in surprise.

With no thought other than to catch up with the child who might be her nephew, Alexandra raced out of the shop and down the street after him.

The boys ran into a dead end, stopped for a moment, communicated with hand gestures, separated, and ran on.

Alexandra stopped a group of soldiers passing by. "Please," she begged, "that boy is my nephew. Help me catch him."

One of the men stared at her. She looked vaguely familiar and her words were English. Perhaps she had escaped. His hand closed over her arm. He smiled. "Come, *mademoiselle*. I will take you to our governor's château."

Alexandra wrenched her arm away. With speed born of desperation, she gathered her skirts and ran. She turned into the street where she had last spotted the Indians. It was too late. They had disappeared. Frustrated, she paused, unwilling to give up the chase after coming so close.

The soldier, followed by three others, rounded the corner. There was no escape this time.

"Please," she whispered, conscious of the curious crowd that was gathering around. "Let me go." The soldier laughed as he gripped her arms, his fingers pinching her skin dreadfully.

Alexandra was about to explain when she saw a familiar dark head towering over the crowd. She stopped struggling immediately. With a helpless sense of inevitability, she waited for the tall figure to shoulder his way to her side. For some inexplicable reason, fate had ordained that they were always to meet when she needed rescuing.

"Well, well," Dominic's silky voice drawled. "What have we here?"

"She is an English prisoner," the soldier explained.

Dominic grinned. "To be sure, *monsieur,*" the mocking voice replied. "She looks to be a most desperate criminal." He sounded amused.

Alexandra looked up through her lashes into the black pools of Dominic Jolliet's teasing dark eyes. Lifting her chin, she turned to the soldier, speaking firmly. "I wasn't trying to escape. Why would I have asked you to help me? If you had only done so, everything would be easily explained."

"Let go of her." Monsieur Brionne pushed his way through the crowd. "The woman is no prisoner. She works in my shop."

The soldier's hand tightened on Alexandra's arm. "I shall take her to the governor," he insisted stubbornly.

"That will do, corporal," Dominic interjected. "As it happens, I know the woman myself. I am Dominic Jolliet, Marquis de Villiers. Surely my credentials are acceptable enough in Montreal?"

The soldier's eyes widened. He dropped Alexandra's arm. "Of course, Monsieur le Marquis," he stammered. "I would have released her immediately if I had known you were acquainted with the woman."

Dominic dismissed the soldier immediately and looked at Alexandra. His mocking eyes took in everything from her simply dressed hair and dingy dress to the limp apron and paint-stained fingers.

"Come with me," he ordered, gripping her arm and pulling her along the street.

"Alexandra." Monsieur Brionne's craggy face looked grim. "Do you know this man?"

"I beg your pardon." Alexandra flushed, ashamed of her breach of etiquette. "Monsieur Brionne, this is Dominic Jolliet, the Marquis de Villiers."

Monsieur Brionne was blunt. "You will keep her safe and return her to my shop, *monsieur?*"

Dominic was startled. No one had ever dared to speak to him in such a tone. "Mademoiselle Winthrop is no longer your responsibility," he replied coldly.

"Please, Dominic." Alexandra placed her hand on the shopkeeper's arm. "The Brionnes have been very kind to me. I owe them an explanation."

Dominic sighed impatiently. A sweet, steamy fragrance drifted from the door of a nearby grogshop. "Very well," he said. "Explain." He nodded toward the shop. "I'll wait for you there." Lifting his flintlock to his shoulder, he disappeared inside, leaving Alexandra alone with her employer.

Less than a quarter of an hour later, she walked into the shop. "A cup of *chocolat* for the lady," Dominic ordered, throwing a coin at the woman who bustled about the tavern.

The smell of cinnamon and chocolate was overwhelming. It had been so long since she had tasted anything so delicious, Alexandra could have drained the cup in one gulp. Forcing herself, she sipped slowly.

Dominic's black eyes laughed at her across the table. "Another cup," he ordered, "and a glass of wine as well."

Alexandra noticed her surroundings for the first time. "How could you bring me here? Are you out of your mind? This is a tavern."

He grinned, appreciating the way her eyes turned a deep gold when she was angry. "Still every inch the English lady, aren't you?" he taunted. "I had hoped your stay with the

Ojibwa would have purged you of your ridiculous notions. Never mind. The wine is for me."

"Where have you been?" she snapped.

He pushed back his chair and stood up. "I'll tell you over dinner."

Alexandra looked down at her skirt. "I'm not dressed for dinner. Tell me now, Dominic. The Brionnes expect me."

"The story is a long one, *chérie*." His eyes were very dark as they searched her face. "Perhaps you misunderstood. You will not be going back to the Brionnes." Alexandra recognized the hint of steel in his silky voice. "You will have dinner with me, now." He held up his hand to silence her protest. "Don't argue, Alexandra. Where we are going, they will make no reference to your hideous gown."

Chapter 19

Once again, Alexandra walked past the stone cathedral, up the *Rue de St. Paul,* and through the narrow alleys to the fashionable section of the city. But this time Dominic was with her and she was curious rather than frightened. It was quite dark when he lifted the knocker of an imposing mansion and let it fall. The door opened immediately. The stern expression on the servant's face dissolved into a welcoming smile.

"Monsieur le Marquis." The man's voice cracked with emotion. "It is very good to have you home."

Dominic grinned. "Thank you, Marceau." His hand rested on Alexandra's shoulder. "I have brought a guest, and neither of us has dined. Is there food in the kitchen?"

Marceau rose to the occasion. Not by the flicker of an eyelash did the majordomo indicate that it was unusual for his master to bring a young lady home for the night. He bowed his head. "We will manage, m'lord."

Again, the grin flashed in Dominic's dark face. "You are a treasure, Marceau. A veritable treasure."

Alexandra's excellent breeding asserted itself. She

smiled brilliantly. "Please forgive us, Marceau. 'Tis dreadful to intrude on you like this with no warning at all."

Marceau was startled, although his wooden expression revealed nothing. He revised his first impression of the woman. Despite the dreadful clothing, she was obviously a lady. Again he bowed. "It is no trouble at all, *mademoiselle.* The Duc de Lorraine is in residence and he rarely eats all that is prepared for him. I'll have the chef attend to it immediately. Perhaps you would like to rest before dinner?"

"That would be lovely." Alexandra smiled once more and Marceau's heart was won.

"Come with me, *mademoiselle.* I'm sure you will find the guest rooms in satisfactory condition."

She looked around curiously. This was Dominic's home and what she had seen surprised her. Instead of the opulent curving arches and excessive ornamentation of the governor's château, the furniture and wall coverings were elegant and restrained, almost deceptively simple. The walls were pale ivory relieved by gilded ornaments and moldings. Tall doors, exquisitely carved, opened into rooms with marble mantels and priceless overmirrors. Aubusson carpets strewn tastefully about only partially concealed the gleaming wooden floors beneath her feet, and chandeliers of the finest crystal hung from the ceiling over her head.

Marceau ushered Alexandra into a small but luxurious bedchamber. A richly carved armoire stood beside the window and rose-sprigged wallpaper covered the walls. Matching curtains draped over the alcove, enclosing the bed against the inevitable drafts of New France. The wooden floor was painted a soft rose, and two white carpets had been artistically placed at each end of the room. A chaise longue, armchairs, several small tables, and a setee—all done in rose and white—completed the arrangement.

It was surprisingly modern and uncluttered. Alexandra

smiled graciously. "Thank you, Marceau. Everything is perfect."

The man bowed. "Dinner will be served shortly, *mademoiselle*. I shall send a maid to show you the way."

An hour later she faced Dominic across a small round table in the dining room. She was pleased with the new custom of dining intimately, within arm's distance of everyone. The long rectangular tables she was familiar with discouraged all but the most necessary conversation.

Dominic ate as he did everything else, efficiently with spare, competent movements. When he had satisfied the edge of his hunger, he pushed his plate away and lifted his wineglass. Leaning his elbows on the table, he looked directly at Alexandra. The black eyes were very intense. "Tell me what happened to you after I left Bowating."

Alexandra was no longer hungry. The deliciously prepared food refused to pass the lump in her throat. How could she tell him of her shameful decision to seduce Red Wing at the Indian camp? After that, would he believe she was innocent of encouraging the governor's attentions?

And yet, Dominic had told her to do whatever she must to stay alive. Had he known all along how it would be? If so, why had he left her alone, and where had he been for such an endless length of days and nights? Alexandra drew a deep breath. Haltingly, she began, telling him only the barest of details, not realizing that the words she left unsaid were revealed to him in the blush of her cheeks, the catch in her voice, the trembling of her mouth, and the lowering of her gold-tipped lashes over haunted eyes.

Dominic's hand tightened on his glass. "I believe I shall pay our esteemed governor a visit."

Alexandra looked at him in alarm. "You wouldn't."

He watched the candlelight flicker across her face. "I really think I must, *chérie*," he replied gently.

"You did nothing when Red Wing offered me the wampum belt," she protested. "Why must you make an issue of Vaudreuil's offer?"

"The circumstances are not at all the same, Alexandra. Red Wing approached you honestly and fairly. He wanted you for his wife. Vaudreuil is a French nobleman and a gentleman. He had no right to insult you in such an manner."

"Will you call him out?" She was surprised that her voice sounded so normal.

Dominic's eyes laughed at her from across the table. "I hardly think it will come to that. He wouldn't risk the scandal."

All at once, Alexandra was very angry. "None of this would have happened if you had come back for me," she snapped. "Where have you been, Dominic?"

Marceau entered the room with a silver pot in his hand. "Tea, *mademoiselle?*"

Dominic waved him away impatiently. "You know I despise the stuff. Why do you keep it in the house?"

"I didn't bring it for you, m'lord," the servant replied frostily.

"Thank you, Marceau." Alexandra smiled enchantingly. "A cup of tea is exactly what I need. It was very thoughtful of you to think of me."

Gratified, Marceau poured the tea and left the room without a word.

Dominic's lips twitched. Alexandra had made yet another conquest.

She sipped her tea and looked at him expectantly. "I'm waiting, Dominic."

He sighed. It had been too much to hope that this conversation could be postponed until their relationship had resumed on a more personal level. He had intended to regain her confidence, to woo her, to make her dependent upon him. This very night he'd meant to take her to bed and rekindle the fires between them. Only when he'd felt she was ready, when his suit had been already won, had he planned to tell her of his meeting with her grandfather and the bargain they had struck between them. Now, looking into the wide golden eyes so intent on his face, Dominic knew he could offer her nothing less than the truth.

"I was on my way to Montreal when Pontiac, War Chief of the Ottawa, found me. He insisted that I stay with his party through the spring."

She released her breath in a long sigh. "I wondered if you had changed your mind. All this time you were an Indian captive."

"Not exactly," Dominic admitted. "I was an honored member of the war party. Even though I couldn't leave, I was treated well." He hesitated. "There is something else."

"Tell me."

"There was an attack on Fort Edward. Captain Doddridge was taken prisoner."

Alexandra's eyes fell before his penetrating gaze. Anthony Doddridge seemed very far away. She wondered why his fate mattered so little to her. "Was he harmed?" she asked quietly.

"No. After the confusion of the battle, I managed to release him. We escaped together to Fort Ticonderoga. When I last saw him, his ransom was being arranged."

Alexandra's voice was so low, it was difficult to make out her words. "Why would you do such a thing for an English soldier?"

"I am not a monster, Alexandra." Dominic was exasperated. Why must she always assume the worst of him? "Have you any idea what the Ottawa do to prisoners?"

"If their methods are anything like those of the Ojibwa, I have some idea."

"Then you should know why I couldn't leave him."

Her expression was very serious when she answered him. "I don't believe I know you at all, Dominic. There are only bits and pieces left of the man I knew in Paris. Now, I see only Dominic Jolliet, the *coureur de bois*. I'm still not sure which I prefer."

"Does it really matter, *mademoiselle*?" The mocking note

was back in his voice again. "You are betrothed to a captain in the English infantry."

Alexandra winced, embarrassed and angry that he still had the power to hurt her. Her eyes met his in a level stare. "You must know how I feel, Dominic. I would have thought our time at Bowating meant something to you as well."

Again she had surprised him. Another woman would never have brought up the subject of their nights in the women's lodge. Still, it was at Bowating that she had refused him. Would he ever know the workings of her mind? "I asked you to be my wife, Alix. Unless I mistook the matter, you intend to go through with your marriage to Captain Doddridge." The dark eyes glinted with disturbing lights. "Was I mistaken?"

She evaded his question. "What has marriage to do with us?"

"Don't be absurd." He shrugged off her question impatiently. "You are an English lady. There can be nothing else but marriage between the two of us."

"You once said that you had never met a woman whose company you could tolerate for any length of time," she reminded him.

"And you answered that a *coureur* isn't home for any length of time," he countered.

Tears collected in her throat. It was impossible to speak.

He leaned forward, eyes intent on her face. "Do you love me, Alexandra?"

"Don't do this, Dominic," she pleaded.

"Answer me."

She shook her head. "I can't."

"The question requires a simple *yes* or *no*," he said reasonably. "If the answer is *no*, I won't trouble you again."

"It will serve no purpose," she insisted.

"On the contrary. It will serve a very important purpose."

Alexandra played with her wineglass, deliberately

avoiding the perceptive dark eyes. He must know how difficult this was for her. How could she explain to a man whose way of life was as foreign to her as the wind-chilled city of Montreal that even a woman in love could not always choose which path her destiny would take? There was more standing between them than the war and Anthony Dod-dridge.

Despite his newfound profession, Dominic was still the Marquis de Villiers, an incredibly wealthy and handsome French nobleman. She had not realized quite how noble until just recently. Dominic was of the blood royal, son to the Queen of France, a man destined by an accident of birth to take his place in history. Every waking moment of his life had been spent in extravagant indulgence. Only his own considerable intellect, coupled with a healthy sense of the absurd, had kept him from becoming completely spoiled.

He came from a world of pomp and glitter, of political intrigue and courtly circumstance. It was a world as different from Alexandra's as any could possibly be. The English nobility took the responsibility of governing seriously. If they benefited from their position, they also paid for it with heavy taxes and service to the state.

From her brief season in Paris, Alexandra knew French attitudes were vastly different. The nobility left the running of their estates to stewards and swarmed to the glamor of Versailles. They revolved like obsequious satellites, bleed-ing their estates and the citizens of France with excessive indulgences. Men and women alike primped and sim-pered, dressed in exquisite colors, wore patches and car-ried muffs. The court was a receptacle of greed, upheld by an unfit monarch under the influence of a frivolous mistress and a corrupt clergy. These excesses were paid for by the sweat and blood of the French peasantry.

The elegant *salons* of Versailles were a hideous contrast to the misery and squalor of Paris. It was common knowl-edge throughout England and the rest of Europe that their

Continental neighbor was a powder keg ready to explode. Rousseau was sounding the horn of political freedom. Voltaire cried out against the tragic abuses all around him. Montesquieu, with his quiet and logical intellect, was wearing away those nobles with a shred of human decency left inside of them. Alexandra shuddered. This was Dominic's world.

She knew that his hiatus from that glamorous existence was only temporary. Dominic belonged in that world and deeply resented the circumstances that had forced him to leave Paris. Because she had been an integral part of those circumstances, Alexandra knew it was only a matter of time before he came to resent her as well. She did not want to be near him when it happened.

Alexandra was the granddaughter of a duke, but she had been raised in an atmosphere far removed from the decadence of London's aristocracy. The early years with her parents had been spent in simple austerity. When she and Julia came to live with their grandparents, life had remained much the same. The duke did not approve of the loose morality of his peers; nor did he believe in indulging the members of his own family. His wife was the only exception. Alexandra had grown to womanhood with no knowledge of the vast wealth she would inherit.

It was not unusual for a gently bred lady to live out her years in the quiet beauty of the English countryside, tending to the duties of her household, with only an occasional excursion into London. Such was the existence the duke had planned for his granddaughter.

Alexandra could no more step into the glitter and debauchery of Paris as Dominic's wife than she could prevent the truth from escaping through her lips. In the end, it would make no difference at all. The outcome would be the same for the two of them, but at least he would know. As for herself, she would have the satisfaction of saying out loud the words she had held in her heart for such a very long time.

"Very well, if it is that important to you, I shall tell you." She wet her lips and looked directly at him. Her voice was firm and sure, without the slightest hint of hesitation. "I do love you, Dominic. I have from the very first." Her face was grave. Now that she had begun, she was determined to hold nothing back. "I love you more than I ever believed I could love anyone. I shall go to my grave loving you."

He sat very still, his features expressionless, as if her words had cast him into a state of frozen immobility.

"Surely you're not surprised?" Alexandra asked in astonishment.

Her words had shaken him to the core. "Good Lord, Alix." He laughed unsteadily. "A man could live with you for a lifetime and never know what you'll say next. After your reluctance to answer me, how could I possibly be prepared for such a confession?"

"I think your reputation with women is a sham, *monsieur*. You seem to know very little about us after all."

Dominic grinned. "Perhaps," he admitted. "Or it could be that you are not like most women."

"I shall accept that as a compliment."

He was on familiar ground now. "It was intended as such."

She smiled with relief. He wasn't making it difficult for her after all. "How can I thank you for coming to my rescue once again?"

He reached for her hand, drawing the small, slender fingers through his own. "There is no need for thanks, *mignonne*. I have every intention of claiming my reward."

Alexandra frowned. "I don't understand."

"We will be married, Alix, with your grandfather's blessing."

She stared at him. "That isn't possible."

"Oh, but it is. Do you really believe that after such a declaration I would allow you to leave me?"

She pulled her hand out of his grasp. "I thought you understood. I'm promised to Anthony."

"The devil take Anthony," Dominic exploded, pushing himself away from the table and leaping to his feet. He towered over her. "I tire of this English paragon. He will never make you happy. We will be wed, Alexandra, and that will be the end of it."

She refused to be intimidated. Calmly, she rose and faced him. "No, we will not, Dominic. You must see how impossible it is. I cannot live here, in a French colony, or even in Paris. My home is in England. Everything I know, everything I need and love is there."

"You said you loved me," he reminded her.

"You are impossible," she shouted, throwing off her mask of reserve. "Will that love last when my countrymen are murdered at the hands of French soldiers? What will become of my grandparents when they learn their great-grandson is an Indian captive and their granddaughter and great-granddaughter are living with enemies. What of your father, Dominic?" She threw caution to the winds and hurled the damning words at him. "And what of your mother? Do you really believe they will allow you to live out your life trapping furs and trading stories with peasants in the wilderness? They are merely biding their time, waiting for an end to your sulking. What kind of life can the two of us have together?"

The coldness in his voice chilled her very bones. "Your sister did not find it so very difficult. You cannot pretend that she and her husband came from the same world."

"My sister is dead," replied Alexandra woodenly. "If she had listened to my grandfather, she would be alive today."

"Perhaps, despite everything, she would make the same choice again."

Alexandra sighed and turned toward the door. "Since we cannot ask her, 'tis a moot point. I'm very tired. If we must continue this conversation, let us do so in the morning."

"It won't go away, Alix." His voice followed her to the

door. "I mean to have you. You'll thank me for it in the end."

He hadn't touched her. He didn't need to. The force pulsing between them was strong enough to propel her back into his arms if she didn't fight against it. She clenched her teeth and, with the discipline born of months in Bowating, walked through the door without looking back.

Chapter 20

The Duc de Lorraine, expecting to breakfast alone, was in the midst of his paper and morning *chocolat* when the door to the dining room opened. His eyes widened in surprise. Forgetting his usually impeccable manners, he remained seated as Alexandra Winthrop pulled out a chair and sat down at the table.

"*Bonjour, monsieur,*" she said politely.

He collected himself and stood. "*Bonjour, mademoiselle.* What a pleasure to see you again."

"I would imagine 'tis something of a shock," she replied.

The *duc's* eyes twinkled. "A very pleasant shock, I assure you."

Marceau entered the room and placed a steaming pot of *chocolat* and a plate of white rolls in front of Alexandra. She thanked him graciously. The stern lines of his face softened. "If you desire anything else, m'lady, ring the bell."

"I shall do so." She lifted the cup to her lips. "The *chocolat* is delicious, Marceau."

He unbent from his stiff formality enough to smile. "I shall bring more," he announced and left the room.

Henri Jolliet bit back a smile. The girl certainly had more than her share of charm. In that, she was not unlike Dominic. "Forgive my curiosity, my dear," he said politely. "How is it that I have the pleasure of your company this morning? If memory serves me correctly, I believe you were a guest of the Vaudreuils'."

"Your memory serves you well, m'lord," replied Alexandra. "The governor and I had a slight misunderstanding. I found employment in a shop on the *Rue de St. Paul.* Dominic found me and brought me here. I hope I do not inconvenience you."

An amused voice interrupted them. "If you must ever earn your living again, Alexandra, try the stage. Your story sounds almost credible." Dominic pulled out a chair and sat down, helping himself to a roll from Alexandra's plate.

She slapped his hand away. "Every word I spoke was true," she protested indignantly.

"Of course." The dark eyes laughed at her. "You merely left out the details."

"Surely I raised you to have better manners, my son," the *duc* reproved him. "Perhaps in good time you will enlighten me as to why this lovely young lady is no longer staying with the governor and his wife."

"I would be happy to do so," replied Dominic. "However, the lady may not wish all her secrets revealed."

"Do as you please" Alexandra widened her eyes innocently. "If you intend to call Vaudreuil out, everyone will know soon enough."

Alarmed, the *duc* looked at his son.

Dominic laughed. "*Touché,* my love. The good governor deserves no less, but I believe I'll spare him. Your reputation would not be served by murder."

Henri interrupted. "I'm waiting, Dominic."

"Vaudreuil offered Mademoiselle Winthrop a *carte blanche*," Dominic replied evenly, keeping his eyes on Alexandra's face. "She declined him and he attempted to rape her. The lying cur told a different tale to his wife and the lady ordered Alexandra from the house." The white line around his lips was the only sign of the controlled anger he held inside. "Without a *sou* to her name, she, the granddaughter of the Duke of Leicester, was forced to impersonate a French *habitante*. For months she worked in the shop of a peasant. Fortunately the man and his wife were kind. I found her in the midst of a group of soldiers. One of them was intent on taking her to prison."

"Did you break the law, *mademoiselle?*" asked the *duc*.

"No," whispered Alexandra. "I thought I saw my nephew with a group of Indians. I cried out in English."

"Ah." The *duc* nodded and looked curiously at his son. "What are your intentions, Dominic?"

"I intend to marry Alexandra," he answered defiantly.

The *duc* took one look at Alexandra's face and spoke quickly. "Your memory is short, my son. Your offer has already been rejected by the young lady's grandfather."

"The circumstances have changed," said Dominic.

"How so?"

Dominic stood and walked casually toward the door. Now was as good a time as any to break the news. "The Duke of Leicester is at Fort Ticonderoga."

Alexandra gasped.

"I saved his life and promised to find Alexandra," he continued. "In return he assured me there would be no further obstacles should the two of us wish to wed."

"He couldn't possibly have agreed to that," whispered Alexandra.

Dominic's mouth twisted bitterly. "Indeed, he did, *chérie*. A desperate man will bargain with the devil himself if necessary."

"You said that Anthony was also at Fort Ticonderoga,"

Alexandra reminded him. "Does he know of this infamous bargain?"

"I don't believe he was consulted," answered Dominic.

The *duc's* eyes moved from Dominic to Alexandra and back again. "Who is this Anthony?" he asked.

Alexandra lifted her chin and looked directly at him. Her eyes were hard and bright and very determined. Henri Jolliet was reminded, once again, of English steel.

"Captain Anthony Doddridge is my fiancé, m'lord. We were to be wed after he served his duty in the colonies."

The *duc* stared thoughtfully at the lovely, flushed face before him. Without looking at Dominic he spoke. "It appears there are serious impediments to your suit, my son. Even you cannot *force* a young lady to marry you."

Dominic set his teeth. "I have no intention of forcing anyone. Alexandra will marry me because she wishes it. Now, if you will excuse me—" He bowed. "—I have an appointment with Governor Vaudreuil."

Alexandra and the *duc* were left staring at the empty doorway. She laughed shakily. "Did he never learn humility, m'lord?"

"Humility is not a virtue among the French aristocracy," replied the *duc* dryly.

Alexandra started to rise. "I cannot stay here," she said.

"Sit down, *mademoiselle*." Surprised at the forceful command, she sank back into her chair. "Am I correct in assuming that you have no feelings for my son?" His eyes did not miss the sudden clenching of her hands.

Her voice was very low. "I did not say that."

"Why, then, do you wish to leave?"

Alexandra turned to him in amazement. "You can't possibly want this union, *monsieur*. What of his position, his rank?"

"There are some who would say that the granddaughter of an English duke is a fit mate for the heir to the House of Lorraine."

She drew a deep breath. "Would his mother say that?"

Henri Jolliet sighed. "If he told you of his mother, my dear, you can be very sure that Dominic's intentions are serious."

"I have no doubt they are," replied Alexandra. "Here, in New France, anything seems possible. But when he returns to Paris, I cannot go with him."

"Are you so sure he plans to return?"

Her palms were wet. She wiped them on the worn folds of her gown. "Are you sure he will not?"

Jolliet shrugged. All at once he looked old and tired. "France is no longer the same country," he replied wearily. "The spirit of the nobility is gone." Alexandra would have interrupted him, but he waved away her protests. "We have a powerful army and navy, but gone are the great commanders of the Bourbon regime. Conde, Turenne, and Villars are dead. Richelieu can no longer be taken seriously. Our king is selfish, indolent, and incompetent; our government ruled by la Pompadour and her favorite, Machault."

Alexandra was fascinated. Henri Jolliet, lost in his private regrets, had forgotten she was there. "*Monsieur,*" she said quietly.

He looked startled and then amused. "I, too, grow old *mademoiselle*. That is why I belong in France. For a long time I hoped Dominic would return with me. Now, I believe it is right that he stay here. It is a new world—healthier, stronger, more suited to young men." He smiled sadly. "Should you decide to wed my son, you will not be living in New France. At this moment, English colonists with muskets and plows, commanded by a young Virginian named George Washington, push at the borders of Canada. Your countrymen number twice as many as ours in a land area much smaller. England cannot help but prevail. It is only a matter of time. I only pray the conquerors will be merciful." Alexandra listened in shocked silence. Henri Jolliet moved in the highest circles of French politics. The queen had been his mistress, the king's advisors his closest friends. Could his assessment be correct? Would England rule all of North America? A sudden thought sobered her. Would Dominic be content to live under English rule?

"Do you want me to marry Dominic?" she asked incredulously.

The Duc de Lorraine's thin lips turned up at the corners. "I would be delighted, *mademoiselle,*" he assured her. "Even if I were not, Dominic must marry someone if I am ever to see my grandchildren before I die. You appear healthy enough to survive the birthing bed."

Alexandra felt the color rise in her cheeks. It was only by the sheerest of good luck that the nights in the women's lodge hadn't reaped disastrous results. Once again, she marveled at how she could have so completely disregarded the possible consequences. Dominic had a terrifying influence on her. In his presence she didn't behave in the least like herself. A lifetime with him was a frightening thought.

With resolution she stood. "Excuse me, *monsieur,* but I must send word to my grandfather."

"I'm sure Dominic has already done so," replied the *duc,* "but a letter written in your own hand would reassure him even more."

Alexandra's smile was strained as she excused herself and made her way to her bedchamber. The message she could no longer avoid sending to her grandfather would hardly reassure him. Indeed, it would be most fortunate if his heart survived the reading of it.

Pierre-François de Rigaud, Marquis de Vaudreuil and Governor of New France, regarded the visitor in his drawing room with a surprised lift of his eyebrows. Dominic Jolliet did not normally call on the Vaudreuils. The Jolliets were French aristocracy, satellites of the crown. Secure in their wealth and position, they socialized where they pleased, refusing to pander to the Canadian born *nouveau-riche* of Quebec and Montreal. The subtle distinction between the nobility of the mother country and that of New France rankled in the breast of the native-born Vaudreuil. He threw out his chest. There was no need for the look of disdain on Dominic Jolliet's coldly handsome face. Were not the Vaudreuils citizens of France the same as the Jolliets?

"I am honored, *monsieur.*" He waved his hand at a nearby chair. "Pray be seated. How may I serve you?"

Dominic did not sit down. Instead, he sauntered across the room and leaned against the marble mantel. Crossing his arms against his chest, he surveyed the buckle of his shoe. "I am commissioned on an errand of mercy," he said casually, as if the matter held little interest for him. "An Englishman at Fort Ticonderoga seeks his grand-daughter. He believes she is here in Montreal."

Vaudreuil smirked. "My dear Jolliet. Every day English prisoners pass through our city gates. They work in our houses and languish in our prisons." With an expert flick of his wrist, he opened a small ornate box and inhaled a pinch of snuff. "Surely you cannot expect me to keep track of them all?"

Dominic stretched out a leg and carefully perused the silk hose covering his muscled calf. "Do you detect a wrinkle near my ankle, Vaudreuil? Come now, tell me. My valet's future hangs on your words."

"Your dress is perfection itself," replied the bewildered *marquis.* Dominic Jolliet did not have the reputation of a fop.

"I really must insist that you look more closely," persisted Dominic, frowning at the imaginary wrinkle. "There. Can you not see it?"

Vaudreuil released his breath impatiently. "I see nothing, m'lord. Truly I do not. If you are finished, I really must excuse myself. Matters of government await. Surely you understand."

Dominic straightened. His night-black eyes lifted to the governor's face. He was a full head taller than the older man. "It is a matter of government that I wish to discuss with you, *Monsieur le Marquis.*"

For some inexplicable reason, Vaudreuil was afraid. He felt the perspiration collect on his upper lip. His voice cracked. "Continue, *monsieur.*"

"The Englishman I spoke of is the Duke of Leicester. His granddaughter, Alexandra Winthrop, was a guest in your home."

The governor smiled nervously. How much did Jolliet know? "My wife was kind enough to take her in," he lied. "The girl is a harlot. She betrayed our trust by seducing Pierre. I ordered her from the hou—"

Vaudreuil never uttered the last word. He found himself against the wall, gasping for air, desperately pulling at the ice-cold fingers of steel choking the life from his throat. Waves of dizziness engulfed him. Then came nausea and finally blackness.

Moments later he regained consciousness and raised shaking fingers to his bruised throat. "Water," he croaked. "Please, bring water."

Dominic reached down and lifted the man to his feet. The governor sagged against the wall, clutching his throat.

"I should kill you now, Vaudreuil, but strangling is too merciful an end and only gentlemen die by the sword." His eyes were cold, his mouth hard and dangerous. "My betrothal to Alexandra Winthrop will be announced within the week. We shall see a great deal of one another, *monsieur.* I'm sure your lovely wife will make my fiancée's stay in Montreal most pleasant." The silky voice lowered menacingly. "If she does not, I'm afraid your political career will seriously decline. Do I make myself clear?"

"What they say about you is true," whispered Pierre Vaudreuil.

"Undoubtedly," countered Dominic. "What is it that you believe to be true?"

"That you are spawned by the devil himself."

Dominic threw back his head and shouted with laughter. Vaudreuil shrank back in fear. "Never doubt it, *Monsieur le Marquis*. Never for one moment doubt it."

Chapter 21

Alexandra stared at the contents of the armoire in amazement. It was filled with an array of costly gowns, silk petticoats, panniers, fashionable wraps, and cloaks of the like she had never seen before. Tentatively, she touched the expensive material. Only the finest dressmaker in Montreal could have fashioned these gowns. Alexandra smiled wryly. Only a few short months ago, the seamstress had refused to employ her. She could still see the haughty face and contemptuous smile. Did the woman burn with angry humiliation at the thought of making clothing for an Englishwoman?

She did not need to turn around to know the exact moment she was no longer alone. Feeling the pull of his presence, she reluctantly turned to face Dominic. He stood in the doorway, his face expressionless, his eyes coal black, wide shoulders filling the entire opening. He was dreadfully handsome. Alexandra chewed her lip, chastising herself for allowing such a thought to creep into her consciousness. Too much was still unresolved between them. It would do no good to weaken now.

"I cannot possibly accept the clothing," Alexandra said stiffly.

A shadow clouded his face, but his words were pleasant enough. "I'll keep an exact reckoning. Your grandfather can repay me when he reaches Montreal."

"You've sent for him?" She couldn't keep the relief from her voice.

Dominic smiled grimly. "You persist in believing the worst of me, *chérie*. Did you think I would not?"

She ignored his question. "When do you expect him?"

"The weather is good. He should arrive within ten days if he leaves immediately."

Alexandra's brow puckered. "He's quite old. Perhaps we should intercept him. It cannot be safe for a man of his years to travel so quickly through the wilderness."

Dominic shook his head before she had finished her thought. "No, Alexandra. He would not thank me for further exposing you to danger. We shall wait for him here."

He closed the door behind him and walked across the room to stand before her. He was very close. Her heart pounded at the nearness of him, but she refused to move away. His hands reached out, carressing her arms. "Do you approve of the clothing?" he asked casually.

Her voice was unusually breathless. "Very much. You have excellent taste."

"I'm glad you think so. Tonight you will have occasion to wear one of the gowns. We are expected at Madame Chevalier's for dancing and a light supper."

Alexandra's eyes darkened. "Don't be absurd," she snapped, pulling out of his grasp. "I can't possibly attend such an occasion. Sentiment toward the English is even worse than it was six months ago." She colored and looked down at the floor. Nothing short of a royal command would induce her to face the Vaudreuils again.

Dominic lifted her chin, forcing her to look at him. "There is no need to concern yourself over the unfortunate incident with the governor, Alix. I assure you, the entire matter is finished. No one else will ever know of it.''

"It isn't only that," she insisted. "The Vaudreuils took me with them on many occasions. The ladies of Montreal do not welcome strangers. It was an experience I have no wish to repeat.''

Dominic's eyes glinted with amusement. "You will find that the fiancée of the Marquis de Villiers holds an entirely different position in society than a guest of the governor.''

Her cheeks flamed brilliantly and she turned away from him. "Please, Dominic. Don't persist in this.''

"Why not?''

She could feel his breath on the back of her neck and knew she had only to turn around and her head would rest on his chest.

"I can't marry you.''

"You can and you will." His lips brushed the back of her neck. The warmth of his body transferred itself to hers. Her skin burned with his heat.

"Please," she whimpered. It had been so very long.

"Please, what?" he whispered lazily. "Please, kiss you here?" His mouth moved to her ear. "Or here?" His lips were now on her cheek. "Shall I stop now, Alix? Or perhaps I should touch you here." One hand stroked her breast while the other flattened against her stomach and pulled her tightly against him.

Her head fell back against his shoulder. Through the thin material of her gown, she could feel the taut muscles of his chest and the tight, rock-hard strength of his thighs pressing against her. She had lost after all. With a moan of pleasure she turned into his arms and lifted searching lips for his kiss.

He stared down at her passion-flushed face. Her lids were heavy and her breath came in short shallow gasps. But there was no regret in the amber eyes. Damning his noble intentions, he cursed under his breath and set his mouth against hers, hard. Her lips opened under his and he lost all semblance of control. Slipping his arm under her knees, he carried her to the bed and laid her on the feather mattress. With sure fingers he unlaced her bodice and pulled it down around her waist. Cradling her breasts in his palms, he buried his head in the valley between the soft mounds and breathed deeply.

Impatient and aching with need, Alexandra arched beneath him and pulled his head to her breast. His mouth encircled her nipple at the same time she found the hardness between his thighs. Her hand closed around it.

Dominic bolted upright in shock and stared down at her, the question in his eyes unmistakable.

She meet his look steadily, without embarrassment, and nodded.

Holding her gaze, he unbuttoned his trousers and lifted her skirts. His hands on the inside of her thigh were warm and sure. The core of her pulsed with desire. She was hot and wet and satin smooth. Sweat beaded his brow. He ached with a painful pleasure that only completion could assuage. Placing his lips against her throat, he slid shaking fingers inside the exquisite warmth.

Her breathing altered. He felt her muscles tighten. Slowly, seductively, his tongue slid into her mouth and out again in perfect harmony with the sensual movement of his fingers. Alexandra moaned and opened her legs. He waited no longer. Moving over her, he claimed what he knew had been his alone since that magic moment three years ago when her eyes had first locked with his.

Much later, when the passion between them had flared and waned once more, Dominic climbed out of bed, adjusted his clothing, and pulled the covers around Alexandra. She raised sleepy eyes to his face and smiled. He caught his breath, wondering if he would ever become accustomed to the richness of her beauty. It was a warm, natural loveliness found in few women he had taken to his bed. Most of the *demoiselles* of his acquaintance looked washed out after the powder and paint from their faces had rubbed off on the sheets.

Already the guilt was eating at him. He should not have taken her when she was most vulnerable and still under his protection. After the first night he had decided to wait until her grandfather arrived in Montreal before pressing his suit. He knew he had an advantage over Anthony Doddridge, and for some perverse reason, it bothered him. He would rather that he and the captain were on a more equal footing and that Alexandra would choose him because of what had always existed between the two of them.

She had willingly given herself to him at Bowating. It was an action a woman like Alexandra would not take lightly. Dominic knew that she would not marry another man with such a deception in her heart. The worthy Captain Doddridge would know of Alexandra's fall from grace before she would even consider going through with their marriage. Dominic was counting on Alexandra's uncompromising honesty to remove the English captain from the picture. He wished it were otherwise. He had intended to make it easier for her by keeping their relationship strictly platonic until the arrival of Leicester. He had not counted on his loss of reason at the scent of her hair and the taste of her skin on his lips.

She would not reproach him for his action. He knew that. Alexandra had a sense of honor greater than that of anyone else he had ever known. She had wanted him as much as he'd wanted her, and because she was so completely herself, she would take the blame. With his last ounce of breath, Dominic hoped that Anthony Doddridge was cast in the same predictable mold as every other Englishman of his acquaintance—stuffy, priggish, outrageously moral, and critical of all behavior with the exception of his own. Definitely not the type of man who would forgive and forget that his future wife had offered her virginity to a lowly *coureur de bois* on the floor of an Indian lodge in Bowating.

"What are you thinking, Dominic?" Alexandra's voice was husky and low, vibrating with what had passed between them.

He rubbed his thumb across her lips. "That I am a most fortunate man. The most beautiful woman in New France is my lover and will soon be my wife."

He expected her to speak, but she merely looked at him with wide, mysterious eyes. Dominic leaned over to kiss her. The bedcover slipped down and her breasts grazed his chest. Her breathing quickened. She looked disappointed when he sat up.

"You see, *ma petite,*" he murmured, caressing a perfectly rounded globe. "It is fire that binds us together. You were born for me, Alix. Never think for one moment that you will find what we have with someone else."

Sylvie Marcheroix stared curiously at the slim, red-headed woman standing at the foot of the stairs. There was something naggingly familiar about her. Something other than the color of her hair, although that in itself was enough to call the attention of every eye in the room. In Montreal, ladies did not step out for the evening without elaborately powdered coiffures. Yes, Sylvie decided, it was more than just the hair that made the woman unusual. It was an aura about her, and the uncompromising line of her back. The set of her shoulders and the regal tilt of her head bespoke generations of family pride.

From across the room, Sylvie's eyes lingered appreciatively on the young woman's features. No wonder Dominic stayed close to her side. A girl with a face like that would not be left alone for long. She was not from Montreal or Quebec. Sylvie knew every debutante in both cities and she was quite sure she hadn't seen her there. Perhaps she was newly arrived from France. It had been over five years since the Marcheroixes had left Paris. The girl would have been too young to have frequented the drawing rooms of Versailles, but perhaps she had been a younger daughter not yet out. Yes, Sylvie nodded emphatically. That was it. The girl was the younger daughter of some obscure French nobleman. She unfurled her fan and started across the room to introduce herself.

"Dominic." She rapped her fan insistently against the brocade-covered shoulder. He turned, eyebrows raised. When he saw who it was, he smiled and lifted her hand to his lips.

"*Madame.*" He bowed gallantly. "I thought you were in Quebec."

Her sherry-colored eyes twinkled up at him. "You thought nothing of the sort. I doubt if my whereabouts ever crossed your mind at all."

"Indeed, they did, *madame.* Your husband has proven himself to be a great friend to my family."

"This talk of husbands and friendship is most unlike you, Dominic. Are you truly reformed?"

The hard line of his lips softened. "Perhaps."

Sylvie did not miss the possessive tightening of his hand on the young woman's arm. "Will you introduce me to your companion?" she asked.

"Of course." Sylvie had never seen Dominic Jolliet look at a woman the way he looked at the beauty by his side.

"Sylvie Marcheroix," he began formally, "this is Alexandra Winthrop, my fiancée."

The name triggered her reluctant memory like cathedral bells on Christmas Day. "*Mon Dieu.*" Sylvie gasped and stared at Alexandra. Could it be? Her startled gaze moved over the wide mouth, the winged brows, and thin aristocratic nose. Of course. How could she not have seen it before? "My dear child." Her hand reached out to clutch Alexandra's arm. "Do you not remember me?"

Alexandra's brow wrinkled. Had she inadvertently offended an acquaintance of the Vaudreuils? The governor and his lady were conspicuously absent tonight. She wondered if Dominic had warned them away. "No, *madame*. I beg your pardon, but I do not."

Sylvie frowned and then pushed her disappointment aside. "No matter. I shouldn't have expected it. You were behind the walls of that dreadful shed with the *petit enfant* and little boy. I am Sylvie Marcheroix, the woman who spoke to you at Fort Niagara. I wrote to your grandfather as I promised."

Alexandra's face paled. She grasped the older woman's hands with shaking fingers. "It is you. I remember your voice. Oh, *madame,* you gave me my only hope. How can I ever thank you?"

"It was nothing, *mademoiselle,* I assure you. A Christian woman could do no less. You must tell me what happened to you. Is your grandfather here?"

"No," replied Alexandra. "But I expect him soon." She hesitated. "My story is a long one, *madame.* Perhaps another time would be better."

"Ah." Sylvie nodded her head in sympathetic understanding. "It shall be as you wish." She brushed the girl's cheek with a soft kiss, murmuring under her breath, "Do not let the cats of Montreal crush your spirit, my dear. There isn't a woman in this room who can compare with you. Even if you were a French aristocrat, they would still despise you because of Dominic."

The color in Alexandra's cheeks deepened. She hated to deceive this bird-like woman with her warm heart and fluttering gestures. But she had given up trying to explain how it must be. Despite Dominic's persuasive charm and Henri Jolliet's kindness, Alexandra could not stay. The looks on the women's faces in the ballroom told her what Dominic refused to accept. She was an outsider, a member of that race whose increasing numbers threatened the very existence of the French colonists. Alexandra could not blame them for hating her. With bare hands, they had carved a life for themselves out of the wilderness. Each year with the change of seasons, they alternately froze and boiled, were attacked by savages and eaten by mosquitoes. The blood of their children stained the snow. No, Alexandra thought regretfully. New France was no place for an Englishwoman.

"Come, child." Sylvie squeezed her arm gently. "Do not look so serious. This is a party." With a brilliant smile, she moved away.

The familiar notes of the minuet interrupted her thoughts. Dominic offered his arm. "Shall we dance, Alix?"

There was something frighteningly sensual about the feel of his hand against the small of her back. His eyes were smoky black in the candlelight. She couldn't tell what he was thinking. Even though he was properly dressed in formal attire, he looked different from the boy she had known in Paris. His face was older, his mouth hard and uncompromising. He no longer looked bored, but neither did he appear content. The powdered hair and satin coat could not conceal the changes of the last two years. The spoiled boy had become a man. As inexperienced as she was, Alexandra knew, without question, that he was a man worth knowing. With heart-stabbing regret, she wished it could have turned out differently for them.

The violins played on. They moved together in the stately motions of the dance. For a fleeting instant, their hands met and a shock flowed through Alexandra's arm. From the slight intake of his breath, she knew he felt it, too.

Dominic was neither blind nor lacking in intelligence. He could predict with shocking accuracy the thoughts behind Alexandra's expressive eyes. The single-mindedness of her convictions disturbed him. Normally, he was not a man who believed in allowing fate to follow its own course. He preferred to steer it in a direction that worked to his own advantage. With the wisdom of a man much older in years and experience, he knew he had come up against something he could not force. If there were to be a future for the two of them, it could not be shadowed by doubt.

Alexandra stood beside him, the epitome of grace in her green-satin gown and upswept curls. Her cheeks were flushed, her eyes sparkled. One hand rested in his. He tightened his arm around her waist and breathed in the delicious scent of her hair. It would serve no purpose to tell her the decision was hers to make. There would be a lifetime for her to find out the power she had over him.

Chapter 22

The brass knocker thudded loudly against the wooden door. Alexandra, about to dip her brush into the rose-colored mixture she had labored over an hour to create, paused. Again the knocker sounded. She frowned. Where was Marceau? Surely he would respond to the imperious demand. A third time, the brass hit the door. With a sigh, she carefully placed her brush on the easel, swept the hair away from her forehead, and walked to the door. She opened it and stared in incredulous disbelief at an extremely large man with bushy eyebrows and an iron-gray wig.

"Grandfather!" she cried and, for the first time in her life, threw herself into his arms. They closed around her in a grip of steel.

"Alix," he whispered, hoarsely. "My God, Alix."

Alexandra felt an unfamiliar wetness against her cheek. She lifted her head and stared in surprise. The lined face was streaked with tears, and he wasn't in the least concerned that she saw them. "I'm fine, m'lord. Truly I am."

Charles Winthrop smiled bracingly. Then his face crumpled. "I've been the worst of fools, my dear. I would give everything I own to have seen Julia before—" He could go no further.

Alexandra squeezed his hand. "She knew you had forgiven her. We were planning to return home together when the Indians attacked." Tears coated her lashes. "She was happy with John, Grandfather. We should be grateful for that, at least."

"And the children?" he asked gruffly.

She shook her head and looked away from the eagerness in the piercing gray eyes. "Travis is somewhere in the wilderness with the Ojibwa. The hunting party never returned to Bowating. Abigail is here in Montreal with an important family. The woman refuses to give her up."

"We shall see about that." Leicester stepped away to look at her, his mouth hardening at her paint-spattered apron and loose hair. "Why are you dressed that way, my love? Have they got my granddaughter working as a servant?"

She laughed through her tears. "I've been painting. Come and see. I'll change in a moment and we can tell each other everything."

"Just a minute, Alix. I haven't come alone. There is a young man waiting outside who wishes very much to see you."

Alexandra's heart pounded. It was difficult to form the words. "Is it Anthony?"

Leicester nodded. "It is."

She wet her lips. Somehow she hadn't expected her reckoning to come so soon. "Perhaps it would be best if I spoke to him alone," she said. "I'll show you to a guest room. Dominic isn't here, but his father is. After you've rested, I'll take you to him."

Alexandra took longer than necessary to settle her grandfather into his bedchamber. Finally, when she could delay it no longer, she changed into a flowered morning gown and descended the staircase to face the inevitable.

Her mouth was dry. She could feel her hands through the thin material of her gown. They were unusually cold. How strange to be afraid of an encounter with Anthony. She had never seen him more than mildly irritated and never at her. Anthony Doddridge was everything she wanted in a husband—loyal, kind, polite and safe, always the gentleman. Why did those virtues, once so important to her, now sound terribly dull?

Dominic's beautiful austere features danced through her mind. Black eyes glinted with laughter and something else that stopped the breath from leaving her lungs. Firm lips, tight with purpose, twisted like quicksilver into a teasing grin. She closed her eyes and saw him as clearly as if he stood before her. The wide shoulders and lean feline grace, the narrow hands and long fingers, the velvet of his touch, the silken danger in his voice, the primitive fury of his temper, the dark archangel symmetry of his face were as familiar to her as the air she breathed, and almost as necessary.

Her fiancé waited in the drawing room, his back to the door. For the first time in his life, Captain Anthony Doddridge was not meticulously groomed. He wore no hat and his scarlet uniform had been exchanged for deerskin breeches and a jacket. His clothing looked oddly out of place with the stiff military boots on his feet. His corn-colored hair, unkempt and tied back with a thong, was his own. Alexandra smiled. Anthony looked most unlike himself. He hadn't heard her come in.

"Hello," she said softly.

He turned immediately and came toward her, hands outstretched.

Alexandra gasped. "Anthony?" She could scarcely believe this gaunt, serious stranger was Anthony Doddridge.

Grasping her hands in his, he searched her face with passionate intensity. "Alexandra, my dear. Are you all right?"

Gently, she removed her hands from the vise-like grip. "Of course. The Jolliets have treated me well."

He sighed and collected himself. "Thank God for that. When you and Julia were taken, we feared the worst."

"The worst did happen, Anthony," she reminded him. "Julia is dead and her children are missing."

"I didn't mean to minimize your suffering," he replied, looking at her elegant gown and fair skin. "However, given the reports of Indian captives, I was prepared to find you in much worse circumstances."

Alexandra's back stiffened. She lifted her chin. "What kind of circumstances?"

Doddridge flushed. How in the hell had their first meeting in over a year come to this? He had nearly died coming to her rescue and she was behaving as if he had insulted her. "I didn't mean to offend you, Alix. Surely, this is not the time to discuss your adventures with the Ojibwa."

"My adventures, Anthony?" She thought of the exhausting trek through the wilderness with a small boy and a baby, fearing every moment that they would die before sunrise. For the rest of her life she would recall Julia's bracing courage and the look on her face as she spoke her last words to her children. Hardly a night passed where she didn't relive in her dreams the terror of that first day in Bowating and the horror of the weeks following her refusal of Red Wing. How dare Anthony suggest that what she had endured fell into the category of an adventure?

Doddridge squirmed before the clear, contemptuous eyes. There was no mistaking the outrage in Alexandra's voice. He sighed once again. "I apologize for diminishing your unfortunate experience," he said. "But you must admit that you hardly appear ill-used."

"I have been in Montreal for months, Anthony. The French are hardly uncivilized monsters."

"Tell that to the colonial settlers," he replied bitterly. "War parties have raided every frontier settlement from

Virginia to the Hudson River Valley. Survivors report that the Indians were Algonquian, primarily Ottawa and Huron, allied to the French. Scalps are highly prized and paid for by General Marquis de Montcalm. His butchery would make your blood run cold."

"Perhaps we are somewhat to blame for that," replied Alexandra thoughtfully.

"Alexandra!" The distaste on Anthony's face was almost humorous.

"We English have never tried to get along with the Indians or to learn their ways," she continued.

"Good God! Why should we?"

"The French *coureurs* have trapped as far west as the ocean. Their colony stretches twice as far as all of ours put together. They couldn't have done it without the help of the Indians. The French live in their villages, marry their women, educate their children. French priests convert them to Christianity." Alexandra's cheeks were flushed with conviction. "We, on the other hand, despise everything about the Indians. We sell them watered-down brandy and a few pitiful necessities of life for a full season's trapping. We fence in their land, chop down their forests, and crowd them farther and farther west to make room for yet another wave of English settlers. Perhaps it's time the English swallowed their pride and admitted they could learn a great deal from the French, Anthony."

"I truly believe you've lost your mind, Alix. Your words are seditious. The sooner we can secure passage to England, the better."

Alexandra stared at him in amazement. When had he become so self-righteous? Would all Englishman appear the same? Perhaps he was right and she had been too long in French Canada. She cleared her throat. "Anthony, there is something I must tell you."

A voice from the door startled her. "Welcome to Montreal, Captain Doddridge." Alexandra turned as Dominic walked into the room. He stopped beside her. Although his words were cordial, he did not offer his hand to the Englishman. "Did you just arrive?"

"Yes," Doddridge replied stiffly. "We came directly here. The duke is resting upstairs, but naturally I wanted to see Alexandra first."

"Naturally." Dominic lingered over the word, drawing out the syllables.

Anthony shifted uneasily. The man made him uncomfortable. He was ashamed of such an uncharitable sentiment, but it was there all the same. Though Jolliet was a nobleman, there was something about him, something frightening and primitive, an untamed savagery, a reckless disregard for the conventions of civilized men. Why in bloody hell was he looking at Alexandra that way?

Anthony clenched his teeth. If only he dared smash his fist into Jolliet's handsome face but his self-preservation instincts were strong. The idea was absurd. This man had saved his life. There were other, more subtle ways of establishing a claim on Alexandra. Deliberately, Anthony drew a deep settling breath. "I must thank you for taking such good care of my fiancée," he said.

"I assure you, the pleasure is mine," replied Dominic.

Doddridge frowned. Neither the words nor the mocking voice were what he had expected. Again he asserted himself. "Now that I am here, I shall take all future responsibility for Alexandra."

Dominic flicked an imaginary speck of lint from his coat and sat down in a chair. Stretching out his legs, he surveyed the captain through heavy-lidded eyes. "You are not married yet, *monsieur*."

The captain bristled. "What does that mean?"

"Only that her rightful guardian is the Duke of Leicester. If he is, as you say, resting upstairs, your protection is unnecessary."

"I intend to marry Alexandra as soon as possible."

Dominic's eyes glinted disturbingly. "You are Protestant, are you not, Captain Doddridge?"

"Of course."

"It will be nothing short of a miracle to procure a special license and a Protestant clergyman in Montreal, *monsieur*."

"I shall surprise you, m'lord."

"Don't be absurd," Alexandra interrupted impatiently. "Your sense of honor is untimely, Anthony. Montreal isn't an English satellite. You've no funds or credit here. How can you possibly support us?"

"If you no longer wish to marry me," he replied stiffly, "you need say nothing more."

Alexandra sighed and walked to the window. In the small clearing at the side of the house, flowers she had never seen before bloomed in pale profusion. The harsh climate of North America did not allow for the brilliant reds and vibrant yellows of an English rose garden. For over a year now, she had considered herself an English rose, incapable of rooting and surviving in foreign soil. Why, then, was she so reluctant to settle the matter once and for all? Was it cowardice or something else that kept her lips sealed? She turned to face the two men, her slender white-clad figure outlined against the dark draperies.

Dominic sat in his chair, legs sprawled out, the black eyes veiled and expressionless. Alexandra wondered, not for the first time, if he already knew what she was about to say. Anthony had not moved. He stood near the mantel, stiff and unyielding. She walked across the room and sat down in an upholstered armchair. Wetting her lips, she began. "There is something I must tell you, Anthony, before there can be any discussion of marriage between us." She looked pointedly at Dominic. "Will you excuse us, m'lord?"

His eyes moved thoughtfully over her face. At last, he smiled and shook his head. "Not this time, Alix. I believe I have something of a stake in this discussion."

"Very well. Listen if you must, but do not interfere."

"You have my word."

Alexandra threw him a withering look and turned her

attention to her fiancé. "This isn't easy for me, Anthony, but it must be said. Under no circumstances should you believe that I no longer wish to be your wife. If, after hearing me out, you still wish to marry me, I shall be more than willing to honor our arrangement. If you do not, I shall accept your decision and no more will be said."

"There is nothing that could change my feelings for you, my dear."

"Please." Alexandra wrung her hands. "Let me finish."

Anthony nodded. "Very well."

"After Julia died, the children and I were taken to the Ojibwa village of Bowating. The French call it Sault Sainte Marie. Travis was adopted into an Indian family. Abigail was allowed to stay with me in the wigwam of Red Wing, the War Chief. We lived there a long time, over six months, I think." Her brow furrowed. "The Indians were very kind to me. I had no contact with white people at all until winter when French *coureurs* came to trade in the village. Dominic was one of them."

Blood throbbed in Anthony's temple. All at once he knew what it was that Alexandra felt obliged to tell him. A killing rage swept through him, blotting out her words, centering on the man seated across from him.

"Did you hear what I said, Anthony?" Alexandra's voice pierced through his red haze.

"Of course," he replied curtly. "Please, go on."

"I still don't know how I could have done such a thing," she continued. Her voice was almost a whisper. "It seems like such a dream, as if it all happened to another person. I didn't believe I'd leave Bowating alive. We just existed from day to day. Still, if I hadn't known Dominic from my season in Paris, I don't think it would have turned out the way it did."

Anthony was startled out of his reverie. "What do you mean you knew him in Paris?"

Dominic answered in a flat voice. "During Alexandra's

first season in Paris, I asked the duke's permission to pay my addresses to her. He denied me."

"*You* wanted to marry Alexandra?" Anthony's expression was incredulous. He stared at the lean, finely etched features of the Frenchman and knew despair. The puzzle had finally come together. Alexandra had agreed to marry him, a second son, a man far beneath her in rank, because she couldn't have the man she wanted.

"There is more." Alexandra lifted her head and looked directly at him. "Red Wing wanted me for his wife. I refused him. From then on, my life became a living hell. Dominic left for Montreal to bring back money for my release. He was captured by a war party and couldn't return." Her mouth was very dry. "When I could no longer bear it, I told Red Wing I would become his squaw." She bowed her head, unable to meet his eyes. "I am not the woman you asked to be your wife, Anthony. And even though I am very sorry to cause you so much pain, I don't believe I would do anything differently if it were to happen again." She drew a deep breath. "Under the circumstances, it would be best to release you from our engagement."

Anthony's face was the color of bleached bone beneath his tan. He felt ill. The thought of Alexandra in the arms of a savage nauseated him. "If you'll excuse me," he said, "I'm tired. We'll finish this tomorrow morning."

"Where will you go?" Alexandra asked.

She looked concerned, almost as if she truly cared. Had he ever really known Alexandra Winthrop? His stomach churned. He really must leave before he disgraced himself.

"There are lodgings in the city where I'll be quite comfortable," he assured her.

Dominic didn't try to dissuade him.

Once the door closed behind him, Captain Anthony Doddridge hurried down the narrow street and turned the corner. Holding his stomach, he doubled over and retched, again and again, into the overflowing gutter.

Chapter 23

The ticking of the clock on the mantel was the only sound in the room. Alexandra was very aware of Dominic's eyes on her face. She didn't dare look up to meet the burning contempt she knew she would find in his night-dark gaze. Why hadn't she told Anthony the truth? Was she such a coward that the words wouldn't form on her tongue? She had betrayed them all. In her twisted efforts to spare Anthony and herself, she had made everything much worse.

Dominic's voice was unexpectedly gentle. "It isn't as bad as all that, *mignonne.*"

Startled, she looked up. He had risen from his chair to stand before her. He took her hands in his own. Warily, Alexandra searched his face, looking for the mockery she knew so well. There was none. Was it pity or sympathy reflected in those dark, unfathomable depths? "What must you think of me?" she whispered.

"I think you have been a long time among strangers, little one," he replied softly. "You have no idea what it is you truly want." His hands tightened on hers and he pulled her closer.

Her eyes moved to his mouth. A familiar weakness invaded her knees. She could smell his heat and the soap on his skin. Everything about him affected her like a powerful drug.

An enigmatic smile crossed his lips. "Why didn't you tell Captain Doddridge nothing happened between Red Wing and you?"

Tears burned beneath her eyelids. "Because I intended it to happen."

"It would mean a great deal to him to know it did not."

She pulled her hands away. "What happened between us in the women's lodge was real enough. What difference does one more indiscretion make?"

Dominic's eyes narrowed as they moved over her face, gauging the sincerity of her words. If she truly believed what she said, Alexandra had changed more than she realized. "Infidelity is common enough in our world, Alix. Distasteful as it might be to him, Captain Doddridge could forgive our relationship. What he will never forgive is your bedding down with an Indian."

"What of you, Dominic?" Alexandra challenged him. "You've introduced me to everyone in Montreal as your betrothed. Why did you say nothing to Anthony?"

He lifted a curl from her shoulder, fingering the silky red-brown strands against his palm. She smelled of flowers. He ached for the right to claim her for his own, to touch her in front of that damned Englishman she called her fiancé, to lift her in his arms, carry her to his room, and bury himself in the warmth of her golden flesh.

"Why, Dominic?" she repeated. "Have you come to your senses and changed your mind?"

"The captain would see my claim as a challenge," he replied. "I prefer not to help him with his decision."

"What will he think when he learns of it from someone else?"

Dominic smiled at her naiveté. "Captain Doddridge and I hardly move in the same circles, *chérie.*"

"Aren't you afraid that I'll tell him?" Her voice was a mere whisper of air against his throat.

"No, Alix. You won't tell him."

"How can you be sure?"

"For the same reason that you lied about sharing the bridal furs with Red Wing." The dark eyes held her motionless. It was as if he could see through her flesh and bones into the very center of her soul. "You want Anthony Doddridge to refuse you. The decision will no longer be yours, and you will have what you want with a clear conscience."

Even a schoolgirl would have recognized the tension in the air. Alexandra moistened her lips. She would ask the question and welcome the consequences. "What is it that you think I want?"

Effortlessly, like wind in the grass, he reached out and pulled her against him. She went willingly, molding her body against the lean length of his. His lips on her throat tore down the last of her defenses. Through a whirlpool of mounting passion she heard his muttered words. "You want me, Alix, however much you deny it. You want me as much as I want you."

Dinner that night was strained. The differences between England and France were evident in the two old gentlemen with opposing loyalties. The duke had broken the news of his wife's death to Alexandra. The thought of returning to the manor house at Leicester without the presence of the small, fascinating woman who was her grandmother left a burning ball in the pit of the girl's stomach. She could barely swallow. Only Dominic remained unaffected by the mood in the dining room. For some reason, just watching the play of his thin, aristocratic hands as they carved the meat into uniform slices had a soothing effect on her nerves. In grateful silence, she listened to him divert the monosyllabic conversation into less-hostile channels. Under his careful guidance, the two old men were actually smiling as they recalled their salad days in the City of Light.

Dominic Jolliet had the charm of a politician. Alexandra looked down at her plate and frowned. Why should he not? The role of diplomat was no game for the Marquis de Villiers, son of the Duc de Lorraine and Queen of France. It was his birthright, as natural to him as breathing. It was that other part he played, that of Night Wind, trapper and backwoodsman, blood brother to the Anishinabe, that was a temporary facade.

"Have you told my granddaughter of our bargain, *monsieur?*" Leicester swallowed the tender chicken and reached for his wine.

The English duke was proving to be a formidable strategist. Dominic grinned. He knew something about taking the offensive himself. "I have," he replied. "The announcement ran in the paper shortly before you arrived."

Leicester's mouth dropped open. His face darkened to a painful red. He looked at Dominic and then at his granddaughter. "You dared to do this without my permission?" he sputtered.

Alexandra could bear it no longer. Leaping to her feet, she knocked over a chair. "Yes, I dared." Her voice, hovering on the edge of hysteria, froze the men in their places. "What of my permission, Grandfather? Did you think of my feelings when you made your disgraceful bargain? Did you think of Anthony?" Her fist slammed against the table, rattling the priceless crystal. "I know what you did in Paris. Does it offend you, Grandfather? Does it horrify your sensibilities to know that the very man you sent away because he wasn't good enough to wed a Winthrop will now become my husband?"

Her hands shook and her cheeks burned with rage. "I'm not a sack of meal or a parcel of land. I'm a woman and I won't be bargained for. Your precious honor isn't worth it. I've been through hell and back again. I've seen my sister's scalp hanging from the blood-stained hand of a savage. I've seen my niece and nephew taken from me without so much as a by-your-leave. I've been kicked and beaten and starved until even you wouldn't have recognized me. I've picked maggots from rotting flesh and eaten it raw. I've lived with lice and filth and dysentery. On my hands and knees I've offered my body to an Indian in return for my life." She ignored Leicester's shocked gasp as the words continued to spill out. "I've lost everyone I've ever loved. Only a monster would refuse me the right to determine my fate. From now on, I'll go where I choose, and with whom, whether or not you give your permission." With a last contemptuous glance at the three of them, Alexandra swept out of the room.

For a long time no one spoke. Leicester cleared his throat and pushed back his chair. His face was ashen, but the training of a lifetime was strong. His manners were impeccable. "Thank you for an excellent dinner, gentlemen. I believe I'll retire for the evening."

Henri Jolliet poured himself more wine and looked at his son over the rim of the glass. "I had no idea Mademoiselle Winthrop had such a temper."

A hint of a smile appeared on Dominic's lips. "Neither did I," he confessed. "Advise me, *mon père*. Is my cause a hopeless one? Shall I give up the chase?"

The duc studied the dark, ruby color of his wine and appeared to consider the matter carefully. Finally he looked up, his eyes bright with laughter. "Only a fool would give up a woman like that. Of all your sins, *mon fils*, I have never considered you a fool. If you do not wed her, I shall ask her myself."

For one startled moment, there was silence. A current flowed between father and son and the dam of long-held resentments broke at last. Dominic threw back his head and shouted with laughter.

Moments later, on his way to the kitchen, Marceau heard

the unmistakable sound of merriment coming from the dining room. Unable to believe his ears, he stepped briefly into the room and stopped, rooted to the floor. The Duc de Lorraine, his head surrounded by a circle of blue smoke, nodded and smiled as Dominic entertained him with a tale from the *coureur's* repertoire.

Charles Winthrop spent a sleepless night. Old nightmares tormented him. Clearly, as if it were yesterday, his son's handsome, youthful face stared up at him from an elegantly carved coffin. The scene changed. Servants moved quickly through the halls, removing all traces of his daughter's stillborn child. He tossed uneasily, twisting the bedclothes into knots. The smell of Anne's blood hung in the air. Now he saw Julia, utterly beautiful, calmly defiant, stating with frightening finality that she would die before setting foot on Winthrop land again. Liane's face materialized before him. A different Liane, hard and merciless, coldly reciting his shortcomings as a husband and father.

New, bloodcurdling images formed in his mind. Julia scalped. Alexandra, bruised and beaten, a suppliant in the arms of a naked savage. Children with unformed faces called his name. A shout broke through his memories and woke him completely. It was his own voice, restoring him to sanity. With a muffled curse he threw back the covers and reached for his robe. He would wait until morning. Then he would seek out Dominic Jolliet. His mind was made up.

"Don't be absurd," Dominic said curtly as he helped himself to another serving of ham. "You have no idea what such a journey would entail."

"I should like to try," the Englishman insisted stubbornly.

Dominic sighed. He pulled out his chair and sat down, applying himself to the excellent ham. "What you ask is an impossibility," he said between mouthfuls. "No one will ever find the boy unless he wants to be found. There are a hundred Indian villages between Montreal and the Red River. Take the infant and return to England."

"The boy is my heir. He is all I have left of my grand-daughter. I must find him."

"Then do it without me. Chief Pontiac of the Ottawas is on the warpath. His prophet has ordered him to kill every white man on sight. Even now, the wampum belt is passing through the northern tribes. Huron, Fox, Saux, Ojibwa, even the Seneca have united to drive the English from Indian hunting grounds. I value my skin even if you don't. Besides—" His contemptuous glance flickered over the duke's portly frame. "—you wouldn't last a week in the woods."

Winthrop flushed. "Very well. I'll find someone else to take me."

"Take you where?" Alexandra stood in the doorway, looking like a breath of spring in a yellow morning gown with wide panniers. Her hair was pulled back from her brow with a yellow ribbon, falling in casual ringlets to her waist.

Dominic stood and pulled out her chair. "Tell your grandfather what a journey into the Canadian wilderness is like, Alix. He seems to think it would be no more difficult than a picnic in the English countryside."

Alexandra sat down and poured herself a cup of choco-late. "Dominic is right, Grandfather. A man your age can't possibly undertake such a journey. You simply wouldn't survive."

"Are you suggesting that we leave Julia's child to grow up among savages?" he asked through clenched teeth.

"Not at all." She reached for a roll and bit into its soft whiteness. "I'll go with Dominic to find Travis."

Dominic's lips twitched. The minx. Did she think she could twist him around her finger the way she did every other man?

"This is no time to joke," replied Leicester.

Alexandra met her grandfather's impatient glance with a level stare. " 'Tis no joke. If you think on it rationally, you will agree that there is no one else."

"An unmarried woman alone and unchaperoned in the wilderness!" Leicester was beyond shock. "Don't be absurd."

"There is no one better suited to go," she argued. "I've traveled through the forests and lived with Indians. Besides, neither you nor Dominic would recognize him."

"It won't be difficult to find a blue-eyed child of seven years among the Anishinabe," Dominic observed dryly.

Alexandra turned on him. "Even if you found him, he would never come with you. He knows me." The golden eyes pleaded with him. "Please, Dominic. Let me do this for Julia."

The duke watched Jolliet waver and recognized the face of defeat. Alexandra was no longer his. Somewhere in that frozen region to the north, he had lost her. Whether she knew it or not, she had thrown in her lot with the extremely attractive and capable young man standing before her. Leicester was conscious of a sense of relief. He need not spend the rest of his life listening to Anthony Doddridge's nervous prattle after all. Something told him that young Jolliet never prattled. Christ, the man had nerves of steel. In the short time he had spent with the Frenchman, Leicester had come to admit with mocking self-derision that there was no one else more worthy of his granddaughter. How strange that Alexandra had seen the quality of the young man's character from the beginning while he, a man of experience, had overlooked it completely.

Dominic walked around the table and pulled her from her chair. Gripping her arms above the elbow, he stared at the clear, piercing beauty of her face. Don't give in, he told himself. Leave, while you can still resist her. Carry your canoe across the mighty falls of the Susquehanna, paddle it down a thousand teeming rivers from the St.

Lawrence River to the Chesapeake Bay. Sleep under a canopy of stars at the farthest edges of the world. Revel in the skilled hands and hungry passions of lithe, brown-skinned Indian maidens. Smoke and drink and eat and sleep whenever you please. Run as far and as fast as humanly possible. Forget this English beauty with her skin like silk and her spine of steel.

But it was already too late. Alexandra's eyes haunted him. Dominic knew he had lost. Tightening his grip on her arms, he gave it one last try. "We are at war, Alix. England has a death grip on our continent. France is losing Canada, and the Indians are desperate. We've made them dependent on us with our weapons, our blankets and clothing. Your generals refuse to give the tribes even the most rudimentary supplies. They cannot shoot enough game to feed their families for the winter." His eyes blazed with anger. "Pontiac has united the tribes. He won't stop to ask which side we support. Julia is dead. Do you wish you to join her?"

Alexandra barely felt the cramping pain of his fingers. Stepping closer, she whispered the words against his lips. "I could not live with my conscience knowing Julia's child is out there and I did nothing. I have seen the worst, Dominic. Whatever happens, I will be with you." Her eyes told him what she hadn't said in words.

His breathing altered and he bent his head to her lips. "Alix—" he groaned.

The duke cleared his throat, acutely uncomfortable with the scene before him. It was obvious from the natural ease of their embrace that the two were on terms of physical intimacy. Good God! A red-skinned savage and a royal bastard. Was this truly his granddaughter? Philippe's child? Perhaps there was bad blood on her mother's side. He refused to dwell on such a possibility. There were details to arrange. Anthony Doddridge must be disposed of, and there was still the matter of his great-granddaughter. The child must be found immediately.

Chapter 24

"I won't allow it, Alexandra." Proud of his rigid self-control, Captain Anthony Doddridge issued the ultimatum. He credited his remarkable rationality to ten years of service in His Majesty's armed forces. What other man would listen to his fiancée's ludicrous proposal with such reasonable calm? "I'm surprised your grandfather would even consider such a thing."

From her seat near the pianoforte, Alexandra watched him pace from one end of the drawing room to the other. "Grandfather has nothing to say on the matter," she replied gently, "and neither do you."

"We are to be married," he reminded her. "That gives me every right."

"Is that the decision you've come to, Anthony? Can you forget the past?"

"I would prefer not to speak of it," he replied stiffly. "The circumstances were beyond your control. You did what you had to in order to survive. No one can blame you for that. I am not so small-minded that I would hold it against you."

"No." She bit back a smile. "You are not in the least small-minded."

"That does not mean I shall stand by and countenance your returning to the wilderness with that Frenchman. It is extremely dangerous." He flushed uncomfortably. "Besides, what would people think?"

"Which is it that you are most concerned about?" she countered.

"I beg your pardon?"

Alexandra sighed. " 'Tis nothing. My mind is made up. We leave in the morning."

His hands clenched in rage. "I would never have believed you could be so defiant. You are not the woman I once knew."

"That is my fault," she said unexpectedly. "I'm afraid I haven't been very honest with you, Anthony. I've always been quite stubborn. I wanted so much to please you that I kept all my character flaws hidden."

Her words appeased him. She sounded more like the woman he had fallen in love with. The tension flowed out of his body. "Alix." He walked to where she sat and took her hands in his. "Once we are home, this will all be forgotten. I know you feel a responsibility to Julia, but there isn't a chance in a million that you'll find the boy. Be reasonable and come home with me now."

Gently, she disengaged her hand. "I'm sorry, Anthony. Everything is arranged." She looked up at his thin, stricken face and relented. "You could come with us."

The image of Pontiac's hideously painted visage appeared before him. Shuddering, he shook it off. "I think not. My obligation to the army does not allow for the sort of ill-timed adventure you propose."

Alexandra caught her bottom lip between her teeth and hesitated. The words must be said. It would be kinder now than later. "Your desire to pursue our marriage plans does me great honor," she began. "However, I believe you need time to consider your decision more carefully. The past weeks have been shocking for you, Anthony. It is possible that, after further reflection, you may change your mind."

"What you are really telling me is that you are no longer sure we would suit," he said bitterly.

Alexandra did not look away. "Perhaps," she admitted.

Doddridge didn't trust himself to speak. With a curt nod, he left the room.

Abigail was no longer an infant. She stood on sturdy legs, one finger in her mouth, and stared at the strangers. The wide brown eyes held no fear, only a natural curiosity for the sweet-smelling woman who held out her arms.

The ache in Alexandra's heart threatened to consume her. Tears filled her eyes and she dared not blink for fear they would spill down her cheeks. Abigail did not remember her. She should have realized that six months was a lifetime to a child. Madame de Champlain was the only mother she knew. The woman wept openly into her handkerchief.

"I had no idea I would have to give her up," the Frenchwoman sobbed. "Little Geneviève is like my own child."

"Her name is Abigail Winthrop," said the Duke of Leicester in his haughtiest voice. "And she is English. You should have known that she would eventually be returned to her own people. Good God, the child isn't a peasant."

"*Madame.*" Dominic took her arm and led her to a white upholstered armchair. "The duke is very grateful for what you have done for his great-granddaughter. Obviously she has been well-cared-for."

Madame de la Champlain sniffed at the conciliatory words. Alexandra was suddenly ashamed. This generous woman loved Abigail, and if the truth were told, the child would probably prefer to stay here in Montreal with her. Alexandra wondered if her grandfather realized the difficulties of caring for a child still in leading strings.

The duke was completely taken with his tiny great-granddaughter. "She is the image of you, Alix," he whispered in awe. "If I didn't know she was Julia's child, I would swear she could be your own daughter."

Alexandra stared in surprise as he knelt down on his knees before the toddler. From beneath his coat, he pulled out a rag doll with button eyes. The child reached for it immediately. Seeing his advantage, Leicester lifted her into his arms at the same time he relinquished the toy. After one serious, wide-eyed stare, Abigail turned her attention back to the doll.

"That's right, poppet," Leicester crooned. "As soon as we find your brother, we'll go home to Leicester. I'll hire a nurse. Not one of those starched fussy ones. No, that wouldn't do at all. I'll find a patient, gentle soul. One who tells stories and laughs at sticky fingers. That's what we need at Leicester. A woman who laughs and tells stories."

Alexandra was in shock. Had the man lost his mind? He was actually babbling. Her eyes met Dominic's. His shrug and answering grin lifted her spirits and dissolved her doubts. Purposely, she walked to where Madame de Champlain sat on her couch. "I thank you from the bottom of my heart, *madame*. Abigail is all that we have left of my sister. She means a great deal to us."

Isabelle La Champlain forgot her tears and stared curiously at the lovely English girl. Geneviève would look very much like her when she was grown. She hadn't known what to expect of Alexandra Winthrop, but it certainly wasn't this. The girl had quality. Madame Vaudreuil had called her a *salope*, but then the woman always did have a waspish tongue. Most likely the girl had refused her milksop of a son. From behind her handkerchief, Madame de la Champlain looked at the lean, chiseled face of Dominic Jolliet. Now, there was a man to weep for. No flesh-and-blood woman could blame a girl for preferring the hard-eyed and dangerous nobleman-turned-*coureur* to Vaudreuil's overly indulged heir.

Isabelle La Champlain reached out to touch the coppery

curls resting on Alexandra's shoulder. "You are very lovely, *mademoiselle*. Perhaps you will write me with news of the child from time to time."

"Of course, *madame.*"

The woman stood. "Take her then, and go quickly. I cannot bear this any longer."

The duke needed no further urging. He wasn't comfortable in the home of a French army officer or, for that matter, in any territory under French dominion. The sooner he had Julia's children safely in England, the sooner he would breathe easily again.

Within moments, he was seated in the Jolliet town carriage with Abigail in his lap. He wondered what her brother would be like. The thought of having a male heir at Leicester lifted the duke's spirits. He felt young again, as if anything were possible. Fixing his penetrating gaze on the elegantly dressed Frenchman seated across from him, he said, "When do you intend to leave?"

Something dark and elemental flickered in Dominic's dark eyes and then it was gone. "Before first light," was his brief reply.

Leicester nodded and stroked the burnished curls resting against his shoulder. "The sooner the better. I want my great-grandson with me."

"What of your granddaughter, *Monsieur le Duc*? Are you so anxious to consign her to the devil?"

The duke's bushy eyebrews drew together in a frown. "Alexandra has made it quite clear she will no longer be ruled by me."

"I wish you wouldn't behave as if I were invisible." Alexandra's even temper was strained to the limit. She glared at Dominic. "You know there is nothing either of you can say to dissuade me. Why must you bring up this unpleasantness now?"

"A self-preservation instinct, *mon amie*. I shall try to change your mind until the very last moment and for every step thereafter."

"It will avail you nothing."

Dominic leaned forward until his face was inches from hers. "Have you considered what will happen if we do not find your nephew?"

"We'll find him."

Deliberately, he emphasized the cruel possibilities. "He may be dead or sold to another tribe. How long will it take before you give up the search? One month? Two?"

"Why do you do this, Dominic?" she asked.

He grimaced and leaned back against the expensive upholstery. "I am trying to save your life, Alexandra. As it stands, I wouldn't give a single *louis* for our chances at this moment."

She stared at him in amazement. "Why did you agree to accompany me?"

His mouth twisted in a mocking smile. "Because I know you. In desperation you would have hired someone else. If there is the slightest chance of our succeeding in this misguided mission, I must be your guide. I haven't spent the past two years in idleness, *ma petite*. Believe it or not, you see before you an exceptional woodsman."

"You are also very humble, are you not, *monsieur*?"

"Humility is not a requirement for tracking, *mademoiselle*."

"What is?"

He struggled to control his temper. Someone in Alexandra's childhood had been very remiss in applying discipline. An occasional swat to her spoiled backside would have gone a long way toward improving her temperament. "Patience and the ability to withstand heat and cold," he answered. "To walk through swarms of flies by day and endure the bites of a thousand mosquitoes by night." The knuckles showed yellow-white through the brown skin of his clenched hands. "A man needs a sharp eye to catch game and a strong stomach that doesn't revolt at meat, stringy and warm with the taste of blood." His eyes held hers, forcing her to remember the horrors of her weeks on the trail. "Strength and a healthy constitution are also necessary. A man must carry a canoe laden with supplies across treacherous rocks slippery with the spray of water-falls and through strong rapids where an inadequate foot-hold can send him to instant death. A *coureur* needs skin that doesn't burn under a hundred sweltering suns. He needs steady nerves, an understanding of natives, and—" He paused for a moment before continuing. "—a passable voice."

It was a full minute before Alexandra, caught up in the poetry of his words, reacted. "A passable voice?" Surely she had misunderstood him.

Dominic grinned. "Why, to out-sing and out-drink every other *coureur* in the forest."

"I see." Alexandra made a point of pulling back the shade and pretending interest in the street outside. " 'Tis most edifying to know your priorities, *monsieur*. I assure you I won't interfere."

"The hell you won't," Dominic muttered under his breath. "You can't help yourself."

That night, Alexandra laid out the clothing Dominic had purchased for her to wear on their journey. She eyed the garments with distaste. Except for the divided woolen skirt and cotton blouse, it very much resembled Indian clothing. There were a buckskin jacket, leggings, and moc-casins for her feet. Space was limited; therefore, she would wear everything at the same time, tying the layers around her in times of extreme heat.

A birchbark canoe would be their sole means of transpor-tation. Because they would walk and portage for most of the journey, excessive luggage would be impossible to carry. Everything they brought with them had to be carried in their arms or on their backs. Food would come from the land. The forests teemed with rabbit, squirrel, and deer. Berries and roots would be steamed and eaten to ward off sickness, and the bark of trees would be boiled for sus-taining tea. In case of bad luck, Dominic carried with him a canister of unappetizing but nutritious beef glue. Several hunks of meat, egg whites, and vegetables were boiled down to a thick paste. The mixture was then sealed into a lead canister which could be melted down and molded into bullets after its contents had been eaten. He also insisted on including a small amount of concentrated soap powder. There was no conclusive proof, he admitted, but cleanliness seemed to prevent recurring illness. They would carry two flintlock rifles between them as well as a healthy measure of powder and ball. Alexandra had not yet mastered the knack of shooting accurately through the long barrels, but her quick fingers could reload with amazing efficiency.

As a gesture of goodwill, Dominic added to his pack a generous amount of glass beads, brass buttons, and powdered vermilion used by the Indians for adornment and to stain their faces and the parts in their hair red. In addition, he carried tobacco, burning glasses, pocket mirrors, and ear trinkets as well as copper and tin strips that could be fashioned into jewelry. These were symbols of friendship and good faith, distributed among the native tribes by the French since first landing on American soil. Alexandra could only shake her head at the shortsightedness of her own countrymen. The British, believing these items to be bribes, refused to take part in this time-honored tradition of exchange. Accustomed to white men bearing gifts, the Indians were offended by British policy. When it came to choosing sides, they consistently took up arms in favor of King Louis of France, their esteemed "Father Across the Water."

After she had washed her hair and the maid had brushed it dry, Alexandra stretched out on the feather mattress, revelling in its luxurious softness. It would be weeks, perhaps months, before she slept in a bed again. Yet, she felt no regret, only a surging sense of excitement. Tomorrow, she would once again battle the forces of nature. She would depend on her wits, her instincts, her wiry good health and sheer determination to survive and succeed. A very large part of her enthusiasm, she admitted to herself, lay in the fact that she would be with Dominic.

Her future with Anthony Doddridge seemed very far away. Deep in her soul, Alexandra believed the English captain would make her the better husband. They were of the same race, bred to the same world. There was no place below heaven for two people as different as Dominic and herself. If Anthony still wanted her when she returned, Alexandra would go with him. But first, there would be days and nights with Dominic. Dominic, whose slow smile stirred her blood to fire, whose burning glance caused her breathing to alter and her heart to drum in an irratic throbbing rhythm; Dominic, whose lightest caress seared her flesh and made her nerves vibrate and ache and sing with anticipation of the promise that lay ahead.

Alexandra had come to terms with the immorality of her decision. Captain Anthony Doddridge did not want a wife who lived and breathed her sensuality. He wanted a lady, an elegant chatelaine of noble birth to grace his home and give him heirs. She had told him about her past relationship with Dominic. Only a fool would assume they would not resume where they had left off. Anthony was no fool. If he still wished to marry her, it would be with full knowledge of what she had done.

Dominic was another matter entirely. Alexandra knew he was completely aware of the smoldering passions she carried within her, hidden away from the world. Indeed, he approved of them. It was Alexandra Winthrop, the woman, he wanted, not the Duke of Leicester's grand-daughter. She also knew that, despite his bold words, he was a man of enormous pride. Once he learned she had decided in favor of Anthony, he would never come near her again.

For Alexandra, his presence had become a need, as necessary to her as breathing. She needed his warmth; his teasing laughter; the quiet strength in his lean, capable hands; his complete and utter disregard for the customs of polite society. She was drawn to him, helplessly, inexorably, like a leaf on the wind. She did not wish to deceive Dominic, but neither could she give up these last few weeks with him. She would live on the memories for the rest of her life.

Chapter 25

Street vendors had not yet taken the boards from their shop windows when Dominic and Alexandra left the city the following morning. Even though it was early fall, the mist hung heavy and cold over the St. Lawrence and the blackness of the sky promised rain. Alexandra was relieved to leave the walled city behind.

By midafternoon they had passed Fort Frontenac, portaged over the falls at the mouth of Lake Ontario, and struck out in a brisk walk through white birch, ash, and maple forests to Lake Simcoe and the Georgian Bay. They camped for the night by the shores of the shining gray water. There was no sign of civilization. Even the promise of free land did not draw settlers this far into the remote wilderness.

Squirrels by the hundred, fat from the bountiful harvests of two seasons, scampered across curving tree trunks and peered from under leafy boughs at the intruders. Dominic took his gun out, aimed carefully, and fired. Within the hour, the savory smell of roasted meat wafted through the air. After dinner, Alexandra gathered enough springy ferns for two mattresses. Wrapping herself in a blanket, she lay down on one of the fragrant piles. There was no moon.

A flash of red disturbed the velvety blackness, glowed briefly, and then disappeared. She tensed. The sweet, pungent aroma of tobacco filled her nostrils. Dominic's pipe. Relaxing her weary muscles, she rolled over to look at the sky. The darkness was alive with moving points of light. She sighed. Sleep was slow in coming. Without warning, the ferns dipped and gave way beside her. Heat rose in her cheeks.

" 'Tis an exquisite night," Alexandra said, feeling a sudden, overwhelming need for words.

Dominic found her hand and silently laced his fingers through hers. A howl rent the silence. Wolves. She shivered and his hand tightened. "Don't worry," he said. "The pack is too far away to concern us. Besides, hunting has been good this season. Man isn't appealing game unless nothing else is available." His voice was warm and smooth and very reassuring.

They lay in companionable silence for a long time. Alexandra's eyes were beginning to adjust. She could almost make out his profile outlined against the night. He looked relaxed, completely content with the world. She had an irrational desire to learn every secret behind that dark, implacable face; to reach into the very corners of his mind and see every thought, every wish and repressed desire. "What would you do if you were somewhere else?" she asked abruptly.

"I beg your pardon?"

"If you could choose your own fate, what would you do with your life?"

The amusement in his voice irritated her. "When have I not chosen my own fate?"

"Surely you can't wish to be here, searching for a child you don't know," she said impatiently. "If we had never met, if you felt no responsibility to help me, where would you be now?" She was frustrated at her inability to make him understand. "You must know what I mean."

Dominic knew exactly what she meant. He also knew that a truthful answer might not be in his own best interests. He smiled against the darkness. A woman who walked without complaint for twenty miles in a sodden skirt carrying a heavy pack on her back deserved no less than the truth. "There is nowhere on earth I would rather be than here at this moment," he said at last.

"You can't be serious?"

"On the contrary. I am always serious."

Alexandra knew better than to argue over such an outrageous declaration. She wanted an answer to something far more important. "Why, then, did you argue against coming?"

Dominic could hear the frustration in her voice. He spoke deliberately, measuring his words as if explaining to a child. "My objections have nothing to do with my feelings for this country or my life in New France. I still believe this is not the time to travel in the wilderness."

"Are you saying that you prefer living here, in this uncivilized place, to Paris?" she asked incredulously.

"Yes."

Gathering her courage, Alexandra braved the question that had bothered her for a long time. "Have you forgiven me for forcing you to leave France?"

He sighed. "You didn't force me, Alix. I left because I couldn't face the circumstances of my birth. As it turned out, leaving France was my salvation. All of this—" He waved his arm in an all-encompassing arc. "—I would never have known. In Paris, gentlemen of my class gamble, drink, and carry on affairs with complacent widows. The most a man can hope for is luck in the card room, an accomodating heiress for a wife, and a beautiful mistress."

"It is not so in my country," Alexandra said, pleased that France was so obviously inferior to England.

"Ah, but it is," he contradicted. "I have been to London,

chérie. Your lords and ladies are soft, their bodies wasted with rich food, a preference for spirits, too many late nights, and not nearly enough to tax the mind. The only area in which England can claim superiority is her government."

"What of her army? Is that not superior as well?" Alexandra was well aware that French losses mounted every day.

"It all comes back to government. Why would a sane man fight for a king and country that considers a peasant of less value than a mule? There is nothing wrong with a French soldier that a full stomach and a plot of land to call his own wouldn't cure."

"Have you become an anarchist, Dominic?"

"I am a realist, Alexandra. Look around you. Here a man is free to be himself, to farm his land or trap his furs, to travel as far and wide as his legs will carry him." His enthusiasm flowed like a current from his hand to hers, the warmth spreading throughout her entire body. Her pulse leaped and her blood sang. Everything within her that chafed at the bonds of convention thrilled to his words. She felt wild and primitive and free, at one with the night and the woods and the intriguing man by her side.

Dominic warmed to his subject. "In the cities of Europe, children are weaned on gin and ale. They die of consumption before their fourth birthdays. There is no hope for anything better. Here, everyone, no matter how small, can become whatever he makes of himself. You ask where I would rather be, Alix? I would go west to where no white man has ever been. The Indians tell of rivers as wide and deeply blue as the sea, of trees so thick a squirrel can travel from the Mississippi River to the Pacific Ocean without ever touching the ground. I would climb granite mountains so high that clouds cover their peaks and gaze upon fountains gushing hot water from the springs of Hades thousands of feet into the air. The Spanish say there are cities with golden palaces and Indian tribes so light of skin they are believed to be a lost race of Welshmen shipwrecked in the New World a thousand years ago." He turned on his side to face her. "If I have any desire to be in another place, it would never be France. My life there is over, Alix. I will not go back."

"I wish I were a man," she said wistfully. "I would go with you."

"If you were a man, I would take you." There was no trace of mockery in the handsome face so close to her own. No disparaging remark protesting that it would be a sorry thing were she a man. He seemed to know exactly how his words had affected her. Her emotions were too real, too sensitive to tolerate anything less than complete acceptance. He moved closer and bent his head. Lightly, he brushed her mouth with his lips. "Good night, Alix."

A strange trembling had taken hold of her body. "Don't leave me," she whispered.

He pulled her into his arms so that her cheek rested against his chest. "I have no intention of ever leaving you, Alexandra."

At Fort Michilimackinac the news wasn't good. Captain Dulac, commander of the fort, reported that Pontiac refused to believe General Montcalm was suing for peace in the name of the King of France. Furious at the abandonment of his French father, the Ottawa chief had incited the tribes north of the Great Lakes and captured nine English forts along the Wabash and Ohio Rivers. The Indians had tasted victory and were hungry for blood and scalps.

Dulac, staring at the lovely, aristocratic face of Alexandra Winthrop, urged them to return to Montreal. Dominic politely refused. "We thank you for your advice, captain, but we must go on."

"I have heard of your influence with the Algonquian tribes, Monsieur Jolliet," the captain protested. "But the woman is English. Leave her with us."

Dominic did not believe that forty soldiers and the wooden walls of Michilimackinac would hold back Pontiac's warriors. Under the circumstances, Alexandra would be safer with him. "We'll manage," he replied firmly.

The village of Bowating was virtually empty. Only a few old men and a handful of women and children were left in the once-bustling village. After questioning one of the inhabitants, Dominic learned that the remainder of the tribe had not yet returned from their summer camp at Lac Île-à-La-Crosse near the Beaver River. It was a journey of nearly one hundred miles, paddling upstream against the current through dense, silent forests. They would be forced to cross wide rivers and portages, always uphill, over a dozen waterfalls. Dominic knew that Alexandra would never last the distance. When he tried to reason with her, to explain that the tribe would be back at Bowating within weeks, she refused to listen and insisted on continuing.

Dominic's face was set in grim lines when he rolled out of his blanket the following morning. The old man had told him that the Anishinabe followed the preachings of the prophet. When Pontiac's wampum belt was carried to Bowating the winter before, the tribe had answered the call. It was not unlikely that he and Alexandra would find themselves traveling the same trail as the war party. After slipping away from the carnage of Fort Edward with two valuable English prisoners, he was not anxious to renew his acquaintance with Chief Pontiac.

The smooth play of muscles across Dominic's naked, sun-browned back and shoulders distracted Alexandra from the hunger gnawing at her stomach. They had not stopped to eat. She knew he was angry and his only recourse was to make her as uncomfortable as possible. The power and beauty of the lean, ropy muscles as they lifted the paddle in a graceful arc and then plunged it down again into the gray water fascinated her. Her fingers itched for her paints. Until one short year ago, she had never seen a man's uncovered body. No portrait or statue could do justice to the masculine power of bronzed skin and sculpted angles and lean planes. Here was perfection in its most eloquent form. She stared for hours, ignoring her clamoring stomach, drinking in the endless rhythm, the synchronized grace, the steady rise and fall of the sun-darkened arms as they rose and dipped, moving the canoe ever northward.

Winged insects, blue-gray and transparent in the setting sun, skimmed across the river. Birds called to their mates, and in the distance, mountains of water tumbled down jagged precipices as they must have since the beginning of time. Alexandra's eyelids drooped and the top of her head felt very warm. The river had narrowed and Dominic paddled more slowly. She closed her eyes and leaned back in the canoe. The next thing she knew was darkness, the flickering light of the campfire, and a warm hand covering her mouth.

Dominic's lips were close to her ear. "Say nothing and don't move." He removed his hand and stood up. In the gutteral syllables of the Algonquian dialect, he spoke, using his Indian name. "My brothers are welcome at the camp-fire of Night Wind."

Alexandra watched in horror as tree branches parted and shadowy figures stepped forward. Hideously painted, half-naked bodies wielding guns and tomahawks stepped into the leaping firelight. Slowly, silently, they circled the clearing until it appeared as if a solid wall of grim-faced humanity separated the fire from the forest. She scrambled to her feet, hands clasped together to prevent their shaking.

Dominic's heart sank as he scanned the dark, implacable expressions of the red men. They were Ottawa. But where was Pontiac? He did not recognize the scarred face of the chief among them. The group was either a war party or a scouting expedition. Whatever it was, he knew their only hope of survival was to pretend friendship with their leader.

"I come to bring gifts and to smoke the pipe of friend-ship with Pontiac." Dominic spoke French this time, gesturing with his hands.

The Indians nodded and conferred among themselves. There appeared to be no leader. Finally, a tall, well-muscled brave stepped forward. Nodding toward the canoe and their bags, he uttered a low, gutteral command. Two more braves ran forward and lifted the canoe to their shoulders. Another reached for the bags with one hand and grabbed Alexandra's arm with the other.

"No." Dominic's voice cracked like a whip in the silent darkness. He leaped forward and pulled her away from the savage, pushing her behind him. The Indian growled deep in his chest and raised his tomahawk. Alexandra lifted her hand to her throat. This could not be happening. Julia's face as she had last seen it appeared before her, the dark eyes sadly resigned. Alexandra moaned and dropped her head into her hands. If Dominic were to die this night, she refused to watch. Long seconds passed. A single exclamation broke the silence. She dared to look up. Dominic was still standing, but the Indian was on the ground, a knife handle protruding from his chest.

An angry mutturing rose from the crowd. The Indian who had first stepped forward uttered a harsh command. Instantly there was silence. He stared intently at Alexandra. Turning toward Dominic, he asked a question she could not understand.

Dominic nodded.

The Indian grunted. Again he spoke and another brave lifted the dead man over his shoulder. "Come," the leader said, this time in French. "We will take you to Pontiac."

"What did he say?" whispered Alexandra much later as she stumbled against him in the darkness.

Dominic reached out to steady her. "He asked if you were my woman."

"Oh." She felt a slow burn in her cheeks and was grateful for the concealing darkness.

"You can tell Pontiac the truth, of course; but I wouldn't, unless one of our captors appeals to you."

It was as black as pitch beneath the trees, but Alexandra

felt the warmth of his grin in the darkness. "I've no intention of telling him the truth," she replied tartly. The last thing she wanted was for Pontiac to claim her as a spoil of war. But neither did she wish for Dominic to learn there was no one on earth she would rather be than Night Wind's woman.

Chapter 26

Alexandra was shocked at her first glimpse of Chief Pontiac. She had expected him to be tall, muscular, and impressive, like Red Wing of the Anishinabe. He was nothing of the sort. Alexandra was only slightly above medium height, but her eyes were level with the bold, button-black ones of the war chief. His head was shaved in the customary scalplock and several earrings hung from each lobe. Blue tattoos covered his hands and he wore the traditional deerskin moccasins. Only his clothing reflected nothing of his Indian heritage. They were the blue coat, white breeches, and cream-colored small clothes of a French military officer, albeit a very dirty version. His face was badly scarred; but beneath the paint, he had narrow, chiseled features. Alexandra noticed that his eyes glittered, and he smiled with a mocking, superior curl of his mouth that did not bode well for their future. When he spoke, it was in the precise, fluent sentences of a French aristocrat.

"Welcome, Night Wind. It is with great pleasure that I offer you and your lady the hospitality of my camp." He motioned toward the fire where several braves were already seated.

Dominic sat down. Alexandra knew enough about the customs of the Anishinabe not to imitate him. She found a comfortable spot under a tree, close enough to hear the conversation and yet far enough away to appear unobtrusive. She prepared herself to wait for hours, if necessary. Indian councils were always executed with a great deal of ceremony. Looking around, she realized with a growing sense of panic that she was the only woman present. Pontiac lit the clay tobacco pipe with a flaming ember. Inhaling deeply, he passed it to Dominic. Alexandra drew a restoring breath and forced herself to concentrate on the conversation.

"I am looking for a white boy," began Dominic. "He is the great-grandson of an important man who will pay for his return. The boy was taken from his home twelve moons ago."

"By which tribe was he taken?" asked the chief.

"The Anishinabe of Bowating."

"Red Wing's tribe is allied to my French Father Across the Water. Why would he take this child?"

Dominic had no intention of explaining that the boy was English. "Red Wing is a wise chief, but the war party was small. A mistake was made."

Pontiac nodded. Such a thing was possible. "We will make an exchange," he said. "I will tell you of the boy and you will help me capture the English fort at Detroit."

Dominic improvised quickly. "The man who seeks the boy wishes to travel across the water before the next moon. I have gifts to exchange for your help, but I must return to Montreal with the child."

The War Chief frowned. "You will help us take back the fort for our French father and send this Major Gladwin back to England. Then we will find the boy."

Dominic saw no purpose in antagonizing the chief. "I have heard that Gladwin is a fair man."

Pontiac grunted. "He is under the thumb of General Amherst. Prices are high and my people starve. Indians are forbidden to trade in gunpowder and rum." He clenched his hands in anger. "How are we to feed our families?"

"France is losing her war with England, my friend," said Dominic gently. "You would do well to listen to the words of the prophet and eschew the ways of the white man. Go back to your old customs. Give up your guns, your metal pots, and your beads. Travel west. Teach your sons the use of the bow and arrow, your daughters the art of dying the quills and feathers of animals."

Pontiac shook his head. "It is too late for that. The only way is to push the English back into the water. The French understand our ways."

"The English are strong. They will not go away." Regret flickered in Dominic's dark eyes. "You cannot hope to win."

The chief stood abruptly. "Then my warriors will die in the attempt. When Detroit is taken, we will search for the boy."

"How far is Detroit?" asked Alexandra as they lay close together under the watchful eyes of their captors.

"As far as Montreal, only in the other direction," replied Dominic.

She lay silent for a long time. "You don't think we'll ever find Travis, do you, Dominic?"

He pulled her into the cradle of his shoulder and brushed a light kiss over her hair. It would do no good to raise false hopes. "No, Alix. I don't believe we will find your nephew."

He felt the wetness through his jacket and tightened his arms around her. Alexandra wasn't a woman who normally indulged in tears. She had not perfected the art of sniffing daintily and dabbing a few perfunctory teardrops from her cheeks. When Alix cried, her eyes looked swollen, her nose reddened, and pink blotches appeared on her cheeks.

Nothing in Dominic's entire experience had the same effect on him as Alexandra's tears. He wanted to soothe and protect her, to destroy the source of her pain, to promise her the world. Fortunately for him, he thought wryly, she knew nothing of her power.

"I'll do my best to find him, *mignonne*. Sleep now. Pontiac's war party will travel thirty miles tomorrow."

Detroit was far from the established settlements of England and France, but it was by no means an uncivilized place. The river flowed from east to west past the fort, which sat on a slope on the north shore, giving it a tilted appearance. The banks of the river rose thirty feet behind the tallest building and the pickets on two sides of the fort ran uphill. Each of the first three streets was constructed on an elevation higher than the previous one. Dominic noticed the military disadvantage at once. A person standing across the river could look over the walls into the fort. Drainage kept the lower south side muddy, and the surrounding region was marshy and full of mosquitos. The stockade shut out the cleansing western breezes.

The task of obtaining information from French *habitants* who had settled up and down along the river was given to Dominic. He found them more than happy to disclose information on the number of English soldiers inside the fort. Reports of approximately two hundred fifty men were corroborated by scouts who had surrounded the village. The odds were against the English. Pontiac had over four hundred Indians as well as the tribes along the river that were allied to the French. Unless the English major could assemble his men quietly and without lights, the Indians would know what the soldiers inside the fort were up to at any given moment. That did not stop them from trying. Their reinforcements had been cut off and no food or water had been sent in for several days.

In the middle of the night, the English soldiers moved

two abreast out of the fort through the east gate. They were as silent as possible, but to Indians trained to the slightest whisper of the wind and rustle of a leaf, the tramping feet and inevitable rattle of arms was deafening. Approximately a mile from the fort, the detachment was split into two groups with an advance guard. They proceeded another mile to the creek. There Pontiac waited for them. His intention was complete annihilation, with no taking of prisoners.

Dominic felt the sweat bead on his forehead as he waited with his musket in the darkness. Alexandra had been sent into the woods behind the swamp. The moonlight clearly lit the road. Pontiac's orders were explicit enough: *When the soldiers reach the middle of the bridge. . . .* Dominic did not particularly mind meeting the English in battle. They were, after all, at war with France and he was very much a Frenchman. It was the aftermath he despised. The blood orgy that followed an Indian victory was more than most white men could bear.

Deliberately, he pushed all thoughts of Alexandra from his mind. He heard boots tramp noisily over wooden planks. Somewhere in the night, he heard a shout, then a scream and a curse. A wall of fire blazed up before him and soul-curdling war whoops rose above the sound of musket fire. Already several Englishmen lay piled on the bridge.

The arc of Indian fire swept the side of the main column. An officer was hit in the thigh. The soldiers panicked and discharged their muskets wildly, confused in the darkness. Major Gladwin, recognizing a trap, faced his men around quickly and gave the invisible enemy a resounding volley of fire. Dominic sighted an English uniform down his musket barrel. Squeezing the trigger, he watched the man fall.

The main body of troops was engaged beyond the bridge. Gladwin gave the order to retreat. Dominic sprinted across the bridge, picked up a fallen musket, and aimed again. Again, the bullet found its mark and a red-

coated soldier hit the dirt. The main body began withdraw-
ing in good order. The Indians were entrenched behind
a pile of cord wood. Dominic joined them and for the
next hour was busily engaged in holding up the English
retreat. Eventually several protecting parties posted along
the way prevailed and the remaining soldiers managed to
crawl back to the safety of the fort. Five officers and eigh-
teen men were killed and thirty-four wounded. Three men
were taken prisoner for blood sport. Pontiac's losses
amounted to seven killed and a dozen wounded.

The Indians found the body of Captain Dalyell, the
leader of the advance guard, and transported him back to
their camp along with their own dead.

"What will they do with them?" Alexandra asked, nodding toward the prisoners.

"You don't want to know," answered Dominic. "We'll
eat and sleep now. It may be some time before you have
an appetite again."

The following day, Alexandra watched in horror as an
Indian cut out the heart of Captain Dalyell and wiped it
across the faces of the prisoners. Sick to her stomach, she
turned away, missing the cutting off of his head and the
mounting of it on a pole. They threw the body into a
nearby stream, and the water ran red with his blood.

That evening, Pontiac invited Dominic and Alexandra,
as well as the leading French residents, to a celebratory
feast in honor of his victory. The meat was rubbery and of
an unusual flavor.

"What kind of beef is this?" asked Alexandra, swallowing
painfully.

Pontiac grinned. "I will show you what you have eaten."
Opening a sack lying on the ground beside him, he pulled
out the bloody head of an English officer.

Alexandra's head swam. Her vision blurred and her
stomach heaved. Falling over into the soft dirt, she retched
and retched until nothing came up but yellow bile. Blessed
darkness consumed her and she knew nothing more.

White-faced, his mouth set in tight, angry lines, Dominic lifted Alexandra into his arms and carried her from the clearing into a shelter of trees. Pontiac's laughter followed them. He placed her carefully on the ground and built a fire. She did not awaken. Perhaps it was best. She needed time to come to terms with the nightmare of her experience. Christ, he needed time himself. Dominic knew that Indians often ate the internal organs of their enemies, but he had never actually seen it happen.

He looked down at the faint blue stains beneath Alexandra's lashes. Her face looked peaceful, devoid of strain, as if she traveled in another world, far away from the gut-wrenching horrors of her waking hours. Dominic did not consider himself a compassionate man. But with Alexandra he was different. No one else had ever inspired the possessive tenderness that he felt whenever he looked at her. It was dangerous to care for someone so desperately. But he knew that in capturing his love, she had made him into something more than he could ever have been without her.

He was terribly thirsty. Checking her pulse, Dominic decided it was safe to leave for a few moments. He walked to the river and knelt. Dipping his cupped hands in the free-flowing water, he lifted them to his mouth and drank. He stank of blood and gunpowder. Hesitating, he glanced over to where Alexandra still lay. She hadn't moved. He slipped off his shirt and leggings and walked into the icy current. The shocking cold numbed his nerves and robbed his lungs of air. Quickly, he plunged under the water, stood, and then went down once again.

Alexandra wakened. It was dark and she was alone. Her mouth felt dry. The moment she reached the bank, she recognized the man in the river. She saw the impatient movement of his hand as he pushed the long, black hair away from his face. She noticed the way it sprang away from his forehead with a life of its own. She saw, as if for the first time all over again, the cleanly chiseled beauty of his arched nose and thin lips, the arrogant high-boned face, the way the strong brown column of his throat moved as he drank, the broad shoulders and taut chest, the flat belly and muscled legs. Her eyes moved down, and her breathing altered. She felt weak and immediately sat down.

He did not realize she was there until after he was dressed. She called his name and his eyes widened. The look on her face stopped the questions hovering on his lips. He sat down and put his arms around her. She burrowed into the hollow of his shoulder and began to cry in deep, soul-cleansing sobs. There was nothing he could do, no solace he could offer but that of silent understanding.

After a long time, her tears stopped, but she made no attempt to move away. She lifted her head so that her lips grazed the line of his jaw. Dominic could feel the change in her mood. He shifted to look down into the wide golden eyes. Their message was unmistakable.

"Alix," he whispered hoarsely.

"Make love to me, Dominic." Her voice had a strange, desperate appeal. "I need you. Now."

His arms tightened. "Are you sure?" The pulsing of his blood heightened to a fever pitch. His veins were on fire. The last few weeks, watching her move, sleeping beside her, touching her skin briefly in passing, had been sheer agony. He could feel himself harden. He wanted her so much he could barely think past the thundering of his heart. It was painful, this wanting. He wasn't sure he was capable of drawing back if she changed her mind.

Her gold-tipped lashes brushed against her cheeks. "I'm sure," she whispered.

His fingers stroked her skin and lingered on her lips. She was so soft. Soft and sweet. He bent his head to her mouth. Instantly, the fire rocked him. Her lips parted, welcoming the possessive thrust of his tongue. Her hands slid under his shirt, and her cool, slim fingers caressed his skin. Dominic knew he was rapidly losing control. With a curse, he dragged himself away and feverishly stripped off his shirt and spread it on the ground. With one arm, he reached to pull her beneath him.

Alexandra knew this would be no gentle coupling. She didn't want Dominic's skill tonight. She needed his passion, his urgency, the raw, heart-stopping violence he held so carefully in check. She ached for the feel of his hands on her skin, for the raging storm of desire in his eyes, for the life-giving act that would erase the terrifying pictures of death and blood stamped into her memory. Tomorrow and yesterday no longer had meaning. Alexandra didn't feel the hardness of the ground or the pebbles under his cotton shirt scraping her back. She knew only the throbbing of her heart, the feel of firm lips and warm hands, and the words she had never heard before, muffled and thrilling, against her throat. When he could hold back no longer and his life and heat exploded within her, she gasped and cried out. Her nails raked his back and her face ran wet with tears of pleasure and pain, mingling with the heartbreak of all she had lost.

Chapter 27

Dominic awoke instantly, his mind completely alert. A voice spoke his Indian name. He turned over and shaded his eyes from the sun. Pontiac's uniformed figure stood over him. Casually, Dominic's hand slipped down to the knife concealed in his leggings. Pontiac grinned. "You have no need of that, my friend."

Unconvinced, Dominic rolled out of the chief's shadow and leaped to his feet. He wet his lips. "What do you want?"

"You and the woman are free to go," replied Pontiac. "I regret that I cannot help you with the child, but Red Wing is now at Bowating. Perhaps he will know where the boy is."

Dominic's eyes narrowed. Something very serious must have happened for Pontiac to make such a decision. Looking at the chief's bland expression and veiled eyes, he knew it would do no good to ask him. Whatever message he had received in the night, no word of it would be revealed to a white man.

Less than a quarter of an hour later, Dominic and Alexandra left their canoe on the banks of Lake Huron and made their way northwest on foot. At noon they stopped briefly for food and water and then moved on. Dominic wanted as much distance between them and Pontiac's war party as possible. More than twenty miles later, an exhausted Alexandra sank to her knees, refusing to travel another step. Dominic unrolled the blankets and gathered leaves for a mattress. One look at Alexandra stretched out, oblivious, on the ground, and he knew he needn't have bothered. She was asleep.

Two days later, they reached the union of the Great Lakes, the Place at the Falls—or, as the Indians called it, Bowating. A cacophony of sound greeted their arrival. Dogs nipped at their heels; children threw stones, and women with sullen faces carrying cradleboards lined the path leading to the wigwam of their chief.

Alexandra was horrified. Good Lord, had it always been like this? She remembered the dirt and the flies and the breath-sucking poverty, but had the people always been so hostile? Her eyes searched one round, brown face after another. Most of them were women she had conversed with and worked beside. Tentatively, she smiled. No one smiled back. Where was Sarah? Surely Sarah wouldn't turn her back on an old friendship.

It seemed an eternity before they reached Min-ni-wah-wah's wigwam. Standing before the familiar entrance, Alexandra could feel her stomach flutter. The circumstances of her departure had been both embarrassing and unpleasant. She was not anxious to meet Red Wing or his mother-in-law again.

Suddenly the skins parted and Red Wing stood before them. His flat black eyes narrowed and then went blank. "Welcome, Night Wind," he said formally. "It has been many moons since last we have seen you." Not by the merest flicker of an eyelash did he acknowledge that he recognized Alexandra.

"I have come on a matter of great importance," Dominic said. "May we come inside?"

Red Wing nodded and disappeared behind the pelts. Dominic turned to Alexandra. "This may be difficult for you. Would you prefer to wait outside?"

She shook her head. Alexandra did not particularly want to enter the wigwam where she had spent so many months, and if Sarah had shown her face, she might have considered Dominic's suggestion. But the Englishwoman was nowhere to be seen. The cold, angry faces of the Indian women left her little choice. "I'm coming with you," she said, stepping through the skins into the wigwam.

It was very dark inside. She waited until her eyes had adjusted to the dimness. Two figures were seated beside Red Wing across from the door. Alexandra recognized Min-ni-wah-wah immediately. The lined face and dark sloe eyes of the old woman were emotionless as they stared back at her. The man rising to his feet was white and strangely familiar. Alexandra racked her brain. Where had she seen him before? Then she noticed his clothing and realized immediately who he was.

"*Bonjour, mademoiselle,*" he said respectfully.

Alexandra held out her hand. He lifted it to his lips. "*Bonjour,* Father Gerard," she replied. "What brings you to Bowating?"

"I follow the French messengers. It is to be hoped that my presence will soften the anger of the Algonquian tribes."

"I beg your pardon?" Alexandra was confused.

Dominic interrupted. "We left Montreal over four weeks ago," he explained. "We know nothing of such news. Perhaps you will enlighten us, *mon père?*"

"Our Father Across the Water has surrendered to the English." Red Wing could not control his bitterness. "We are to lay down our arms and call our enemies brothers."

Alexandra gasped. So, it was true. Dominic had predicted correctly after all. She allowed the meaning of the words to sink in. The English were now masters of the New World. She should be elated. Strangely, she was not. The only emotion she felt was sympathy for the inhabitants of New France. Would they leave their homes and return to Europe? Or would they accept their conquerors and make the best of their new lives? She thought of the proud, capable citizens of Montreal. Probably the latter, she decided. Those who had braved the Atlantic crossing, experienced frostbite and starvation, built homes and buried children as they carved out a living from this savage land would never return to the narrow confines of the Old World. She looked at Dominic. Except for a certain tightness around the mouth, his expression told her nothing of his thoughts. He was staring at the priest.

"Is this true, *mon père?*"

"I am afraid so, my son." Father Gerard lifted his black-frocked arms in a helpless gesture. "The king has decided that this continuous war with England is draining the royal treasury." He sighed. "His royal majesty is losing popularity. Another tax increase would invite revolution. He is merely acting precipitously."

"He is selling us down the river, you mean." Dominic's control had broken at last. For a long time he had known this would happen, but hearing rumors in Indian lodges and around *coureur's* campfires and even in the damask-hung drawing rooms of Montreal's nobility was one thing. The actuality was another altogether. "This country is ten times the size of France with only a fraction of its population. It is rich in minerals and resources. There is enough lumber to build a million Versailles, enough gold and silver to fill the treasuries of Europe. Are we to give it all up because a mincing fool cannot discipline his spending habits?"

"Softly, softly, my son," cautioned the priest. "You forget of whom it is you speak."

"I forget nothing, Father," replied Dominic bitterly. "I know our good King Louis. I've watched him humiliate his wife, his children, his servants, and anyone else around him who displays the least modicum of good sense." His dark eyes flashed with contempt. "I'm surprised at your loyalty, Father. The King of France is no friend to the clergy."

"Perhaps not. But then, this has been my home for twenty years. Now, that I am no longer a citizen of France, I can look more kindly on her king."

"How fortunate for you," replied the mocking voice, "that France no longer claims your loyalty. There are more than a few of us who cannot subject ourselves so easily to English rule."

Red Wing leaned forward, his eyes on Dominic. "You are angry, Night Wind?"

"Very angry."

"You will join with us against the English?" Red's Wing's eyes glittered triumphantly.

Some of the rage left Dominic's expression. He drew a deep breath and pondered his answer. When finally he spoke, his words were clear and controlled. "It is no use, my friend. The English are strong. Stronger even than the armies of France. If you anger them, the life of your tribe, your women and children will be in great danger."

"The Anishinabe have always been allied to the French. Will the English not wish to avenge the blood of their brothers?"

"The English know very little about the tribes, Wiskino, Bird-of-the-Red-Wing. To them, one is very much like another. If you trade with them and do not make war, they will not harm you."

"Is that what you would do, Night Wind?" Red Wing persisted. "Would you make your peace with them?

"I?" Dominic looked surprised at such a question. "If I were an *indigène*, I would have no treaty with white men. I would take my tribe far north, past the Lake of the Woods. I would teach them in the old ways so that they need never again trade with the whites."

Red Wing looked skeptical. "We need gunpowder and blankets."

"Your ancestors used animal skins and the bow and arrow."

The broad, handsome forehead of the Indian chief was creased in concentration. Finally, he sighed. "You have given me a great deal to think about, Night Wind. I will pray to Kitche Manido and seek council with the elders."

"It is the message of the Delaware Prophet," Dominic reminded him.

The chief frowned. "Our ways are not the ways of the Delaware." He looked at Alexandra and his forehead cleared. "Why have you come to Bowating with Al-ex-an-dra?"

Deliberately, Dominic forced himself to relax and recite the words he had practiced over and over again. "Alexandra's heart has been sore," he began. "The vow she made to the spirit of her sister has not been fulfilled."

Red Wing nodded. He was familiar with honoring vows made to the dead.

"The English boy who came with her when she first arrived at Bowating is her sister's child. To fulfill her promise, Alexandra must take him back across the water to the home of his ancestors."

Min-ni-wah-wah spoke for the first time. "The boy has been adopted. He no longer wishes to return to the English."

Red Wing silenced her with a wave of his hand.

"I have brought gifts for his family." Dominic reached into his sack and held up the beads and tin. "I also bring gold, much gold, for the tribe of Red Wing to make up for the loss of the boy."

"All prisoners are to be returned." Father Gerard reminded Red Wing softly, but with authority.

Dominic shook his head at the priest. This was his battle. He needed no other help.

"How much gold?" asked Red Wing.

"Enough to buy supplies for the Anishinabe of Bowating for five winters. Enough to last until your braves master the ways of their ancestors."

Alexandra held her breath. She was caught in the web of Dominic's silky, persuasive voice. As always, she marveled at his exquisite skill at negotiation.

Finally, the chief nodded. "I will send for the boy and his family. They will decide."

"Be sure to tell them the child must be returned eventually," said Father Gerard. "It is part of our agreement with the English. If they wait, they will lose the boy and have no gold to show for it."

"Are they here in Bowating?" Alexandra's voice was edged with excitement.

Red Wing nodded. With a smooth fluid movement, he rose to his feet. "Come." He held open the skins at the door. "I will take you to the boy."

Alexandra stared in dismay at the dirty, lice-infested child standing outside his adoptive mother's wigwam. His slight body was thin and scarred, and even though Alexandra knew little of children, she felt instinctively that he was much smaller than a normal seven-year-old. Thin, symmetric blue lines had been tattooed into the flesh of his arms and again at his wrists. His hair was rank and dark with bear grease and stuck straight up from his head like porcupine quills. He said nothing at all. If it hadn't been for the snub nose and brilliant blue of his eyes, Alexandra would never have believed this surly, ill-favored child was Travis. He stared at her, hostility evident in every trembling muscle of his slight frame.

She knelt in the dirt at his feet. "Travis." She spoke English. " 'Tis Alix, your aunt. Don't you remember me?"

The boy's eyes were mutinous and his lip stuck out in stubborn defiance. Alexandra turned to look over her shoulder at Dominic. "What have they told him?"

Dominic spoke a few cryptic words to the sad-faced squaw who hovered a few feet away. She mumbled a low, incoherent answer. Alexandra's knowledge of Ojibwa was functional, but only if the speaker enunciated clearly. Dominic translated. "She told him you have come to take him across the water to live with white men."

Alexandra frowned. "Why does he look at me like that? 'Tis almost as if he hates me."

"Try to understand, Alix," Dominic explained. "This is the boy's home now. He's buried the past. Children adjust quickly. He's accepted this woman as his mother."

"She is not!" Alexandra protested. She could feel the heat of the afternoon sun burning the planes of her cheeks and the tip of her nose. "How dare you suggest that he's forgotten Julia."

A whisper of sympathy glinted in the night-black eyes. "Would you rather he had pined for her? Perhaps sickened and died?"

"Of course not!" she replied, stung at the injustice of his question. "But surely he must prefer his own life and to be with his own people?"

"Children do not recognize the differences between races. The Anishinabe are his people. You are taking him away from all that is familiar to him."

Her eyes were the color of flashing topaz, brilliant in their righteous indignation. "Surely you can't expect me to leave him here?"

"I expect a small particle of compassion for a child who has already lost one set of parents," he said impatiently. "Give him some time to get used to the idea of coming with us."

Alexandra clenched her jaw. "I don't have time. Pontiac and his Ottawa war party used it all up. We should have been back long ago. Grandfather has probably given us up and sailed for England."

"And what of the estimable Captain Doddridge?" Dominic's voice was dangerously soft and the mocking light was back in his eyes. "Do you believe he has abandoned you as well? Or perhaps you only wish it."

"How dare you?" The burning of her cheeks had nothing to do with the sun.

He exhaled slowly, working to control his temper. "Enough, Alix. I'll tell the boy to prepare himself. We'll leave in the morning if you insist."

She nodded and lowered her eyes, refusing to meet the accusing blue stare of her nephew. From beneath her lashes she watched Dominic kneel before Travis. He gestured as he spoke, curving his arm in an arc and touching the boy several times on the chest.

She glanced at the small dirty face and surprised a stricken, almost panicked expression in his sharp, too-thin features. It disappeared so quickly that she thought she had imagined it. There was nothing of fear or surprise or anger in the stoic mask of Julia's son. He stood stone-faced, his narrow arms crossed forbiddingly against his chest.

Dominic had finished speaking, and still the boy said nothing. After a moment, he turned away and disappeared into the wigwam behind him. His Indian mother followed.

Alexandra stood completely still and chewed the inside of her lip. She had hoped to speak with Travis, to remind him of the words she had told him never to forget. Never once had she considered that in one short year he would forget the life he had been born into and become completely Indian. She sighed. It was a difficult task she had set for herself.

Silently, she walked beside Dominic to the *coureur's* lodge. It was empty this time of year, and the sweet grass growing knee-high on the banks of the shining lake water provided a comfortable place to spread their blankets. Alexandra had never missed her sister more than she did now. What would Julia do if she were here at this very moment? She sat down on her blanket and stared out at the mists gathering on the lake. A blue crane skimmed across the surface, its massive wings dipping in the eddying current. A tern called out in the darkness, and loose vees of migrating ducks darkened the late-afternoon sky. Against the silver-peach-and-rose sunset, the breathtaking outline of spruce, silver birch, and maple trees were silhouetted in blurred splendor. Only when she rubbed her eyes to bring it into focus, did Alexandra realize she was crying.

A warm hand found the nape of her neck. "Don't, Alix," Dominic murmured. "I can't bear to see you cry."

"You think I'm selfish." Her tears were falling in earnest now.

"Hush, *mignonne*." His hand worked miracles against her skin. "You know nothing of what I think."

She wiped her nose with the edge of her blanket and sniffed. Dominic smiled. Only someone as naturally lovely as Alexandra would care so little for appearances.

"It isn't for me that I must bring him back," she said. " 'Tis for Grandfather and Abigail and Travis, too. What kind of life would he have here? He'll thank me when he's grown, you'll see."

Dominic pulled her into the circle of his arms. His breath was warm on her forehead and there was a hint of laughter in his voice. "I fully intend to see just that. Don't cry anymore, Alix. Your nose is red and it doesn't become you in the least."

He heard her muffled laugh against his chest and smiled with relief. It was the worst kind of helpless torture to hear Alexandra weep.

Chapter 28

"What do you mean he's gone?" Alexandra's face was pinched and white and her voice unusually shrill. The Indian woman shrugged impassively, but there was the faintest glimmer of triumph in her slanted black eyes. Alexandra's fury was close to the erupting point. Her fingers itched to slap the brown, smirking countenance.

Dominic stepped forward. As if he could read her mind, his fingers curved around her arm in a bruising grip. "Losing your temper will get you nowhere," he murmured under his breath. "Let me handle this."

Alexandra bit down hard on the inside of her mouth. Quick tears sprang to her eyes. She kept her head down, furious with the unsympathetic squaw and her own lack of control. Where could Travis be? How he must hate her for taking him away. Surreptitiously wiping her eyes with the back of her hand, she listened to Dominic speak.

"Yellow Moon has been a good mother to the white boy," he began courteously. "His grandfather will reward you for caring for him." He held out a handful of blue beads and several pieces of tin. "These are only a few of the gifts he sends to you."

Yellow Moon reached out a greedy hand for the baubles, but Dominic shook his head. "There is no white child in your wigwam. I cannot give away the gifts of the white man until he is turned over to me."

The squaw frowned. Her black eyes glittered. Alexandra was sure she would succumb to the glassy temptation of the beads. Instead, she stiffened and shrugged, the mask of indifference settling once again across her broad features. "The forest is large and my son is small," she said. "He did not tell me where he was going."

Dominic stared at her thoughtfully. The woman was skilled at hiding her emotions and he wasn't sure she told the truth. Still, it was possible. The boy had been more upset about leaving his adoptive family than anyone realized. Dominic knew that six months from now Travis Graham would be so immersed in his own culture that his year with the Ojibwa would seem like a dream. If there were the slightest doubt that the boy would have a better life as the grandson of the Duke of Leicester, Dominic would have given up the chase at that moment. Whatever the squaw knew, she would keep to herself, no matter what the bribe. He handed the beads to Alexandra and shook his head regretfully. "She wouldn't help us even if she knew anything, Alix. We'll have to find the boy on our own."

Alexandra's golden glance beseeched him. "Is that possible?"

"I wouldn't have wagered half a *louis* on the odds of finding him in the first place." He rubbed his thumb across her cheek. "We'll find him, *mignonne*. Don't worry."

Several hours later, Dominic knelt in the spongy dirt on the side of a stream and traced the faint moccasin print of a small child. Less than two feet away lay the spoor of a large cat. His mouth tightened and a faint white line appeared around his lips. Resting his flintlock against a tree, he waited for Alexandra.

She came up beside him. "What is it?" He pointed to the footprint and watched her eyes light up with relief. "Is the track fresh?" she asked.

"It is."

"Then he can't be far away." She pulled at his arm. "Do let us hurry, Dominic."

"I want you to return to the village, Alix," he said. "We are less than four hours away and our marks are still fresh. I'll bring the boy back when I find him."

"Don't be ridiculous." She laughed, a clear, bell-like sound in the stillness. "Why on earth would you ask such a thing? Travis is moving south. There is no need to return to Bowating."

He sighed impatiently. "Must you disagree with everything I say?"

"Not at all," Alexandra replied slowly. "I just don't understand your reasoning."

He didn't want to alarm her but he had no choice. "Look there." He pointed to the droppings. "A mountain lion has the boy's scent. I've got to move quickly. Even so, I may be too late."

Her face paled and she spoke through stiff lips. "You can't know that. Perhaps the cat knows nothing of Travis. Or perhaps he's already had his fill of meat."

"I've seen his tracks, Alix. They began before the stream. A cat won't cross running water unless he's stalking prey."

She moved ahead of him. "I'm going with you."

"Why won't you understand?" he shouted at her. "You can't keep up. I'll be worrying about the both of you."

Ignoring him completely, she walked on, leaving him to stare at her stiff, unyielding back.

Cursing, Dominic dropped his pack, reached for his flintlock, and began to run in a loose, loping stride. He passed Alexandra and called back over his shoulder.

"When you lose sight of me, look for my tracks. I won't stop until I find him."

She nodded. Stooping to tie up her skirt, she walked back for the pack he had dropped, shouldered it, and trudged after him.

Dominic heard the snarling screams of the frustrated animal long before he actually reached the spot where Travis was wedged in a crevice between two large boulders. The mountain lion was enormous, a hissing, angry, tawny-colored feline with hooked claws and yellow eyes. Cheated out of its prey, the animal paced back and forth before the fissure in the rocks, stopping occasionally to take an angry, futile swipe into the enclosure where Travis lay huddled.

Dominic lifted his flintlock just as the cat caught his scent. The lion turned away from Travis. With a deadly roar, he ran straight toward the rifle. Bunching his muscles, he sprang. Dominic knew he had but one chance. Marking a spot dead in the center of the animal's chest, he squeezed the trigger and then dove for the shelter of the bushes. The cat dropped within inches from where he had taken aim.

Drawing a deep, reviving breath, Dominic stood and walked to the crevice. The opening was too small to admit more than his head and shoulders. There was no movement inside. When his eyes adjusted to the darkness, he could make out the boy's outline huddled into a ball with his face pressed against the stone. Speaking softly in the gutteral tones of the Ojibwa, Dominic tried to coax the child into a response. For a long time there was nothing. At last, when the *coureur* had almost given up, Travis moaned and turned toward the light. Dominic smiled reassuringly and reached out his hand. "You are safe now. The lion is dead."

Tentatively, a small hand reached out to grasp his larger

one. Dominic frowned. The child's grip was surprisingly weak. Either he was starving to death or he had been injured. "Are you hurt, little warrior?" he asked.

Travis nodded and gestured toward his leg. Dominic sucked in his breath. Blood oozed from several deep slash wounds in the boy's right thigh. From the condition of the wound and the dark color of the blood, it was obvious that it had occurred some time ago. If it wasn't treated immediately, it would fester.

"Can you crawl to the opening, Travis? I can't reach far enough inside to carry you."

The boy nodded. Dragging his injured leg, he laboriously worked his way toward the light. When he was close enough, Dominic pulled him into his arms. He was terribly thin. Taking one look at the child's dry, cracked lips, Dominic turned back toward the stream.

Travis drank his fill of cold water and allowed Dominic to bathe his wound. He was nearly asleep when the sound of leaves rustling in the underbrush brought him to instant attention. Someone was coming. He sniffed the air. It wasn't an animal, but he couldn't place the scent. Through lowered eyelids he peered at the woman who stepped into the clearing. The *coureur* walked over to her, held her arms, and spoke in low, calming tones. She gasped and covered her mouth.

Travis closed his eyes. He had seen enough. Alix thought he didn't remember her. But he did. She was his aunt. His mother's sister. She'd come to stay with them after his father died. She had brought him books from England, danced and laughed and played with him all through that summer before the Indian attack. She had made his mother smile again after a long, cold winter without smiles. He didn't hate her, but he did want her to go away. Travis couldn't leave Bowating. Not without his mother. She wouldn't know where to find him if he left. He would wait until his mother came for him. Forever, if necessary.

"Will he die?" Alix's hushed whisper carried no hint of the hysteria she was desperately trying to control.

Dominic stared at the flushed cheeks and labored breathing of the small boy. "I don't know. We'll take him back to Bowating."

"No," she burst out. "We'll take him on to Montreal and find a real doctor."

"Indian medicine may be better in this case, Alix. Not many white doctors have experience with mountain lion gashes."

"You can take care of him," she pleaded. "Remember what you did for Abigail?"

"It isn't the same thing at all. Abigail had the fever. This isn't a white man's disease. Indian shamans are familiar with animal wounds."

"They'll bleed him," insisted Alexandra, "and even I can see that he mustn't lose any more blood. Please, Dominic. Surely you know what to do."

He hesitated. She was right. By the looks of it, the child might not reach Bowating. It was probably better to treat him immediately. "Find the brandy in my pack," he ordered Alexandra. "I'll build a fire."

With a sigh of relief, she hurried to do his bidding. Dominic was already blowing the embers into flames when she returned. Grasping the handle of his knife, he held the blade in the center of the heat until the metal glowed white hot. "I'll have to drain the wound," he explained. "He'll need a large stick to bite on and some brandy to dull the pain."

"I'll help you," Alexandra offered.

He smiled grimly. "That you will. I need you to hold him down."

Cold sweat beaded on her brow. "Dear God," she prayed under her breath, "please don't let me be sick."

Years later, when Alexandra recalled that evening and the endless journey that followed, it wasn't the horror of seared flesh that she remembered or the wicked gleam of

Dominic's knife as it cut through the swollen, foul-smelling flesh. It wasn't the heaving of her own stomach or the hateful, incessant flies that buzzed around the gaping wound or even the forceful bucking of the small body under her hands. It was the courage of the seven-year-old boy bonded to her by ties of blood. Not once did he cry out or flinch or try to pull away. When Dominic held the hot knife against his leg, his body jerked once, the stick beneath his tongue cracked, and mercifully, he slid into unconsciousness.

Beneath the haze of her nausea, Alexandra was more than a little proud. Despite his slight body and small bones, Travis had steel. Winthrop steel. His mother's steel. The Duke of Leicester would not be disappointed in Julia's son.

"He'll rest tonight," said Dominic. "Tomorrow is soon enough to start back to Montreal." He stood and walked to the edge of the stream where a dark green shrub grew close to the water's edge. Using his knife, he dug up several roots and rinsed them in the water. "Boil some water, Alix. Slice the bulbs and then steep them in the hot water. The Indians use it to slow the bleeding."

"Does it work?"

Dominic shrugged. "Sometimes, with luck. It can't hurt. I may have to lance the wound again before I sew it up."

Obediently Alexandra found the cooking pot in his pack. While the water heated, she sliced the root into uniform wedges. It smelled spicy. Tentatively, she chewed the corner of a thin slice. It was crisp and cool and unusually pleasant. A small tingling sensation began in the back of her throat. It grew stronger and her eyes watered. Suddenly her entire mouth was on fire. Dropping the knife, she rushed to the stream and stretched out flat on the ground. Scooping sloppy handfuls of water into her burning mouth, she drank and drank. Finally, the fiery feeling disappeared. Embarrassed she sat up and looked accusingly at Dominic. "You didn't tell me it would taste like that."

He grinned. "I didn't expect you to eat it."

"It can't be good for him," she argued.

"On the contrary. The water leeches out the burning taste. When it's cooled a bit, hold his head and try to get some down his throat." He looked up at the sky. "It's nearly dark. Are you hungry?"

Alexandra shuddered and shook her head.

He nodded in agreement. "I thought not. It would be nothing short of a miracle if you had an appetite. Keep an eye on the boy. I'll try and sleep now. Wake me later and I'll sit with him until morning."

Twice during the next several hours, Travis woke with a burning fever. Alexandra took off her shirt, dipped the edge in water, and washed his face, chest, and hands. With tears streaming down her cheeks, she listened to the delirious babbling of her nephew. This child who had traveled through miles of dangerous wilderness, who had had the presence of mind to outwit a ravenous mountain lion, who had borne terrible pain with incredible courage, now cried out for his mother. In the language Alexandra thought he had no memory of, he begged his mama to hold him, asking her why she hadn't come for him, pleading with her to take him home. With dawning horror, Alexandra realized Travis didn't know of Julia's death. He thought she had abandoned him. With trembling lips and burning eyes, Alexandra eased his head into her lap. Caressing his brown cheek, she looked up into the star-bright heavens and begged her sister's forgiveness. "I'll never let him suffer again, Julia," she whispered. "I promise you that."

The white moon was round and full and the glittering lights from a million stars lit the clearing to daylight brightness. From his blanket near the trees, Dominic woke to the agonizing cry of a child in pain. He heard his mumbled words, nearly incoherent but unmistakably English, and he saw the expressions appear and change across Alexandra's face. First pain and then guilt and, finally, regret. Throwing aside the blanket, he stood and crossed the clearing to sit down beside her. He reached out to trace the tear tracks on her cheeks.

"I should have told him Julia wasn't coming back," she said in a choked whisper. "I was so caught up in my own grief, I didn't realize he didn't know."

"It was probably kinder that you did not. The hope of reuniting with his mother may have helped him survive."

A thick mist had settled over the water, cooling the air and chilling her skin under her jacket. Dominic's voice was a warm and healing beacon in the darkness.

"I must tell him the truth."

He squeezed her hand. "You'll find a way, at the proper time."

"Will it hurt him if I tell him now?" Her golden, cat's eyes were filled with purpose.

Dominic's grimaced. "It may be the only way we get him back to Montreal without a struggle. If the boy is waiting for his mother, we'll have a devil of a time convincing him to come with us."

Alexandra did not tell Travis of his mother's death until much later. The following morning his fever was lower, but he did not waken when Dominic lifted him into his arms. It wasn't until nightfall that he could be coaxed into taking a few sips of sustaining broth before he fell asleep again. The wound appeared to be clean, but it needed to be stitched. Dominic had performed such a procedure once before, but one look at the child's pale face convinced him that it would be better to wait for a proper surgeon. He only hoped it wouldn't be too late. Travis did not look as if he could last much longer.

Chapter 29

Three days later they reached Montreal. But it was a Montreal very different from the one they had left over one month before. Red-coated soldiers marched through the streets, their bayoneted muskets held at exactly the correct military angle against wide, confident shoulders. Polished boots reflected the pristine white of their breeches, the sun-burned strength of their stern, no-nonsense faces, and the unmistakable glint of disdain in their hard gray eyes. "We are Englishmen," those eyes said. No army on earth is as efficient, as capable, as powerful, or as worthy of commanding your obedience.

Off duty, they hovered in taverns, at the posting gate, in the shops, even at the very gates of the governor's château, waiting for an infraction by French sympathizers. Like mosquitoes, thought Dominic, preparing for their next blood meal.

Alexandra watched the forbidding set of Dominic's shoulders with trepidation. Like a spark against tinder, she knew his nerves were on edge, anticipating—no, relishing—the inevitable moment when his barely checked temper could vent itself in an act of explosive wrath against this intolerable invasion of his country. She only hoped it wouldn't occur with Travis in his arms.

Unbelievably, they made their way up the *Rue de St. Paul* to the door of Dominic's home without incident. Alexandra breathed a sigh of relief when Marceau's kindly face ushered them inside.

"May I say that we are very glad to see you, *Monsieur le Marquis.*" He wasn't able to disguise the trembling of his voice.

Dominic's grin was a flash of white against the darkness of his face. "Come, Marceau. Don't tell me you doubted that we would return."

"Of course not," the man hastened to reply. "It is only that you have been gone a very long time, m'lord."

"We had an unexpected delay. Fetch a surgeon, Marceau. Mademoiselle Winthrop's nephew is in need of his services."

Marceau bowed. "Yes, m'lord. I shall send a servant immediately. Your father will be very pleased to hear of your return."

Dominic did not stop, but walked directly to the stairs. "Leicester's need is greater. Tell him that his granddaughter and great-grandson have arrived. Prepare him for the boy's illness."

"As you wish, m'lord."

Alexandra sank wearily into the nearest chair. "When you are finished, Marceau, could you possibly arrange for a bath in my room?"

"It will be taken care of immediately, *mademoiselle.*"

She smiled her lovely, genuine smile. "What would we ever do without you?"

"Fortunately, *mademoiselle*, it is unlikely that such an event would ever occur."

"Thank God," murmured Alexandra, closing her eyes for a brief respite.

The next thing she knew was the incredible softness of

a feather mattress under her aching muscles and light streaming in from around the edges of drawn curtains. A servant poured steaming water into a wooden tub, and the delicious scent of baked bread and fragrant coffee drifted up from a low table to her appreciative nose.

She sat up in bed. "Is it morning already?"

"*Oui, mademoiselle*," replied the servant. "You have slept half the day away. Will you bathe or eat first?"

The tempting rolls were too much. "I shall eat first and then bathe and wash my hair. Is my grandfather awake?"

"For hours," replied the maid. "He is sitting with the little boy, who has also had a bath."

Alexandra gulped down the coffee and gasped as the scalding liquid burned her tongue. Poor Travis, at the mercy of her grandfather after all he had been through.

She did not linger in her bath, but even so, her hair needed washing. The thick mane was then brushed dry and pulled back from her brow in an intricate twist at the nape of her neck. Lunch was served on a tray in her room and finally several gowns brought out from the armoire. The green silk she preferred needed pressing. It wasn't until several hours later that Alexandra presented herself to her grandfather.

When she opened the door to Travis's bedchamber, an astonishing sight greeted her. She blinked and looked again. It couldn't be. The enormous bed was entirely taken up by three figures curled up together. The duke, propped up by several pillows, held Abigail in one arm and a very blond, very dark-skinned boy that could only be Travis in the other. On a tray at the foot of the bed were the remains of what looked like the kind of repast the duke abhorred— warm milk, toast, and strawberry jam.

Abigail's sticky fingers clutched the lapel of his expensive coat and Travis's berry-stained mouth was stretched in laughter. Alexandra noticed for the first time that his front teeth were missing. His hair looked very fair against his great-grandfather's shoulder. Her eyes burned with the effort of holding back tears. It was going to be all right after all. Julia's children had worked a miracle. Laughter and young voices would echo through the halls of Leicester once again.

"Alexandra," the duke called out. "Don't just stand there. Rescue me."

"You don't deserve it," she pretended to scold. "Just look at your coat."

He looked down at the evidence of bread crumbs and jam sprinkled across the fine brocade and grinned. "It was well worth it, I daresay. Look at this boy, Alix." He tilted his head to look down at Travis. "He's the very image of your father but with more spirit than Philippe ever had. Why do you suppose that neither of Julia's children look like her?"

"Probably because they had a father," replied Alexandra dryly. "I don't believe Travis looks like anyone in our family. He looks like his own father. You do remember James Graham, don't you, Grandfather?"

"Not if I can help it," returned the old man.

"There is something else you should remember," continued Alexandra. "Julia and James were very much alike, Grandfather. They were proud and very brave. Perhaps you can now understand the kind of courage and defiance it takes to live in this wilderness. It would be most unusual if their children did not inherit those qualities as well."

Leicester stared silently at the lovely, implacable face of his granddaughter. He recognized the thinly veiled message for what it was and made a vow to himself. He would respect the independence of these children God had seen fit to give him. With Alexandra and Travis and Abigail, he would return to Leicester and live out the rest of his life in peace.

"What of yourself?" he asked gruffly. "Will you come back to England with us or stay here?"

"That depends on Anthony," she replied.

He studied her carefully and opened his mouth to speak when a strand of Abigail's baby-fine hair made its way into his mouth. He frowned and pulled at his tongue, much to the delight of the two children in his arms. When the hair was finally retrieved, he had forgotten what he was going to say.

"Has Dominic come to see you, Grandfather?"

"Yes, early this morning." His bushy eyebrows flew together. "Why do you ask?"

"That really isn't any of your business," she said smiling sweetly and turned to leave the room.

"See here, missy," her grandfather roared. Travis's lips tightened and he curled one arm around a whimpering Abigail. Appalled at the children's reaction, Leicester gentled his voice. "You won't be able to see him just now. He has a visitor from France. A lady."

"Really?" Her voice was clipped and polite, nothing more.

The duke relented. "His mother is here, Alix. No one else knows her identity other than Lorraine and myself. I shouldn't have told you, but I know how you feel about young Jolliet and I can't bear to see you hurt. I'm not really the monster you think I am."

Quickly, she walked to the bed and leaned over to kiss his cheek. "Thank you, Grandfather," she whispered. "You've never been a monster to me."

The duke stared at the door for a long time after she left. He had always believed it was Julia of the dark eyes and black hair who had taken after his beloved Liane. That nagging feeling of familiarity he had experienced when he had first seen Alexandra again in Montreal crystalized into piercing awareness. The straight back and direct gaze, the lovely low voice, the slender sharp bones, the lovely heartbreaking smile could only have come through the bloodlines of Liane de Bouvier.

* * *

The silence in the elegantly appointed salon was oppressive. Marie Leczynska looked at the lovely moldings on the cream-colored walls, at the apple-green draperies and the exquisite Aubusson carpet, at the casual arrangement of tasteful rococo furniture and the priceless hand-painted vases. She looked at the paintings, the chandeliers, the candles, the settees—everywhere but into the cold, accusing eyes of her son.

Dominic leaned against the mantel, his arms crossed against his chest. Except for his brief formal greeting, he had said nothing at all since he'd entered the room. Marie had known from the beginning that her task would not be an easy one, but until this moment she had not realized quite how bitter he had become. Taking a deep breath, she lifted her head and looked directly into the eyes so like her own. "I have come a long way to see you, Dominic," she began.

"One can only wonder why the Queen of France would come on such a fruitless errand."

A wave of red crossed her cheeks. "Is it hopeless then? No matter what message I bring, you intend to refuse me?"

"Yes." The single word, stabbing and final, hung in the air between them.

Tears gathered in the black pools of Marie's eyes. Her lips trembled, but she did not look away. "Why do you hate me so, Dominic?"

He laughed humorlessly. "Need you ask?"

"I gave you what I could."

"That was precious little."

"You had Henri and the duchess." Her voice broke. "Your life was much better than that of my other children. A queen cannot be a mother, *chérie*."

"I didn't need a mother, *ma mère*." The last two words were drawn out in biting contempt. "What I needed was the truth."

"Henri thought it was better to wait."

"I should have known you would place the blame elsewhere."

She lifted her hands in a helpless gesture. "Has it been such a bad life, my son?"

"Don't call me that." The hurt he had never intended to reveal was reflected in his angry words. Wetting his lips, he struggled for control. "All of Paris knew what I should have known from the beginning," he explained. "As the legitimate son of the Duc de Lorraine, nothing is impossible. A byblow of an adulterous queen is something else entirely."

"How dare you judge me?" Marie's face flamed an angry red under her face powder. "You know nothing of my life."

"I suppose that is my father's fault as well," he shot back.

"You condemn me for one indiscretion in thirty years? Are you so perfect, Dominic?" Her expression changed. "If this is all because of the English duke's granddaughter, I shall never forgive you."

"I don't recall asking your forgiveness."

"Mon Dieu" she gasped. "You must love her very much. Will you stay here and marry her, in this land that is now England's?"

He didn't answer. Instead, he walked to window and pulled aside the heavy draperies. The sky was gray and the streets wet with a fine autumn rain. He was weary of talk. The conversation had taken more out of him than he'd realized. More than anything in the world, he wanted to confess. To tell this striking, dark-eyed woman that he was not perfect. That he had taken another man's woman to his bed. That he knew the pain of loving where he had no right to love. That if he were only slightly less principled, he would have left Anthony Doddridge to the soup pots of Pontiac's warriors and returned to Montreal to marry his fiancée. He told her none of it. Instead, he turned around and spoke courteously for the first time. "I'm sorry, *ma mère*. This sparring serves no purpose. Why did you come to Montreal?"

Marie was taken aback. This meeting had been a surprise. The Dominic Jolliet she remembered had been cooly polite, impeccably mannered. This stranger was not at all polite. There was a sharpness about him, like the edge of a finely honed knife blade. He was larger somehow and leaner, and his coppery hawk's face reminded her of the stern, stoic features of the Indians she had seen prowling the streets of Montreal. Perhaps her mission had been doomed from the start. Paris, with its mincing, perfumed aristocrats was not large enough for the new Dominic Jolliet.

"I had hoped to persuade you to return with me to Paris. With my influence and that of your father's, you could move in the highest of political circles. The king needs men who have knowledge of the world outside France. Lately, his decisions have not been wise."

Dominic laughed shortly. "If throwing away French lands is an example, I agree."

"Then you'll come home with me?"

Dominic shook his head. "No."

"You are not an Englishman, Dominic. Living here under English rule will not suit you."

"I know."

His mother frowned. Gathering her courage, she crossed the room and placed her hand on his arm. "We have colonies in the West Indies and in South America. But the girl is English. She will not be happy living under a French flag."

Dominic did not reply. He stared out the window, his back to her.

"What will you do?" Marie whispered.

"I don't know, *ma mère*. I truly don't know."

Preparing herself for rejection, Marie held her breath.

Slipping her arms around his waist, she rested her head against his back. His hand came up to cover hers. Tears of relief and happiness and regret welled up in her eyes and spilled over onto her cheeks, wetting his shirt.

Chapter 30

The *Fleur de Lys* sailed into Montreal Harbor on a cold, miserable day in late November. By special arrangement it would stop at the port of Boston for an exchange of prisoners and from there sail on to France. The Duke of Leceister arranged passage for his entire family. Travis, completely recovered under the excellent care and enormous amounts of food urged on him by his doting great-grandfather, was eagerly anticipating the voyage. The change in him was miraculous. Alexandra was sure he had grown two inches in a fortnight.

She watched her grandfather's spirits improve as the date of their departure approached. Not even the fact that he and Alexandra would have sole care of Abigail for the entire sea voyage daunted him. He had every intention of hiring an Englishwoman in Boston to act as a nurse for the child; but if none were to be had, he would make the best of it.

Anthony Doddridge had already been ransomed back to the English and was on his way to Portsmouth on a British frigate. He would wait for Alexandra in London, his letter read, and there they would decide their future. She was both frustrated and relieved that their inevitable confrontation would be delayed. Anthony's letter was brief and courteous, leaving no clue as to the state of his mind. A tiny, rebellious ember simmering in Alexandra's mind flickered into flame. Neither Anthony nor her grandfather had considered the possibility that she might remain in America with Dominic. Of course, she had given them no reason to believe she wouldn't be returning with them and Dominic seemed to have lost interest in her entirely.

After his mother had returned to France, he had left Montreal rather abruptly, giving no explanation for his departure. If Alexandra had not come upon him just as he was leaving, she doubted that he would even have said goodbye. He had been gone for over a month and the ship was leaving in two days. It was an impossible situation. Dominic would never be content to live out his life in an English colony and she longed for the clipped speech of tasteful drawing rooms and the green, softly rolling hills of home. Perhaps it was better this way. Goodbyes were too often painful ordeals.

Surprisingly, there weren't many French colonists who chose to leave their walled city on the St. Lawrence with its cobbled streets and steep, dark roofs. Despite the unwelcome presence of British soldiers garrisoned on every corner and in the government buildings, the citizens of Montreal appeared to take it all in their usual pragmatic stride. Alexandra had stopped in to see the Brionnes and was shocked to see them conducting business as if their city were not in the hands of the enemy. Waiting until the British officer had counted his change and left the shop, Alexandra clutched Madame Brionne's arm. "How can you bear to see your city overrun like this, Madame?"

Madame shrugged and bit down on the British coin. "English gold is as valuable as French gold, *chérie*. I'll not refuse it."

"What will you do now?" Alexandra asked.

"Now?" Madame looked puzzled. "Why, I shall prepare a good corn chowder for my husband. Will you join us, my dear?"

Alexandra shook her head impatiently. "No, thank you. My grandfather expects me. I meant where will you go now that Montreal belongs to England?"

"Go?" Madame Brionne's dark eyes widened. "Why should we go anywhere?"

"Because New France no longer exists." Alexandra was sure her French was not clear enough. The woman could not actually mean what she said. "Those Frenchmen who have fought and been killed by English soldiers will now fight *with* them," she burst out passionately. "Your taxes will go to an English king. Your sons will march and die in England's wars. If I were you, I would return to France. How can you even think of staying here?"

Madame Brionne reached out and took the young woman's hands in her own. Her smile was warm, her eyes bright with understanding. "Monsieur Brionne and I have lived in Montreal all of our lives. We have never seen France or the territories west of the mountains that also belong to your king. Why should we leave our home because a new monarch claims it as his own? When you have lived for as long as I have, *chérie,* you will know that one ruler is much like another. When the city settles down and your soldiers return home, Montreal will be no different than it was before."

The Duke of Leicester was jubilant at dinner that evening. He lifted his glass in a toast. Tomorrow they would sail for home. Only Henri Jolliet noticed Alexandra's pale cheeks and lack of conversation. Wisely, he refrained from commenting. He had an idea that the cause of her despondency had everything to do with the maddeningly elusive behavior of his son. Dominic had been gone for over a month and it didn't look as if he would return before Alexandra's ship sailed. The *duc* sighed. He hadn't wanted an English marriage for Dominic; but the more he came to know Alexandra, the more he realized that she was the right woman for him. Two years ago, Dominic had recognized something in the English beauty that stirred his heart and left him cold to the lures of other women. Fate had given him another chance and now he was throwing it away. Jolliet pushed back his chair and excused himself. He had suddenly lost his appetite.

Alexandra leaned back on her hands and held up her face to the sky, loving the kiss of the March sunlight. From her place at the crest of the hill she could see for miles across the valleys and knolls of Leicester land. The tapestry of dark green and light gold and breathtaking blue against the lichen-covered walls of the manor house was the same as it had been since the fourteenth century when Edward the Hammer had granted an earldom to the first Charles Winthrop. For four hundred years, an unbroken line of male Winthrops had ruled Leicester. It would all end with her grandfather.

Alexandra thought of Travis's piercing blue eyes, his flashing smile, and the sudden, impatient way he had of throwing his head back when he was annoyed. She laughed out loud. He was the image of his father. Unless she was mistaken, the future lord of the House of Leicester would be a great improvement over those of the past. Alexandra had told Travis of his mother's death before leaving Montreal. He had accepted the news with the same courage that had caused him to set out alone in the Canadian wilderness. With a child's understanding of the world, he considered her murder an act of mercy, far less reprehensible than either Alexandra or her grandfather had seen it. After solemnly listening to his aunt's tale, he asked to be excused and spent the rest of the evening playing quietly with Abigail.

Unbuttoning the jacket of her riding habit, Alexandra pulled the pins from her hair and combed her fingers through the silky strands until it lay like a curtain of burnished copper across her shoulders. For months now, she had been consumed with a strange restlessness as if the high ceilings and spacious rooms of Leicester Manor were confining her in too small a space. She sighed. For over three months she had pushed aside her memories, refusing to dwell on the impossible. What a coward she was. She had lived long enough to know that pain never went away until it was properly faced. She closed her eyes and for the first time since her return to England deliberately revived the memory of Dominic Jolliet.

As clearly as if he stood before her, Alexandra pictured the tall, spare body; the dark, coppery skin; the thin, firm-lipped mouth; the thin blade of his hawk's nose, and the probing, night-black eyes. She saw him as he had last appeared before her, leaning against the mantel in his drawing room, one buckskin-clad leg thrown carelessly across the other, his arms folded across his chest. How had he acquired that air of confidence, that easy assurance, that quality of capable command that men such as Anthony Doddridge could aspire to for a lifetime and never hope to achieve?

The sun was warm on her head. She could feel its comforting heat on the bones of her face. But in the pit of her stomach, she felt only a cold darkness. How could she have thrown away the priceless gift he'd offered? How could she bear a future without the presence of Dominic Jolliet?

She must have fallen asleep in the pool of drugging sunlight because suddenly an amazingly lifelike image materialized before her. Only this time, it wasn't the mocking *coureur de bois* who invaded her consciousness, it was the Dominic Jolliet of Paris. Splendid in a black-velvet coat with dazzling white small clothes and knee breeches, he stood before her in all the elegant severity of a gentlemen from Versailles. Alexandra sat up and rubbed her eyes. The image did not disappear. She began to tremble. Not if her life depended upon it would she have been able to command her useless limbs. She sat on the ground, helplessly staring up at the man whose face had haunted her dreams for nearly four years.

For a long time Dominic was content merely to look at her. She was the same and yet she wasn't. The clear, lovely bones of her face and the subtle autumn coloring would be hers forever. It was her expression and something around the eyes that bothered him. The young vibrant girl he knew from Paris was gone. She was a woman now. A woman who looked as though she had suffered great pain and was suffering still. Dominic frowned. He would choke the life out of Anthony Doddridge if he had caused that look of wary hurt she was trying so hard to conceal.

"I've come a long way, Alix," he said gently. "Aren't you going to speak to me?"

The tears crowded her throat at the sound of that beloved voice, and for moment she found it difficult to speak. "I can't believe it's really you," she said at last.

"Believe it," he said crisply.

"You are looking well." Her eyes moved hungrily across his face, asking a thousand questions, the golden depths revealing everything her polite words left unsaid.

"Thank you." Dominic was amused. He could play the game as well as any.

Alexandra flushed. He was deliberately making it difficult for her. She stood and brushed off her skirt. Taking a deep breath, she looked directly at him. "Why are you here, Dominic?"

He was no longer amused. The black eyes were deadly serious. "I came for you, *mignonne,*" he replied simply. "If you recall, we are betrothed."

"What I recall," said Alexandra sweetly, "is a man who left Montreal with no word of his whereabouts for months." Her hands clenched. "You might have written."

"Have you forgotten that in the wilderness, a man is not always master of his own fate?"

"Why did you leave at all? You knew Grandfather had plans to leave. Nothing was settled between us. What was I supposed to do?"

He reached for her, but she stepped backward. "Was I wrong to come?" he asked. "Do you want me to go away?"

"I want to know why you allowed me to leave?"

Dominic studied her carefully, noticing the trembling mouth and clenched hands. She was nearly undone. He held out his arm. "If you'll walk with me for a bit, I'll tell you."

She looked down at his outstretched hand. It was long and sunburned and beautifully formed, the hand of a French aristocrat, the hand of the man she loved. She placed her own in it and felt his fingers close around hers.

Gently, he pulled her close to his side and walked. He looked out across the breathtaking beauty of the English countryside. "No wonder you love it so," he said admiringly. "I've never seen anything quite like it."

Alexandra's thoughts flew back to a land of granite mountains, smoky-blue with morning mist; thundering waterfalls; miles and miles of spruce and maple and silver birch, dark and solemn against the backdrop of a flaming sunset. "There are other places as lovely as this," she replied. "They are different, perhaps, but every bit as beautiful."

"So they are." The expression on his face was unreadable.

She stopped, forcing him to look down at her. "Are you afraid of me, Dominic?"

He grinned. "Always. You've a shrewish temper."

"I do not," she protested, "and even if I did, you wouldn't be afraid of it."

His smile faded and something dark and disturbing flashed briefly in the black eyes and then disappeared. The time for dissembling was over. He would tell her the truth and she would decide for or against him, but first he had to ask. "Have you and Captain Doddridge settled things between you?"

"We have." The long, golden eyes told him nothing.

"May I ask what you've decided?"

"Anthony condescended to overlook my indiscretions in New France."

"I see." Dominic dropped her hand. His voice was very cold. "When is the happy occasion?"

"There isn't one. I decided that we would not suit. Our engagement is at an end."

His lips curved in a brilliant smile. "You are truly a witch, Alix. Did you enjoy making me wait for that?"

She smiled and his breathing altered.

"I did," she replied. "It isn't often one can catch you unawares. But I shall become quite adept at it in the future."

"Do you mean that?" There was no laughter or mockery in the dark eyes that held hers. Only a question and a bright, irrepressible flame.

"You've come five thousand miles for me, m'lord," she teased. "How could I possibly refuse you?"

He threw back his head and laughed, the loud, boyish laughter of the boy from Paris. "When did you know?" he asked her at last.

"When you handed me your handkerchief in the Royal Gallery at Versailles."

He drew her into his arms and buried his face in the fire of her hair. "I know quite well when you fell in love with me, *mignonne*. What I am curious to know is when you decided to marry me?"

She smiled into his shoulder. "When you didn't try to stop me from coming home."

"Ah." She could feel him nod. "I guessed correctly, then. I thought once you returned to England, you would find that you missed me after all. I waited as long as I could stand it."

"Where shall we go, Dominic? Surely you don't mean for us to stay in England?"

He traced the delicate bones of her cheeks and chin. "Will you mind very much leaving England?"

"Not if you are with me. But, Dominic, you can't wish to live in Montreal now that it is an English territory."

"I wasn't thinking of Montreal." His voice carried a current of excitement that she'd never heard before. "I want to go west. I want to explore, Alix. I want to share the excitement of untouched lands, paddle down waterways that have no end, walk among animals that have never known the scent of man. I know now that I can never be content living the life of a country gentleman. I am a *voyageur*, my love. Will you come with me? Will you paint the pictures that we see?"

A curious trembling had taken hold of her. She had never voiced the longing inside her, never imagined that a woman could answer the *coureur's* call to roam the wilderness. This was what she had yearned for, freedom and adventure, to pursue her craft whenever and wherever she pleased, to share her life with a man who expected no more and no less than she was. She thought of Bowating. Sarah was there. Sarah with her even serenity and her calm acceptance of fate. She would see Sarah once again. All at once, something occurred to her. "Will we have children, Dominic?"

"That lies in the hands of God, Alix."

"But do you want children?" she persisted.

He ran his finger down the tip of her nose. "Yes, I do. But not until after we are married."

She blushed. "How can we raise children in a *voyageur's* canoe?"

"Far to the south, there is a lovely city called St. Augustine that now belongs to Spain. In the winter months we can make our home there." He grinned. "Winter is a good time for having babies."

Alexandra's clear laugh floated across the valley. Men

really were ridiculous creatures. "Babies sometimes make unexpected appearances, Dominic."

His eyes widened in mock horror. "Not our babies, Alix. Every red-haired minx will be properly behaved. I'll see to it."

Still laughing, she pulled down his head and kissed him. His lips softened and moved over hers, and then, there was no more room for laughter.